Books by Ki Longfellow

China Blues
Chasing Women
Stinkfoot, a Comic Opera (with Vivian Stanshall)
The Secret Magdalene
Flow Down Like Silver: Hypatia of Alexandria
Houdini Heart
Shadow Roll: A Sam Russo Mystery Case 1
Good Dog, Bad Dog: A Sam Russo Mystery Case 2
The Girl in the Next Room: A Sam Russo Mystery Case 3

Follow Ki Longfellow on the Internet:

Blog kilongfellow.wordpress.com
Facebook Ki Longfellow
Twitter @KiLongfellow
Official Website www.kilongfellow.com
Sam Russo www.eiobooks.com/samrusso

The Girl in the Next Room

by
Ki Longfellow

A Sam Russo Mystery

Case 3

Eio Books

This is a work of fiction. Though based on the known facts of people and places mentioned, the events and characters inscribed herein spring from the author's imagination. No descriptions of public figures, their lives, or of historical personages, are intended to be accurate, but are only included for the purposes of writing a work of fiction, and are not necessarily true in fact.

Copyright © Ki Longfellow 2013
All rights reserved.

Published in the United States by

Eio Books
P.O. Box 1392
Port Orchard, Washington, 98366 U.S.A.

www.eiobooks.com

Library of Congress Cataloging-in-Publication Data

Longfellow, Ki
The girl in the next room : a Sam Russo mystery CASE 3 / by Ki Longfellow.
    pages cm
  ISBN 978-1-937819-05-7
1. Russo, Sam (Fictitious character)--Fiction. 2. Private investigators--Fiction. 3. Murder--Investigation--Fiction. 4. Staten Island (New York, N.Y.)--Fiction. I. Title.
  PS3562.O499G57 2013
  813'.54--dc23

                                                  2013002043

Cover designed by Shane Roberts
Book designed by Shane Roberts

Dedicated to Carole Lombard & Pan Zareta

(And to you, Matt Greenfield, to you)

The Girl in the Next Room

A Sam Russo Mystery

Case 3

I was calling on my new neighbor, the goober in room 4-C. 4-C was old Nate's room before old Nate curled up his toes and died. When the new guy answered my knock, it was like watching a rock roll away from a hole. The rat inside was enormous. He had a glass of something brown in one hairy paw and a glass of something less brown in the other. I figured one of 'em was a chaser.

About then his smell came out and punched me right on the nose.

I stood there, Jane at my side, trying not to inhale. I said, "Hello. My name is Sam Russo."

"So?"

"I live in 4-A."

"So?"

"I wondered… have you seen Holly?"

"Who?"

"The girl in 4-B. That's the room between us."

"Girl? Beat it bub, before I give you what for. Or her, if I *did* see 'er." With both hands full and a wet smoke stuck in his wet mouth, there wasn't much he could do to keep his pants up. They were dungarees: old, encrusted with filth, and slowly sinking.

I thanked a slammed door.

Goddamn you, Nate. Dead, you're a pain in the ass. You let this guy into my building. Here for a week now, he played his radio half the night. Obviously fond of a drink or ten, coming or going he'd slam between the stair rail and the wall. He dropped his used butts on the stairs. A coupla times he didn't make it to the top, and we were supposed to step over him. I admit it: I stepped *on* him. As for Jane, she never missed.

But worse, much worse, he was sharing the bathroom.

With Nate newly underground, Holly and I'd had a nice long run with just one or the other of us in it, but now, like Joe Louis and boxing, our run was over. I was thinking of moving. Out of Stapleton. Off Staten Island. But then, I was always thinking of moving.

Manhattan was only a ferry ride away. If I couldn't get off Staten Island—yet—I could at least find a room with a better view of New York City.

But Jane and I were sailing pretty close to the wind money wise. And then there was Holly. I didn't want to leave Holly alone in a room next to the room with a guy like the new guy in it.

Holly who? I didn't know her last name. I didn't know her first name either. I just knew the one she used. Basically, I knew sweet diddly about Holly in 4-B. Where she came from. What it must of been like for her growing up. Who her people were. Why someone as smart and funny as she was worked the streets. And why, of all places, did she work them in Stapleton? Holly could do better than Staten Island. Even I could do better than Staten Island.

What I did know was that Holly hadn't come home for two days and three nights. The first day wasn't bad. For one thing, it was the first Saturday in May and I was glued to my radio listening to the Kentucky Derby. I can't remember when I named myself Sam but I can remember when I decided that the day the Kentucky Derby ran each year was my birthday. Of course this meant my birthday fell anywhere from the 1st to the 7th of May, but I liked that part. It messed with my horoscope. On this year's birthday which, as it happened, fell on May 7th, I'd put my money on a colt called Capot, but Ponder, a "come from the back of the pack" closer, took it with a run called "relentless." Ponder'd been dead last and then he was suddenly a rip-snorting first. But hey, I figured losing a few bucks to listen to an unexpected win by the son of Pensive—the horse who should of taken the Triple Crown in '44—was well worth my loss.

On Sunday I began to worry. And Jane began to worry as much as me. Holly'd missed not only the Derby—something she'd promised to try now we were pals—but my birthday. It wasn't like her to break a promise. Also, I liked to think she'd remember I was getting old.

Twenty eight. Thirty wasn't far off.

When we'd pass Holly's door, Jane'd stop and sniff all along the bottom edge. Doing that, her tightly curled tail would unfurl.

It was the tail that did it.

After our latest scrape, the one in Manhattan where Jane got another scar to go along with her growing Sam Russo knife and gun collection, and I'd been *this* close to being Russo soup, I'd taken only "safe" cases. No one was famous, we never got covered in oily mud, it just about covered the rent, and no one died. Just ugly little human nature stuff. No matter the job, jealousy and greed lay at the bottom of most of it— and a sort of basic human fear lay at the bottom of jealousy and greed. I'd find myself standing around knee deep in some mess someone had made of his life, or her life, or in the lives of others, or all the above—usually all the above—and wonder what they were scared of. It all boiled down to who the hell knew? That was the problem. None of us really knew what we were doing, or why.

It was making me sick. But it was better than making me dead. And twice as better for not making Jane dead.

My Manhattan adventure down two different rabbit holes still worried me though. I'd tripped over who did it, even survived the fall, but I never did discover all there was to know. I might of learned more—I was sure there was a *lot* more to learn—but a neat black hole through the killer's neat black brain put a stop to that. That brain contained a whole lot of things I wish I'd learned. Too bad I wasn't going to learn it.

Mrs. Willingford was off in California somewhere, buying a shiny new racehorse. And if I knew Mrs. Joker Willingford, which I did, sort of, she was also busy bumping into good-looking strangers and blocking doorways with her hats.

Anyway, for a few months there, it'd been just me and Jane and a lot of getting to know Holly. We'd spent our idea of Christmas together. For Holly that meant a small hurtful tree and a present for Jane and one for me. I suppose the tree hurt because it was the first one I'd ever sat by on a Christmas Eve listening to Bing sing Christmas carols. Where I'd grown up—the Staten Island Home for Children—we celebrated Christmas like Scrooge celebrated Christmas.

Holly gave me a book. Holding it was like holding a paving stone. Reading it was like wading out into a swelling sea and practically drowning there. *Raintree County* was some book. Jane got a new leather collar. Attached to the collar was a metal disc. The disc said JANE, and under that was my Saint George 7 phone number.

"In case she gets lost," said Holly.

"Jane's never lost," I said.

"Never say never," said Holly.

Jane said something in her own language neither Holly nor I understood, though we were both working on it.

Jane and I gave Holly a silver locket. It wasn't shaped like a heart. I might be that sappy but Jane wasn't.

We'd actually laughed, Holly and I. And Jane. When Holly wasn't working the Victory Boulevard edge of Tompkinsville Park, or singing in the Green Garter, she was great to be with. We went to the movies a lot. We liked the same movies, the same radio shows, the same books. Besides my Christmas present, Holly'd borrowed a few things from the Stapleton library I'd never of thought to read if she hadn't. I could of done without a strut of a guy called Hemmingway but Scott Fitzgerald and Charles Dickens really had something to say.

Because of Holly, I was getting elevated.

Jane and I liked her. We both liked her a lot.

So where was she?

She'd better not be dead. Besides liking her, my being a Private Investigator was turning out the most dangerous job in the world. Two big cases in '48, Summer and Fall, each a mess of multiple murders, and each almost winding up with me or Jane dead. Or both of us at the same time.

Did Holly's disappearance have something to do with me?

If so, I was through as a private eye. For a PI, I was the bunk. I wasn't Poirot with his little gray cells whirring around in his head, working out whodunit all by his lonesome. I

wasn't Bogie playing Sam Spade or Philip Marlowe. Bogart
didn't really have cases exactly, they were more like sticky
situations where he'd get hired, get sapped, get kissed by a
great looking skirt, get sapped again, or for variety, pistol
whipped, and somehow turn out right side up in the end. I
wasn't your ordinary real life police detective—which did
not include my old friend Lino Morelli because Lino Morelli
wasn't ordinary. Lino, detective with the Staten Island
police, was dumber than a sack of Idaho spuds. I mean your
real ordinary police detective who took fingerprints, tapped
phones if he was lucky, had files and files of convicted and
yet-to-be-convicted bad guys to look through and finger. I
wasn't anyone I'd ever heard of or read of or seen on the
silver screen. I was Sam Russo, and if Holly was dead, I'd
rather not know she was dead.

As I said, we liked her.

So maybe we ought to move out first thing in the
morning. Then I could go on with my life believing Holly'd
been off visiting her old mom somewhere, say over in small
town New Jersey, or maybe even in upstate New York—a
place she'd come home from just as my cab was turning the
corner. And Jane and I hadn't looked back.

Only I wouldn't move out in the morning. I wouldn't go
anywhere until I knew about Holly.

I got the call at dawn. Fell out of my Murphy bed to
answer it. Knocked Jane off her personal pillow. I'd been
dreaming of Mrs. Willingford. We'd taken a whole floor at
the Plaza which somehow became one enormous room and
we were dancing like Rogers and Astaire. Only I was dressed
like Ginger, all white and black froth. Gorgeous, really. The

frock, not me. And Mrs. W was dressed as a jockey, whip included. No time to let that one sink in, I was listening to Lino Morelli on the end of my line.

He was saying, "Sam? You awake?"

"Uhh?"

"Good. You remember the nance I saw in your room that day last November? The time I came to tell you about the giant floater?"

I was suddenly awake, so awake my grip on the phone came this close to cracking the thick black plastic. Jane growled. Jane didn't like Lino. But then, who did?

"Yes," I said through terrified teeth. *She's not dead. She can't be dead. Don't tell me she's dead, you miserable little weasel.* "What about her?"

"She's in intensive. She's askin' for you. Get over here. Fast."

I couldn't bring Jane. They didn't allow dogs in hospitals. It killed me to shut the door in her surprised face, but I did it.

2

The Staten Island Public Health Service Hospital looked like an ancient pyramid rose up out of Bay Street. It was the kind of thing you'd see in a National Geographic magazine devoted to Mexico. I was sprinting through the emergency doors where Lino was waiting, and then tripping all over him so he'd move faster and take me to Holly.

They had her in a ward. Not for women. For men. But the way Holly looked, she couldn't have cared. Holly didn't look like she'd care about anything ever again.

Three nurses were sponging her down, getting her ready for a doc.

I pushed through them, reaching out to hold her hand. Warm, her hand was warm, and that warmed me. A little. "What happened to her, Lino?"

All I got was a shrug. I got more from the cop leaning on the wall with his hat pushed to the back of his huge head. The padded shoulder of his greasy jacket was staining the white paint. "Probably just what someone thought it deserved."

I was on the greaseball faster than Jane would of been on the greaseball. Lino was almost as fast. Lino may be dumb, but he's strong. He got me off the creep before I could get myself into real trouble.

"For crying out loud, knock it off, the both'a ya," he said, "Can't you two see we got us a damsel in distress here?"

Holly'd been found in a canvas duffel bag dumped near

the public latrines in Tompkinsville Park. She'd been thrown away with the trash. When the wino who opened the bag got a good look at his loot, her naked body was so soaked in dried blood, he thought he'd found a painted manikin.

She still had her pink silk purse. Inside, she still had a tube of bright red lipstick, her favorite Pan-Cake in its little green enamel compact, a jar of the pricey cream she used on her face and for Jane's scars—Holly swore it could make them fade—and five dollars and seventeen cents. Someone had tried to throttle her, someone with big hands, or maybe Holly had a delicate neck. The skin of her neck looked like a police blotter. Around her swollen neck, hanging between the dark blue thumbprints, was the silver chain off the locket Jane and I had given her, but no silver locket. And she was still alive, although if not for getting found, she wouldn't of been for much longer.

She'd been worked over. Maybe even tortured. Her scalp was bloodied from hanks of hair being yanked from her head. There were small deep cuts on her arms and her legs, some on her belly. The deepest was in her groin, a hair's breath from—let me put it this way: for a girl, she was hung like Flynn.

I hardly recognized her face. It'd been a lovely face. As delicate as a girl's. For a boy, she was a beauty. Hell, for a girl she was a beauty.

Sorry, *had* been a beauty.

Someone had been through her purse—maybe more than one someone. One of those had to be Lino. I figured if he could, I could.

I'd seen Holly carry this purse. It usually looked stuffed. Now it looked ransacked. But I knew about the bottom. It wasn't an expensive purse—I ought to know, I'd bought it for her at Macy's—so the bottom was stiffened by a piece of covered cardboard. Under the cardboard Holly kept what she valued. No driver's license, but then, like me, she had no car. Her bigger bills from her better customers. And a piece of paper, born snoop that I was, I'd always longed see.

Her birth certificate.

Holly's registered birth name was Baby Shauer. If it'd been me, I'd of changed that one too. He'd been born in Tottenville, an old town at the other end of the island. I'd never been there, never needed to go. But I supposed that answered the question: why Staten Island? Like whoever I'd been before I became Sam Russo, Baby Shauer was a homegrown islander. I couldn't say when Holly herself was born. Probably when she made it to the northern end of the island and could see the spires and lights of Manhattan. Like me, she hadn't gotten there yet. Maybe to visit as I had done, but not really off island. Born in early December, she was twenty-two years old which explained why the draft never got her. Her father's name wasn't listed. Her mother was a Viola Shauer, age at Baby Shauer's birth: 16. Occupation: waitress. Or so it said.

I put Holly's birth certificate back where it belonged. And then I sat. I sat by her side for two days and two nights, only taking enough time to rush back to the corner of Victory Boulevard and Bay Street and up four flights of stairs to room 4-A so I could feed, water, walk and apologize to Jane, before rushing back to sit some more.

They'd sewed her up, everywhere, cut off what was left of her long hair, hair she once could do anything with. It all depended on who she'd decided to play out on the streets;

lately she'd taken to tight shorts with a tight bib top and her
hair in two ponytails either side of her head. They'd slathered
her scalp wounds with something that smelled like it should
work, snapped her nose back and hoped the bandage would
keep it there, wired her broken jaw. There wasn't anything
they could do for her neck: the black bruising, the thumb
prints, the swelling, aside from make sure she could breathe,
that she'd keep breathing.

I slept in a hard chair. I brought food up from the hospital
canteen. I drank a lot of coffee, smoked a lot of Luckies out
on the fire escape at the end of Holly's hallway. I watched
the nurses on a male ward take care of her. I watched the
orderlies and the cleaning crew. I watched her girl friends
come, mostly street walkers. I knew some of them, knew
their names, and they knew me.

They came in all shapes and sizes: young, older, one or
two pushing forty. Some were as lovely as film stars. Some
could give Margaret Hamilton painted green a run for her
money. Some were colored girls. One was Chinese or near
enough. No matter what they were, they wept over her,
they left her flowers and cards, they thanked their lucky stars
it was her and not them. Who could blame 'em for that?
When it's our skin, we tend to want to keep it.

Holly was a lady. She deserved all the medics could do.
If they ever tried not giving it to her, they had me to deal
with. I wasn't budging.

I held her hand. Her hands were hot, her fingers were
cold. I didn't think about that. I talked to her. I didn't know
if she heard me, but I talked to her.

She'd already heard a lot of my war horse stories so I told
her a race horse story. Not one about when he was racing, but

one about how he lived when he was finished racing. I told her as much as I knew about Man o' War: the half a million people who made the trek to Faraway Farm just to say they'd seen him, the great ones he sired like War Admiral who got whupped by another great called Seabiscuit who was Man o' War's grandson. The friend he made in Will Harbut, his colored groom, who had a grand southern way with words. I talked for over an hour. I talked until I came to the part that made me stop talking. I suddenly remembered how it was when Man o' War died. I knew the exact time—a year and a half ago, November 1, 1947, at 12:15 in the afternoon. I knew the exact time because I'd been listening to my radio and whatever the hell I was listening to got interrupted by the announcement. It was about as somber as FDR telling us the Japs had just bombed Pearl Harbor. Will Harbut, his best friend, had died less than a month before, and when I heard that, it hurt, but when I knew the big red horse Will called "Mannie Wah, de mostest hoss" had passed away on Faraway Farm in Kentucky, I cried. This was before I'd met Jane, so I was all alone and I sat in my room and I cried for one hell of a long time. I remember I thought about his last month without Will Harbut talking about him, without Will Harbut showing him off, and wondered if he'd died lonesome and pining.

All of a sudden I thought of Jane. How long did dogs live? How old was Jane? Fuck.

Holly woke up on the second day. And when she did, the eye she opened was blood red.

I was there. Just me. No doc around. No nurse. No Lino. No cop of Lino's. And I was scared.

I was out of my chair and bending over her, pushing a

loose bandage away from her battered face, being careful not to touch the stitches in her cheek and her forehead, the notches in her arms, the knife wound in her lower belly: deep, serious, operated on, her bandaged nose, the wired jaw, her left eye still swollen shut.

"It's me, Holly. It's Sam."

She tried to smile. She tried to say "Sam." She couldn't do either. A tear rolled out of her good eye, her beautiful once green eye.

I smiled for her. I smiled like an idiot. "You're fine. You're alive. Everything's healing. And when you go home, Jane or I or the best nurse money can buy will be with you day and night."

All I got for that was more tears and a single word, "Flowers."

"You bet, baby. They arrive from friends every hour, on the hour."

Doped to the gills on morphine, Holly wasn't a fool. She could tell she wasn't going to be fine. And even if one day, she was going to be OK, she'd probably never be the Holly she was.

"Was it a mugging, Holly? Was it rape?"

She couldn't shake her head. Shaking her head hurt her.

"Don't move your head. Just squeeze my hand. Tell me what happened. Who did this to you, and why? Where *were* you all this time?"

She did her best to turn her head away from me, did her best to curl up while she sobbed. And I sat in my chair and watched and waited and seethed inside. So many did so much to deserve what they got. That wasn't the law, it was just the truth. But not Holly. I swore right there that I'd find out what and who and why and even where, and when I did, there'd be hell to pay for whatever had happened to my Baby Shauer. It didn't matter if I never felt like Bogie again, Sam Russo was going to do something about this.

Forget pride, mine or Holly's. I wired Mrs. Willingford. She wired back more than enough money to pay Holly's medical bills as I knew she would. A telegram came with the dough.

```
BEVERLEY HILLS  MAY 8 1949
SAM RUSSO
STAPLETON, NY
SORRY ABOUT YOUR FRIEND.  IF SHE'S
YOUR FRIEND, SHE'S MY FRIEND.
CAN'T GET BACK THERE YET BUT I'M
WORKING ON IT.  DON'T DO ANYTHING
I WOULDN'T DO.  THAT LEAVES THINGS
WIDE OPEN.  JOKER SAYS CROSBY'S DEL
MAR RACETRACK IS ALL ACES.  BUT STAY
CLEAR OF THE BEVERLEY HILLS HOTEL.
IT'S A DUMP.
KISS JANE FOR ME.  L.
```

The L stood for Lois. I was surprised to see it there. Mrs. Willingford was never anything but Mrs. Willingford. I wouldn't have it any other way. And, so far as I knew, neither would she.

I'd never tell Holly about the money. She'd assume I'd paid for her. And then she'd spend the rest of her life trying to pay me back.

That wasn't a problem for now. That was a problem for later.

3

And when Holly was well enough, which wasn't all that well but the hospital was out of ideas, I took her home. Meaning I took her to my room where she got the bed and the private care and I got the floor. With Jane.

Before she came, I looked round my room. What would Holly need? She couldn't read yet, so books were out. A new radio would be just the thing. Who was I kidding? I wanted a new radio as much as I was sure Holly needed one. So I went down to Bay Street and bought a top-of-the-line Philco.

Like Durante said to Mrs. Calabash: thank you, Mrs. Willingford— wherever you are.

The nurses weren't round-the-clock, but the two who came, one for a three day straight shift, the other for four, started at eight in the morning and stayed until six in the evening. That gave me plenty of time to do some digging.

On the night she'd disappeared Holly'd sung at the Green Garter. She didn't have Piaf's voice, she didn't even have Doris Day's voice, but she could put over a song with the best of 'em. Sometimes, on her best nights, she could move you like Billy Holiday could move you. From deep inside the nerve.

It was Saturday, the 14th of May, and just as I knew he'd be, Mickey Cates was holding down his personal bar stool at the Garter on Hannah Street. When he wasn't out killing some poor sap for some damn reason, and not getting caught at it no matter how hard Lino or I tried, he was knockin' 'em back at the Garter.

Mickey Cates was so Irish he was green. He drank Irish whiskey. He spoke with a pronounced Irish lilt, not that I'd heard him speak more than twice. Because of Cates, the Garter stocked a lot of Irish tunes on its Wurlitzer. If I'd heard Dan Sullivan and his Shamrock Band once, I'd heard 'em fifty times. That wasn't too bad, but the polkas—the Irish polkas I was learning to hate with a fine red Italian feeling.

The Irish were also a chatty bunch. They liked to clot together with other Irishmen over from the Olde Country. But Cates was a loner. Me, I thought he was a real live hired gun out of his time and out of his place. Wyatt Earp would of known him. Wyatt Earp would of shot him. Not being Earp, all I could do was keep an eye on him—which is why I knew he'd be right where he was because I checked on him at least once a month for going on two years now. When I was in town, I went looking for Cates. I can't say he ever hid.

And every month I hoped I'd hear someone had killed him. But so far, what with Earp twenty years under his personal California tombstone, no such luck.

I tipped him a nod like I always did and Cates tipped me a nod like he always did, and then we ignored each other. But I knew he knew exactly what I was doing every minute I spent there just like I knew exactly what he was doing.

We had this routine and it was working fine.

The place was pretty quiet for a Saturday, but then it was still early in the afternoon, maybe around one, maybe a little later. Later, a lot later, the joint would be jumping. Strippers, sailors, salesmen, souses, snowbirds, and lesser sorts like Cates: the best of the worst the island of Staten had to offer. It didn't matter. It wasn't who was on my side of the bar, but who was on the other side. I'd come to see the guy serving, the guy who'd been working on Holly's last good night.

His name was Sal. Sal wasn't the best bartender who'd ever mixed a drink, and he wasn't the worst. What he was was the ugliest. Sal Ploverman was so ugly it was hard not to look at him. One beady eye rode high on his face, the other hung low. If he had a nose, I don't know where he kept it. Far as I could tell he breathed through a hole that was almost, but not quite, above his mouth. His mouth was OK, so far as it went, but his teeth were all headed in their own individual directions. None of this was Sal's fault. It wasn't his parent's fault. All this was Hitler's doing. A perfectly reasonable looking Sal Ploverman'd been in a Sherman tank rolling through the rubbled streets of the city of Cologne when some German kid managed to lob a grenade inside the open hatch. And there went Sal's face, a leg, and one finger. He was lucky. It was half a leg. And the finger was a pinky.

Looking like he did, you'd think the Garter wouldn't want him dishing out drinks. Might turn a few stomachs. But Sal owned the place. Like his daddy had before him, and his grandma before that. The Green Garter was a Stapleton landmark. Although when me and my fellow inmates were kids, and had managed another of our escapes from the Staten Island Home for Unwanted Brats, I remember it being the Ploverman Five & Dime. Paul Jarrett and Lino Morelli and me did our first shoplifting there. Small stuff, penny candy mostly. Once, Paul got away with a Lone Ranger pocket knife. But he would. He was that kind of kid. Funny, sneaky and lucky. As for Lino, who'd grow up to be a cop, a police detective no less, he was our look-out. Lino had a natural whistle on him that beat us all hollow.

Anyway, Plovermans was just a front for the speakeasy through a secret door under the fabric counter. A real blessing Paul didn't know that or he'd of worked out some scheme for getting us in. One that would wind up with me and Lino in the clinker and Paul back at the "Home" telling the other kids all about it. Makin' 'em laugh. Brother, Paul Jarrett could make 'em laugh. For just one moment I wondered if he was doing as well up north at Sing Sing. I hoped so. Even after he shot me, three whole times, he was still a funny guy.

"Sal," I said, choosing a stool closest to the stage.

"Sam," he said, pouring me a beer before I'd asked for one. That was OK. It was just what I'd ask for anyway on a cloudless spring day in downtown Stapleton.

"Where's Jane?"

"Nursing Holly."

"Right," he said. "How's Holly?"

"About how you'd expect after what she's been through."

Sal scratched his missing chin with his good hand. "Right."

"Sal," I said, "I know you've gone through this before, but I have to ask again—"

"Hell, I been wondering when you'd get here and ask. So fire away. The cops ain't half as interested as you might think."

"'Cause she's a he?"

"I'd say, yep. An' 'cause she does what she does. Which

ain't what she does here. What she does here is half my business. Things ain't been the same since."

"You see anything that night? Anything different from any other night she was leaving and you were closing up?"

"Yep. An' I been waiting to tell you about it."

"So tell me."

"I saw a car the likes of which I ain't never seen in Stapleton before. It was parked right where on Hannah Street Holly'd have to walk past it to go home."

"What kind of car?"

"Just told you. I ain't never seen one before. 'Cept it was in two colors not just one color like a normal car. An' Holly, she just slams on her own brakes, you know? Like she was looking at rent for a year. And she says somethin' to someone in the car and someone in the car says somethin' back at her, so in she gets an' off she goes. An' the next night she don't show up to sing. An' the night after that. You wouldn't believe how many regulars asked where she was."

I drank my beer and I thought. Holly's body had finally made it home; it was safe at my place. But the real Holly hadn't actually come back yet. I had to wait 'til she did before I could ask her about that car.

A voice to my left was so unexpected I felt my stool rock. The voice was soft and slow and easy on the ears. It said, "Lagonda."

I turned and looked straight at Mickey Cates. He didn't look at me. He didn't look like he'd said a thing.

"Lagonda?"

I had to strain to hear Cates's answer. "It was the last thing Bentley designed for Aston Martin. And under its bonnet doesn't it purr like a whole basket of wee kittens? A

2580cc twin overhead cam straight 6 engine, it has."

I wasn't one of those small town kids who grew up bent over the bewildering engine of some old car. Or lying on my back under it. I wasn't even one of those kids who clothes pinned playing cards to their bicycle spokes. I was a city kid, an orphan, poorer than dirt. Raised, if you could call it that, by Florence and "Mister" Zawadzki, a one-of-a-kind husband and wife horror act—all this was gibberish to me. But from the green light in Sal's lopsided eyes and the reverence in Cates's green voice, I knew it meant a bunch of pistons and plugs as special to them as the great Man o' War was special to me.

"T'was blue with wings of a darker blue color. Two rode in it. And though both wore good suits and had better haircuts, there was a queer small feel to 'em."

I understood that. I also understood this was the most I'd ever heard come out of the mouth of Mickey Cates. But forget that. Cates wasn't the bad guy now. The bad guys were the two in the car. And the question was: who the hell drove a rare and imported Lagonda around Staten Island?

4

Holly never looked in a mirror. The one I had for shaving was hidden away. Her compact lived in a Prince Hamlet cigar box where I kept odds and ends, like my war medals.

She couldn't talk yet, but she could write. Not a lot, and she needed help, but it was more than she could do in the first few days. So when I asked about the Lagonda parked near the Green Garter and the two men in it, she scribbled a reply.

?

"A big car, Holly, a big blue colored car with darker blue fenders Sal saw you lean into on your way home from the Garter."

?

"What's the last thing you remember?"

Sal.

"Nothing else, nothing at all?"

Lino.

"When did you see fucking Lino!"

Hospital.

"Oh. Right. That's it?"

It.

"But that could change?"

?

Sighing, I leaned over and turned the knob on my Philco. Today's nurse, called Bertha or Beverley or Bathsheba or something beginning with a B, had it dialed to *Mary Noble,*

Backstage Wife. Fuck that. This was the day the Preakness Stakes ran.

I pulled up my chair, pulled up the only other chair I owned for Jane, fluffed up Holly's pillow, added coal to the stove, poured myself a shot of good whisky, fought off my desire for a Lucky, and then we all three of us listened as Capot took the second leg of the Triple Crown away from Ponder. Holly held my hand the whole time, squeezing when Capot—Ted Atkinson up, both horse and jockey chock full of beans—got pressed for the lead by the good horse Palestinian. Capot still flashed across the finish line first, breaking the track record when he did. Only a voice on the radio and the roar of the crowd, I could still see the rain and the mud and Capot's brown mane and brown hooves flying.

I'd lost a ten spot on Capot in the Kentucky Derby but won $25 bucks in the Preakness. So I was ahead a tidy fifteen clams on the colt I'd had my eye on since he was a two-year-old. That is, I would of been that much ahead if I didn't count Jane. Jane picked out her choice with her small black nose. She lost two and a half dollars on a nice little bay called Halt, which he didn't exactly do but he might as well have.

Holly was asleep when Jane and I left. I stood and watched her for a minute. Somewhere under the sewn-up cuts and dark bruises, the jaw wires and all the white bandages, I had a sense of Holly swimming back—maybe not to me, and certainly not to Staten Island, but to life, the one I knew she hoped to live. I knew about that life. She'd told me about it often enough. One of these days, Holly intended to go to Hollywood. Naming herself Holly was only a first small step. And once there, she intended to sing and dance and act her way into the American heart.

"After all, darling," she'd once said, "do you really know what's squashed under Mae West's corset besides Mae West's fat?"

She had me there. Before she'd said that, I hadn't given it a thought. After she said it, I found myself wondering from time to time.

But Mae hadn't had her face smashed in. Mae, dick or no dick, had a chance. Looking at Holly, it broke my heart.

On the way out the door to my room, I said to Bessie or Beatrice or Brunhilda or whoever, "Lock the door after us. Even if no one's coming for her, I don't like the chump in 4-C."

Today's nurse looked at me like it was me who lived in 4-C. Mrs. Willingford's money paid for the best. I'd bet the farm the woman built like Marjorie Main and holding her ground like Marjorie Main had never seen anything like my place before. But I doubt she'd think the Beverley Hills Hotel was a dump. You had to be as stinking rich as Joker Willingford to come up with that one.

"Of course," she snipped.

Before Jane could nip a leg like a bomb casing, I caught hold of her Christmas collar and pulled her back.

"Come, Jane. The game's afoot."

And when we were out in the hall with the door closed and both of us were inhaling four floors of boiled cabbage— it was feeding time all over Stapleton—I yelled at the door, "LOCK UP, YOU OLD BAT!"

Jane twitched an upright ear at the sound of a bolt slamming home.

The Staten Island Police Station was on Richmond

Terrace which was, to me and most everyone I knew, just more of Bay Street where it curved west with the island. A gray bulky shoulder of a three-story building and on each floor a row of small gray stingy windows facing the gray waters of the Upper Bay. When I'd first seen it, before the war when my oldest friend Lino was still a cop on a beat, it had a tree. Like so many things now, the tree was gone. Pity about that. I remember liking that tree. It did something to the building. That tree gave the place some heart.

Now it just looked like a packing crate.

Inside I went straight to Staten Island's idea of a Detective's Headquarters Division: one room, six desks, a wall of file cabinets, constant static from some dispatcher somewhere taking complaints. I listened for a minute. One caller wanted a cat shot. One sounded like he could use an exorcism. One was put on a speaker. I guessed he was a regular—the language rivaled Mrs. Zawadzki for foul. As for the lug with the big head who'd called Holly an "it," he could be anywhere. If he was, I'd do something. Most likely what I'd do was ask Jane to do something, but then I thought better of that when I remembered what could happen to Jane. Jane was a dog. The fathead was a man. His fellow fatheads were certain that the worst man on earth was worth more than the world's most noble animal. This really got my goat. Especially when I thought of some of the horses I'd known, but a whole lot more when I thought about Jane. How many times had she risked her life for me? How many times for the jockey she'd loved before me, the one who'd got himself murdered up in Saratoga Springs?

Who else could I say that about—including me?

The lug wasn't there. Lucky for all concerned.

Lino Morelli had his polished Florsheims up on his own littered desk; it was the one in the back closest to the toilet. He was drinking laced coffee and eating a meatball sandwich. No paper in his typewriter, his phone wasn't ringing, the nearest cop was asleep on a wooden bench, his hat over his face. All I had to do was walk four feet to my left to look at a wall crammed full of wanted posters.

I stood, lit a cigarette, and watched Lino eat—and he let me stand there.

It was easy to take his daily crust. It was easy because Jane had tiptoed around behind him and pissed like a perfect lady on a jacket fallen from a peg on the wall.

Jane didn't like Lino. I think I've said this before.

When he was finished showing me who was the boss and who was the chump who solved most of his cases for him, he gave me a big greasy meatball smile. "How's tricks, Russo?"

"Tricky, Morelli. You getting anywhere with my neighbor's case?"

"You mean the fru…"

"I mean Holly, the girl beaten, stabbed and strangled within an inch of her life and dumped inside the borders of your town like a sack of New Jersey's garbage."

Lino spread his hands. "It's like this, Sam, he didn't croak, did he? An' we got so many big cases, we— "

"If you had a big case, you'd be banging at my door faster than— "

Lino's head swiveled on his neck, his hooded eyes darting everywhere. Who knew who was hiding under his desk? In a file cabinet? Under a hat pretending to be asleep? If there was one thing he didn't want broadcast, it was his always calling on me.

You ask me, I'd make book every man, woman, child and their cow living in the mixed-up mess of streets and hills and vacant lots and dying docks on the northernmost tip of Staten Island knew that Police Detective Lino Morelli was dumber than Gracie Allen. They knew Gracie was an act but Lino was the real deal. They may not have known about me, but they knew someone had to be solving his cases. As for the guys he worked with, they handed out hints like mints to anyone who asked: look no further, they were trying to say, I'm your man.

Me? I didn't care who got credit for what. I didn't care about the medals and the bonuses and the front page of the Staten Island *Advance*. Working Lino's cases was how I learned my trade before and after the war. And coming to see him now was how I learned Holly was my case and my case alone.

But since I knew that already before I came, the visit was mostly for show and for the slim possibility Lino had learned something.

Lino knew less than I did.

I was turning away when he stopped me. "You pick something up, you bring it on home."

I bothered to turn my head. Jane didn't even pause. She was already pushing on the pebbled glass door. In a minute, maybe less, she'd get it open on her own.

I flipped my butt in the general direction of his ashtray. It missed. "Sure, Lino. Like always."

"That's my Sam," said my old friend Lino, stubbing out my cigarette before there was yet another hole in his desk. "Like always."

He grinned that same grin he'd grinned since we were

kids: sly, sure of his ground, amused by how he saw me. I let him look. He thought I'd always be there, always take care of him, always know my place in his shadow.

Who cared what he thought. Always was over.

I bought another pack of Lucky Strikes off the newsie outside the main doors to the station and surveyed my kingdom. Beyond Richmond Terrace, the Staten Island ferry was just leaving for the lights of Manhattan. A few blocks over, the old Orpheum Theater was showing a rerun of *Knock on Any Door* plus *Champion* with Kirk Douglas. I'd skipped the Douglas movie—as a kid I'd been beat up enough without watching a coupla men knock the crap out of each other— but I'd rushed off with Holly and Jane for *Knock on Any Door*. Of course I'd rush—it was a Bogart movie. Bogie wasn't a PI in it. He played a lawyer. But at least his guilt-ridden lawyer was a slum kid. And who could forget one of the greatest lines ever heard in a film?

"Live fast, die young, and leave a good-looking corpse."

Half the guys I served with on Luzon did exactly that, all except leaving behind a good-looking corpse.

Jane stood at my side, her head up, her ears erect, her tail in a tight curl over her back, her red and white coat perfect. What a couple we made.

I meant that.

I thought about Lino's jacket and smiled.

5

I'd turned ten the day Twenty Grand won the Kentucky Derby. Paul Jarrett and Lino Morelli and me and some new kid named Albert, we'd all shimmied down our rope of twisted sheets and run off to spend the time before the race jumping off the old Stapleton pier.

Back then the Staten Island Home for Children looked like somewhere Bela Lugosi would hang his cape. The last time I saw it, about a year ago now, it still did. The window we shimmied down from was in an actual turret. The "Home" had four turrets, one at each corner. Paul said if King Kong ever turned us over, we'd be a table. I remember thinking that was funny.

What wasn't funny was how high the window was. It was five stories up.

Speaking of Twenty Grand. All over the walls of Room 4-A were photos of horses. Twenty Grand was right up there with Colin and Man o' War and Pan Zareta and Ben Brush and Zev and Gallant Fox and Dan Patch and Roamer and Longfellow and so many more. There was also a snap shot of me and Magpie. There'd never been a better mare than her, none braver under pressure.

The stuff I brought home from the war I kept where I kept Holly's compact, but not that picture of me and Magpie. We went up on my wall in a gold frame that set me back thirty bucks.

Anyway, the point of this story is Lino Morelli. I found

out who Lino was that day, the real Lino, the stripped bare
Lino.

Jumping off the Stapleton Pier wasn't like trusting our
lives to Flo Zawadzki's old sheets, but it was still a risk. The
water underneath was dark and it was oily and under the
water were rocks. There were crabs down there, big ones,
and barnacles that could rub your skin off. Once in awhile
the water was covered in pinky yellow suds, runoff from all
the German breweries. And once in awhile it smelled like
the boy's toilet Flo would force some girl to clean whenever
she thought of it—which wasn't often.

And sometimes there were shadows down there not
even Jarrett, our cut-up and teller of tales, could make a
joke out of.

But, hell, we were kids. Even dumber, we were boys. So
we jumped. One at a time. Two at a time. And then the last
time, all four of us together. Albert was farthest out on the
pier. That was the best place to be. The water was deeper.
And the worst place. Most of the shadows were there.

I came up. Paul came up. Lino came up. And then we
waited, three heads bobbing in Upper Bay waters, for Albert
to come up.

Albert didn't come up. And he didn't come up some
more.

I looked at Paul. He looked surprised. I looked at Lino.
He looked scared. Really scared, like the kind of scared that
shows the bone under the face and the dark at the back of
the eyes.

Paul and I dove at the same time. I don't know what
Paul was feeling, but I was feeling sick. Death didn't mean
a lot to me at ten. At ten, nobody died. But they could

disappear. At the Staten Island Home for Children, children disappeared all the time. If they were little, like real little, I assumed they'd got adopted. If they were older, I assumed they ran away. If they were real trouble, I assumed they were moved to another Lock-up for Lost Kids. I never assumed they died.

But if Albert disappeared, I might get in Dutch with Mister. Get smacked around. Get locked in a closet. So I dove.

Paul and I went down at the same time and we came up at the same time and neither one of us had Albert with us. I remember Paul's face as clearly now as I saw it then. No longer surprised, he was as spooked as me. I didn't know back then what I know now, which is that Paul knew all about dying. So I didn't know he was sure Albert was dead.

And where was Lino who'd come up with us when Albert didn't?

Lino was back up on the pier, kicking his skinny sunburned legs over the edge, and watching our efforts— I'd say "with interest" if he'd looked interested. He'd sure stopped looking scared out of his wits.

I yelled, "Help us!"

And this is what Lino said, "Nah. Why should I? You guys'll find 'im."

Paul was already back under the water and I would of been too if I hadn't seen Albert dragging himself out on the rocks a little ways away.

So that was Lino. Morelli on the half nutshell. Why risk himself when someone else would do whatever needed doing? But worse, he was too chicken to risk himself. Paul Jarrett was a lot of things, some of them pretty bad which was why he was sitting out his time on Sing Sing's Death Row, but Lino was an out-and-out coward.

Ever since, I expected nothing of Lino who expected everything of me.

I knew I was on my own here. If Holly was drowning, I was the only one who'd dive.

First thing, find that Lagonda. How hard could it be? There weren't many of them in the entire world, much less in the great state of New York. Holly was that rare thing in her world: loved. Most of the girls who'd visited Holly, loved Holly. I'd make book most of them knew she wasn't a she. But if there was a working girl who didn't love Holly, she'd know better than to peach to the cops and pushers and pimps. Holly might get a beating out of it, she might get a night in the clinker, but the girl who snitched would get worse, much worse, from Holly's sisters in arms.

So that's where I'd start. Me and Jane would stand around with the girls who stood out in the cold along Victory Boulevard. They all knew about Holly, and every single one of them would have ideas about what happened to her. All I needed was just one of those ideas to add up.

I also needed a nurse to stay with Holly past six o'clock. No self-respecting hooker hooked before suppertime.

So first I had to bribe the one who was there. Beulah maybe, or Bertina.

"Listen to the radio, read a book, better yet, read to Holly." It cost me a pretty penny—OK, so it cost Mrs. Willingford—but we came to a deal. She'd stay on, even if it took all night. The way things were, it could take all night. It was Saturday night in Stapleton. Holly's friends were in and out of cars, in and out of interesting "hotels" on Bay Street, in and out of alleys, it might take some time to find just the right friend.

Jane and I struck gold at three in the morning.

The friend's name was Big Ivy. Unlike Holly's name, unlike mine, that was probably not a moniker she'd made up for herself. None of my business. Big Ivy suited her. With her big painted mouth and her small painted eyes and all those teeth, she looked like Carmen Miranda without all the fruit. Looking like Carmen Miranda got her a certain kind of john—one with a sense of humor.

"A snazzy foreign car in two colors? Yeah, I seen it. I seen it more than once. Last time was about three months ago when Lucinda used to work my spot with me. Whoever was in it didn't ask me to take no ride, but they asked Lucinda. But that's Lucinda for you. Pretty as a picture. And young. So you gotta expect she gets a lotta free rides. You know, come to think, I ain't seen Lucinda since. So I guess she's back in Brooklyn where she can get more action. You saying she ain't?"

I said I didn't know what I was saying, except the night Holly went missing someone had seen her lean into a Lagonda.

"A what?"

"The foreign car Lucinda took a ride in."

"I thought a Lagonda was one of them funny buildings they got in Japan."

"That's a pagoda."

"Pagoda. Lagonda. It's all Greek to me. But I gotta tell you how much I like that dog you got there. I could use a dog like that. Oh boy. You gotta scram now. I think I see me my favorite john."

We scrammed, Jane and I. Right over to a tree near a lamppost which by now was deserted. Holly's friends were thinning out.

OK. So the Lagonda had been round Tompkinsville Park more than once, more than twice. And a girl named Lucinda who'd been here, wasn't here anymore. She hadn't come back in a duffel bag, half dead. She hadn't come back at all. She'd been pretty and young. Unlike Big Ivy, but just like Holly.

Fuck.

It looked like someone might be killing Ladies of the Night. As usual. They were always an easy target for gutless nutcases. But this time they were *my* Ladies of the Night. I mean, whether I liked it or not, it was my town, my island.

I looked down at Jane and she looked up at me. Of the two of us, Jane looked fresher and brighter and cleaner. I said, "You got it made, being a dog. 'Cause I gotta say, this really boils my blood. It makes me ashamed to be human. Even worse, to be a male."

Jane smiled. It sure looked like a smile.

As I said this, I came to my senses. I remembered it wasn't only men who were boils on the butt of humanity. I remembered some of us were women named Mrs. Zawadzki. And some of us were called Lady Macbeth.

How the hell was I going to find that car? Lino would just root around via departments various until he found its plate and then the name and address that went with the plate.

Without my good friend Lino's say so, no one was giving me that kind of information.

So now what?

So now I had to hope my good enemy Mickey Cates

would talk to me.

If I were him, I wouldn't. Not after how long I'd dogged him for the killer he was.

"Jane," I said to the best friend I had in the world, "when we see Cates, no growling, no biting, not even a dirty look. And do you think you might conjure up one of those smiles?"

All I got was a look.

6

After four hours fighting the floor on a floor mat, Jane and I were driven out of a disturbing dream of a small woman in a huge sweater chopping me into a Russo stew. Well, *I* was in the middle of a dream like that. Fuck knows what Jane was dreaming about; all four paws were twitching. It was Stapleton and its damn church bells that woke me. Not only Stapleton, but New Brighton, St. George, Tompkinsville, Clifton… damn, every single burg tipping towards the sea had some sort of church. The island had always been big on churches and the churches had a real thing about bells.

Jane needed her walk. She needed to make a deposit in Tompkinsville Square which wasn't a square but a triangle. I needed a cuppa coffee which I bought from the soda jerk kid in the ground floor Rexall and drank while Jane did what she did in the park. Close to a whole year with me, she was on good footing with a lot of grass, the dirt behind particular bushes, several favored paving stones, all the whores, three or four old ladies, and about half a dozen bums.

By eight a.m. we were tending Holly. Today's nurse changed her dressings—I peeked, not bad, and I knew bad after Jane was sliced up—while I fed her. Holly's breakfast was gruel. The way I grew up, I knew gruel when I saw it. But runny flavorless gruel was about all her throat could take.

Jane lay on the bed, rested her head on Holly's arm, careful not to touch any of her bandaged cuts, never taking her eyes off Holly's face. Neither of Holly's nurses could of stopped her—and I'm here to say they tried.

Mrs. Willingford's hired nurses were turning out OK. Neither was what you'd call charming. Or even pleasant. But if Holly thought she was female, then to them that's what she was.

For that, they were gold in my book.

I'd decided if they could behave, I could behave. And we all got along just fine. Up to a point. The point was my room. The old pot bellied stove, the tin bathtub holding up the table, the toilet down the hall, the creep in 4-C, the horse pictures all over the walls, what I liked to call my drapes which if you touched 'em, could send up an impressive glot of dust, a dog in the "sick room" not to mention *on* the sick bed—none of this was up to their usual standards. But the hell with that. They wanted her in a private nursing home. I wanted her in my place.

A day or so back, we'd all turned to Holly. Someone had thought to ask her. I admit it wasn't me.

Holly wrote: *Sam's.*

I knew it. And I couldn't help smiling about it. Sam's it was.

Holly was still in terrible pain, she was still doped to the gills, and she still couldn't say more than a few words at a time, but we were getting somewhere. I leaned over and turned off the radio—fortunately I'd already heard the first episode of *Richard Diamond, Private Detective*, a singing gumshoe no less, so I knew who dunnit.

"You got into an expensive car, Holly. Do you remember that?"

A head nod.

Hey. We were getting somewhere.

"Do you remember who was in it?"

Another head nod.

"Two men, right?"

A yes.

"Two men in nice clothes. Maybe rich men?"

Another yes.

"Their names? Do you know their names?"

No.

"Did you go somewhere close? In Stapleton or Clifton?"

No.

"Then Manhattan?"

No.

"The other way? Bayonne? Or south?"

"Souf."

Holly had begun to cry. Holly crying made Jane sit up, cock her furry head and yodel deep in her furry throat. It made her nurse push me aside. "Leave her alone, Mr. Russo. She's still in no shape to talk about this. Honestly, can't you see she's in no shape to talk at all?"

But Holly held up her hand. She was intent on talking around her wired jaw, her swollen face awash with tears. The pain must of been something because Holly wasn't a crybaby.

"'Errr's 'aitlin?"

The words weren't clear but we heard them.

Nurse B, leaning close, said, "I think she's asking for someone."

Holly nodded her head. "'Aitlin. 'Id oo fin' 'er?"

I knew who she meant. She was asking about Caitlin,

a little brunette she went on her walks with, in and out of the park. Caitlin, who lived, I think, not too far from the house of horror where I grew up—somewhere on Jersey Street near Castleton—was almost as lovely as Holly, a sweet young dark haired thing in a nice freckled package. Once or twice, we'd taken her with us when we went to the movies. Not my movies, but the kind Holly and Caitlin liked: June Allyson or Kathryn Grayson movies, dizzy stuff like that.

I'd thought: hell, if she'll go to mine I'll endure a few of hers.

Another thing. Caitlin was female. I think.

"Caitlin got in the Lagonda too, Holly?"

A nod. Vigorous and painful.

"Where did they take you two? Do you know?"

A shake of her head.

"Was it far?"

Again, a nod.

"A city?"

No.

"Into the countryside?"

Holly shut her eyes.

"She's tired, Mr. Russo. I must insist you leave her alone now."

For once, I agreed. I rose from my chair by her bedside, Jane at my heels, but turned back. Holly was trying to talk.

"'Ig 'ouse."

"A big house in the countryside south of here? On the island?"

Nodding, Holly tried to smile. Her smile about killed me.

Time to go back to the Green Garter. Time to talk once more to Sal. But really it was time to try and talk to Mickey Cates. He might not talk back, but I was counting on the idea that he would. I hoped he'd talk because he'd think if he was to give me a little something I cared about, I'd give him a little something. For instance, I might stop dogging him. He was wrong. No matter what he gave me, even if it turned out to be the latch key to the big house Holly'd been taken to, when this was all over—and I'd survived it—I would still be on him like the fleas that were never on Jane. This was another odd thing about Jane. I couldn't say why, maybe because she scared 'em, but fleas didn't bite African dogs called Jane Russo.

Anyway, Cates was a cold blooded killer. If Murder, Inc. was still in business, no doubt Cates was a valued employee. Killers like Mickey Cates didn't get a pass.

But I had to try to get to him. If anyone knew the ugly underbelly of the Isle of Staten, Mickey did.

Sunday at noon and there they were, Sal sweeping up the glass from the usual hell of a Saturday night, Mickey on his personal barstool nursing a beer. In a dark back booth a coupla dubious customers were bent over doing something dubious. But who cared? There were always a coupla gumboils just like 'em in every strip joint I'd ever seen.

I sat myself down on the stool right next to Cates, the one nearer Sal—although what I thought Sal could do if Mickey took it into his noggin to slug me I couldn't say.

Jane, as usual, made things a little more even steven. Just as Mickey was swinging his heavy Irish head my way with its mane of curly Irish hair—no way would I call the swing friendly—from a crouch, my dog hopped up onto the barstool on the other side of him. Mind you, these were padded barstools which swiveled. Her momentum should of spun her right off. But it didn't. She landed like a frog on a lilypad and stuck there, where she then gave Mickey Cates her full attention, eyes squinting, eyeteeth shining. It was no friendlier than his would of been if he weren't so damned impressed.

So was I.

As for me, I'd practiced my suave the whole way to Hannah Street. If I hadn't walked through the door as composed as Bogie in a tight spot, I was close. I felt like a friend I'd made a few months back, the actor Jimmy Stewart. Jimmy's calm could calm a mob.

Forgot to mention, Jimmy'd sent me a postcard from somewhere he was stuck filming what he wrote was "a stinker." Besides himself, it starred Joan Fontaine and a chimpanzee. Out of respect for a great guy, I didn't go see it. But I did pin the postcard on the wall near the ice box. It now sat propped against the table lamp near Holly's head where she could see it whenever she wanted. Holly loved Stewart. I'd already told her soon as she was fightin' fit again, I'd introduce her.

And I would.

But for now, Jane and I were bookending Mickey Cates. Sal and his broom had moved towards the door. Whether to keep watch or beat a fast getaway, I didn't know.

In for a penny, in for a pound. I said, "In the Lagonda, those two guys— "

Mickey didn't say a thing, just turned his beer round and round on the bar top. He had beautiful hands.

"—they took Holly somewhere in the center of the

island, some big house. They also took a friend of hers, a working girl called Caitlin. You ever hear of her? Caitlin?"

Nothing. Just that cold glass going round and round in those deadly hands.

"Holly came back, Mickey. Beat all to hell, strangled and stabbed and left for dead. Never going to be Holly again, not my Holly and not her Holly, but she came back. Now Caitlin—"

I had his attention. I knew I did. His hands had tightened on the glass and the glass had stopped turning.

"What are ye sayin'?" That voice, his musical voice was as cold as death.

"Caitlin didn't come back."

Mickey swung his stool towards me so fast, even Jane, who'd leapt from stool top to bar top, couldn't of stopped him if he'd meant me harm. Good thing he didn't mean me harm.

"Where is the lass?"

"If you mean Caitlin, I don't know. That's why I came. To ask for your help."

A moment passed, two. He stared at me until he chilled the bones in my face. If he wanted, I was a dead man. If he was feeling good, I was a cripple.

He said, "Whenever ye call, I'll come. Whatever ye need of me and mine, is yours."

Hard work, but I kept my mouth from falling open.

7

Cates was as good as his word. All three of us, me and Mickey and Jane, were out the door of the Garter and into a neat black Mercury coupe with red upholstery.

As a throwaway kid who didn't know cars from beans, I'd grown into a man who knew horses like I knew my own heart, but still didn't know cars from beans. But this car I could get to know.

Jane seated in the back, her white paws crossed, her haunches ready for anything, her chiseled head right off an Egyptian tomb, Mickey drove us south, right out of Stapleton on Victory Boulevard. I had no idea where we were going, but we were getting there fast, a lot faster than the law allowed. Somewhere we turned off Victory, and were instantly into wooded farmland.

It was like we were invisible. I didn't see a cop once, not even one walking a beat. As for one riding a horse or even a bicycle, we didn't see any of those either.

Cates didn't say a thing until we were well past anything that looked like a town, and turning onto a dirt road heading toward an old white farmhouse and an old red barn. There was a thin curl of smoke leaking out of the farmhouse chimney.

"You keep yer yap shut unless I tell ye to talk. Got it?"

"I got it."

He jerked his thumb towards the back seat. "And that?"

I turned in my seat. "You heard the man, Jane. No

talking."

For that, I got a hum from Jane and a look from under the brim of Cates' hat I can only describe as "one more word out of this boyo, bedad, and it's him for the pot."

My Irish was as fluent as my French—or, for that matter, my English.

We weren't half way to the wide front porch, rockers included, before the barrel of a rifle appeared in a first floor window. And a second barrel poked through the open barn door. I knew those rifles. I'd seen a lot of 'em during the war. They were M1 carbines. I'd had one myself. I'd know the look and sound of 'em anywhere. They weren't so hot against tanks, but for flesh and bone they were just the ticket.

Mickey stopped, stepped in front of me, whipped off his hat and held up his left palm. The barrel in the window disappeared, though not the one in the barn. Around that same moment, the front door of the house opened. As it did, Jane and I heard a horse neigh in the barn. There was the dull thud of a hoof against wood. The horse was acting up. Probably didn't like the carbine or the man. My bet was on both.

The genius in the barn had a high piping voice. He may have had the weapon but that voice was sharp with fear. "Shaddup, ya crummy nag."

The next sound wasn't a thud, but a long shrill whinny, accompanied by a yelp of pain from the gunslinger.

I hadn't met the horse and I hadn't met the genius—but I already liked the "nag."

There were four fat faces sitting around the kitchen table. Compared to Mickey, they looked harmless enough. White shirts and braces, jackets off but hats on in the house, two big ashtrays spilling ash on the checked red and white oilcloth, a fug of smoke that was barely breathable, what they were sure to call "gats" in shoulder holsters, four pairs of shiny black shoes. In front of each was a plate of something eatable. I couldn't tell what it was but it smelled like they'd all live through it.

As soon as Jane walked in, the fattest of the four fat men smiled. It was an engaging smile, one you could believe in if it weren't for the holstered gun. And the knife strapped to a leg big enough and round enough to string phone wire from.

"Mickey," he said. The way he said it sounded surprised. But not too wary. Not enough to make me any more jumpy than I already was.

"Mullan," said Mickey. "Behan. O'Brady. Donnelly."

Each nodded the best they could with all that fat under their Irish chins. And here I thought the Irish were thin wiry fellas.

Mullan said, "Sit yerself down, Mickey. Sit yer friend down. The dog herself has already made a wee home."

I glanced at the dog herself. Jane had gone straight to the wood-burning stove and was now posed near it. It was her sphinx pose and she was good at it. She'd chosen not only the warmest place in the kitchen, but the best place to keep an eye on all of us. It was also midway between two doors.

Mickey made no move to do more than stand right where he was. "I won't, thank ye, Mullan. I've come about Caitlin."

In an instant, the whole room changed. The four men seemed thinner, the air thicker. The smile on Mullan's face fell into his plate. The other three, only one had a name I'd caught—Behan—sat as still as headstones.

"And what is this about Caitlin?" said Mullan.

"She's gone. Your man here is looking for her."

"Your man" meant me. I stood taller, pressing my back on the heavy air.

"What do ye mean, she's gone?"

"Tell himself what ye mean, Russo."

All those eyes turned on me, including Jane's. The three scarred bullet holes near my heart began to ache. The headache I'd fought the whole ride here, suddenly won.

I told them what I meant. "I have a friend called Holly. Holly has a friend called Caitlin. The Saturday night before last, they both got into a Lagonda. When Holly got in, the car was parked on Hannah Street near Bay. I don't know yet where Caitlin got in. Two well-dressed men were in that car. Six days ago Holly was found in a sea bag in Tompkinsville Square. She'd been stabbed, strangled, and beaten almost to death. There's no doubt she was meant to die. Caitlin hasn't come back. Dead or alive."

The silence in this farmhouse kitchen was loud enough to hurt my ears. And it went on for a long time.

Mickey finally broke it.

"Yez heard the man. What's to be done?"

Mullan turned his now sad eyes full on me. "And ye, who are ye?"

"A private eye."

"Who do ye work for, gumshoe?"

"This time I work for me."

"What about the police?"

"The cops don't give a fig about Holly. I expect you

know why. I won't be going to the cops for anything. But I care. I care about Caitlin too. We all went to the movies together. We ate popcorn. I mean to do something about this."

"Ye could die doing something, me lad."

"I suppose I could. But Holly's my friend. When a man's friend almost gets killed, he's supposed to do something about it."

"Ah, I see ye know yer Bogart."

"A hobby of mine."

"Has Mickey told ye who Caitlin is by way of being?"

"Mickey isn't fond of talking. At least not to me."

I got a smile from three of the four fat Irishmen. So far, this whole thing had felt like a court martial or getting sent down to Mister's office—again—for stealing his ciggies. A warm nose shoved itself into my hand and with that, everything was different. Just the feel of Jane's nose changed it all, down to the smell of the place.

I said, "Cates brought me here. I'm not dead. There must be a reason."

"The reason is Caitlin."

"I figured."

"Our Mickey here, he's after being in love with the wee poor girl."

I snuck a look at Cates. His ears were red.

"But she won't have him. Prefers to walk the streets. This is never a good thing for a man's heart. Some men might stop her, permanent. But not our Mickey. He just drinks and nurses his eternal hopes."

With a terrible tooth rattling scrape, Mickey pulled out a chair and sat in it. That left just me and Jane, still standing, still being stared at.

"Funny thing about Caitlin is we all have this feeling for her. Every man at this table, every man in this house, married or not. So when ye say Caitlin is gone, every man hurts. How can we help ye to help our Caitlin?"

"Find that Lagonda."

"Done."

"You know Caitlin. You know what she does and where she lives. Get out the word, look for her everywhere."

"Done again. And what shall ye be after doing, Mr. Russo?"

"Waiting for Holly to remember more about the two men and the big house. And when she does, I might need a few hands——"

"Done for the third time. Ye need us, ye go to see Mickey. We learn something, we'll be telling Mickey."

And that was that. Mickey drove Jane and I back to my place as silently as he'd driven us away.

This time I paid attention. If I had to, I could find that farm again. Not that anyone'd be there. An hour after Cates and I were gone, the tires of his Mercury blowing back dust and grit, it was a dead cert that house would be deserted, angry horse and all.

I awoke from another dream. This one was about four fat men holding up the world. None of them looked like Atlas, all of them looked like Irishmen. The world they carried was square and each man had a corner resting on the slack fat of his naked white back. They were talking, but not to each other.

I'd understood every word when I heard it, but getting woken by a mouthful of sharp teeth made it all suddenly sound like gibberish. Which I think it was.

Jane was nipping my ear.

My eyes flew open to that light that comes to the corner of Bay and Victory in downtown Stapleton just before dawn. It's a cold light, weak and dreary and gray. Something about it drains the blood from a man's heart. In a light like that, who would wanna wake up?

"Fuck off, Jane."

Jane gave me a few minutes. I used them to listen for the sound of Holly breathing, to know she wasn't sleeping Marlowe's Big Sleep, when Jane nipped me again.

And then I heard what Jane was hearing. The slightest tapping at my chamber door.

Someone was out there, in the hall, on the other side of 4-A, gently rapping.

It wasn't the hairy beast from 4-C. He wouldn't tap or rap, he'd pound. It wasn't Detective Lino Morelli. Lino'd rap with his knuckles and if that didn't work, hit it with the butt of his gun. It wasn't Mickey Cates or any of his Irish friends. They'd kick the door in. It wasn't Jimmy Stewart. He wouldn't disturb a man at an hour like this unless that man or his dog was on fire. And it wasn't a raven.

I suddenly knew who it was.

I kept still for a few seconds more, mainly to soothe myself with the sound of Holly breathing. Her broken nose was healing. No more snoring. I'd never tell her she snored. I didn't tell her it wasn't the same nose she and I were used to. I didn't tell her it bent to the left now. She'd already had about all she could take. But the rattle was less. I waited for the day I could joke about it. That could be a long time coming, but I'd be there for it.

Jane was on our side of the door, tail curled over her back, staring. She knew as well as I did who was out there.

"Sam? You awake, Sam?"

I was awake all right, I just wasn't dressed. But what the hell—a person visits a person before dawn, a person gets what they get.

I swung open the door in my skivvies.

One of those hats, the foreign perfume, and that woman swept into my room. The rich one. The great looking one. The pushy one. The one who'd adopted me—sort of like I'd adopted Jane, now that I thought about it. Right behind her came her "chauffeur" Woody, cleaned and pressed, with a large covered basket over his arm.

I smiled at the man who'd once saved my life—another story for another time. I got a good humored nod in return.

"Love the outfit," said Mrs. Willingford, "and so does Woody. Set the basket on the—oh! Is that a table? I think it's a table. Set it there, Woody, and then wait in the car. We won't be long."

What did she mean by "we"?

"What do you mean by 'we'?"

"Jane, my darling dog, wait 'til you see what I brought you. All the way from California."

Jane was dancing on her pure white toes, a smile on her pointy mug as wide as any I'd ever seen for me. But then, Jane approved of Mrs. Willingford. There weren't many I could say that about. I approved of Mrs. Willingford as well. But at—I glanced at a Big Ben clock barely visible on what I liked to think of as my bureau—five in the morning?

Mrs. Willingford fished some sort of chew toy out of the basket and offered it to Jane. Jane sniffed, thought about it, then opened her mouth slowly. When it was opened just wide enough, she took the toy between her teeth as carefully as I'd pick up a cactus.

"Holly's asleep," I said, "right over there."

"I know Holly's asleep. That's why I'm whispering."

"OK. I get that. And thank you. But why are you here? And why so early?"

"Because that's when Joker's private plane landed at your airport. Have you ever seen your airport? It has one dirt runway and half a hanger."

"You exaggerate."

"I do not. Don't touch the basket. Aside from a few things for Jane, I've brought all that for your friend."

"Brought all what?"

Mrs. Willingford was unpinning her hat, unpeeling her gloves, looking for a place to sit down. "She'll love it all. The latest in everything, straight from I. Magnin. I'd like a cup of coffee, please."

"The drugstore's still closed."

"Then for heaven sakes, make some. I've been flying about in a small noisy airplane for hours. Where's your bathroom?"

Oh fuck. The bathroom.

"Do you really need it now?"

"What kind of question is that? Of course I need it now or I shouldn't have asked."

"In that case, come with me."

I took Mrs. Willingford to the bathroom, a rather grand name for what had become of the small room Holly and I once had to ourselves. One look, and we were back in my place.

There was no more mention of bathrooms.

"When does the nurse arrive?"

"Eight."

"We can't wait for that. I certainly can't. Leave her a note. Where's your telephone? I know you have a telephone. Aha! There it is."

By five thirty a.m, Holly had been carefully loaded into a private ambulance, as had Jane. I had to do the best I could finding a seat. By six thirty a.m., we were in Mrs. Willingford's Park Avenue apartment. Holly was tucked away in a huge bed in a huge room that had more medical stuff in it than the average hospital.

Mrs. Willingford waved at it. "Joker's old. And careful. He says if he's going to die, which he's not sure he'll bother doing, he's dying here, in his own home. Surrounded by his Chubb safe. With his gentleman's gentleman in the next room."

"His——"

"His valet. Blackwell is also our butler. He cleans dentures like nobodies business. We have a room just like this in all our homes."

"And they each have a safe?" I was holding Holly's hand. Jane was licking her foot. The foot was poking out from under silk sheets. Even Holly's feet were small and delicate.

In at least one way, the gods had been good to Holly. Getting born the year Bubbling Over won the Derby—it suddenly occurred to me: Bubbling Over, what a perfect name for Holly, for the way she'd been, for the way she'd be again if I had anything to do about it—had kept her far away from the horror of war and from being someone called Baby Shauer fighting in it.

Holly'd woken up as three big guys in white had gentled her down our four flights of stairs, fallen asleep in the ambulance once we were on the ferry, woken once more for her grand entry into a massive white building on Seventy First Street where it crossed Park Avenue.

I didn't know it yet but I was getting my first look at what real money could buy. Enough bedrooms and bathrooms for each of the kids in my cheery dorm back at the Olde Alma Mater: a library, a ballroom, a whole bunch of wood-burning fireplaces, a rooftop garden with a private bungalow—a butler and valet called Blackwell, as proper as William Powell's Godfrey, and a lot of black faces running around doing whatever they were told to do.

And I thought we'd abolished slavery.

To be fair, there were a few white faces in the crowd.

I was covering Holly's foot with a blanket made out of

what seemed spun gold when the guy right out of all those Dr. Kildare movies walked in. And if it wasn't him, it was his twin.

"Ah," he said in one of those movie doctor voices, "and this is the patient?"

Jane was at his ankles which he pretended not to notice, but he noticed all right, and I was making sure I got in the way. "All right, Mrs. Willingford, who's this character and what's he doing here?"

"This character," she said, removing one less than perfect yellow rose from the vase by Holly's bed, "is Doctor Jacob Bloomberg, the best plastic surgeon Joker's money can buy. Not that there's much of a choice. Plastic surgeons are thin on the ground. Lucky for us this is New York City. They tend to clot here."

Bloomberg, who'd been preening, stopped. "I've served in the war, Madam. I studied in England."

If Mrs. Willingford heard him, she gave no sign. "Dr. Bloomberg's going to give your friend back the face she once had, perhaps even improve things a little. Although I can tell she's already a beauty." She waved the rose at me. "You rascal, Sam."

No point in explaining Holly to Mrs. Willingford. She'd find out soon enough.

Holly wasn't asleep. And if she had been, she wasn't now.

"Oh darlings," she said round her wired jaw, "ask him to remove my mole while he's at it, would you?"

Dr. Bloomberg, who carried a little too much weight around his middle and was just a little too short to replace the guy who played Dr. Kildare, gave her a smile filled with perfect teeth. "When we're through, young lady, you'll look better than new." He turned and waved us all away, especially Jane. "I'd like to speak with my patient now. If you'd all be kind enough to step out of the room and give us some privacy?"

No one moved.

Holly turned her green and pleading eyes on us. They were both green again, although the bruised one looked smaller than the unbruised one.

"I'd really like this, Sam. I really need it. Please?"

That did it. What Holly wanted, if it was in my power, Holly got. I'd never envied Mrs. Willingford's money before, but I did now. There were some things money could buy.

I looked at her and she looked at me and I knew that mole was a goner.

Me and Mrs. W. obeyed Dr. Bloomberg. Jane didn't. Jane wasn't budging. I had to pick her up and carry her out yodeling in protest.

A half hour later, attended by Blackwell the butler, a guy dust wouldn't land on, we were sitting around on some dead queen's living room furniture drinking coffee out of cups a mouse would have trouble with and eating cream puffs—which wasn't easy when you're also admiring Mrs. Willingford's legs. Admiring various parts of Mrs. Willingford was something I usually did when I got the chance. I'd also been telling her all I knew about what might have happened to Holly and what *did* happen to me when Mickey Cates introduced me to his fat friends, New York City's Irish mob. Or maybe only Staten Island's Irish mob. Around about here somewhere, Mrs. Willingford gasped. "A Lagonda? Good grief, one of Joker's friends has a Lagonda. He talks about it all the time. Isn't that right, Blackwell?"

"Perfectly true, Madam."

"You bet it is," she said, beaming at Blackwell, "believe you me, when that boob shows up, with or without his Lagonda, I get scarce real fast."

I spilled coffee out of my tiny cup. Blackwell was wiping it up almost before it could land on the queen's footstool. "What color?"

"I presume you mean the car?"

"What color is the damn car?"

"It's blue, dammit yourself, with darker blue fenders. If I were an art critic, I'd say it was something from Picasso's Blue Period."

9

The year I'd decided I'd been born, the great Man o' War should of won the Kentucky Derby. He didn't win it because he wasn't entered in it. He wasn't entered because his owner, a fella named Samuel Doyle Riddle, didn't much like what he called "the west." Kentucky was his idea of the west.

Another damn Irishman, Riddle was in the wool business as well as the horse business.

I'd bumped into Mr. Riddle at Belmont once, right after the Belmont Stakes, the race he'd won with War Admiral. By "bump into," I mean just that. I was seventeen, cocky as all get-out, and racing through the crowd to make a bet before the next race went off. I knocked the old man's hat off, stepped on his spats, came this close to tipping him over a railing.

He wasn't nice about it. The woman he was with, at least fifty years his junior, wasn't nice about it either. They both claimed I'd done it on purpose. The woman said I must be a pickpocket, and a damned bad one. I came this close to getting thrown off the track until the guards found I had only enough money on me to place a small bet and no more. I guess they figured a pickpocket ought to carry more cash.

Standing in the middle of the Willingford sitting room, its white ceiling high over my head with a leering pink-cheeked cupid in each corner, I'd just met Joker Willingford. I don't know why, but it felt like I was looking at Samuel D. Riddle with his once white hat rolling along the racetrack turf along with all those cigarette butts and bad bets.

Joker was about as old as I'd expected him to be: old. If he could've straightened up, he'd of come up to my nose. I also expected him to be as frisky as his horses. I was right about that one too. One thing I hadn't expected was the limp. Mrs. Willingford never mentioned a limp.

First thing he said to me was, "What kind of a dog is that?"

I had my hand out, expecting a handshake from the husband of Mrs. Willingford. Mrs. Willingford was lying back on some sort of couch lighting a cigarette with an enameled lighter the size of my only pan. She had a small blodge of cream on her nose. And she wasn't making a move to smooth things along. Jane had finished her third cream puff. Her nose was spotless. She sat perfectly still on one of Joker's antique chairs and squinted at him.

"Egyptian."

"Looks it. What got to her? Looks pretty chewed up."

I dropped my hand and lit my own cigarette. I used a book match from the Green Garter. "Stabbed and shot."

"Mrs. Willingford told me some about that."

I was thinking: even Joker called his wife Mrs. Willingford.

Joker was saying: "All in the line of duty. I like that in a dog. I'm a horse man, myself."

A horse man? The old man leaning on a silver topped cane in a Park Avenue joint big enough to house half of Stapleton owned Joker's Special Blend, one of Kentucky's biggest distilleries. Owning a place that made booze allowed him to afford a Kentucky horse spread called Beeswing Farm where one of America's leading stallions, Jokers Wild, stood at stud for more money per pop than I'd seen in my whole life.

I said, "I know. I've met Fleeting Fancy."

"Great filly, ain't she? Whadda sprinter. Kinda like Mrs. Willingford here."

Mrs. Willingford had nothing to say about that. But if I knew her at all, and I thought I did, Joker would pay in some exquisite way for calling her a horse. I could think of her as a horse, and the worst one I'd ever heard of, but I couldn't say it.

It was time to take some control here. So far, all the running'd been made by Mrs. Willingford—and now Mr. Willingford was in the lead. For the first time in weeks I thought about Bogie. Would he stand for this? The fuck he would. I'd laugh except it wasn't a laughing matter. It hadn't been funny even once since Holly went missing.

I flicked the spent match in the general direction of an ashtray. It missed but I liked that. It made me look like I was one of those "devil-may-care" kind of guys. In the silence since Joker's last words, I'd just stood there smoking and staring at him.

I said, "You have a friend who owns a Lagonda."

"Yup. Sure do."

"My friend Holly got into a Lagonda one night and the next thing anyone knew she was nothing more than a pulped and bloody mess in a sack. I need to know who your friend is."

"Oh my god. Is she dead?"

"She's in one of your bedrooms with a Dr. Bloomberg. She'll live but not as the Holly she was."

"In one…?" Joker took one limp forward, then stopped. "Your doing, Mrs. Willingford?"

Mrs. Willingford looked up. The cream was still on her nose. She was still as beautiful as Fleeting Fancy. She did not smile. "We can afford it."

"Who said we couldn't? But you don't think William would do such a thing?"

"I have no idea what little Billy would do," she said.

"Well, I do. Nothing. William Ransom Cunningham III hasn't done a blasted thing since he was born. Except spend his Daddy's money."

Time for me again. "Mr. Willingford, do you know how many Lagondas are presently running around New York?"

"One?"

I had no more idea than he did but I was sure one, especially one painted like the one Holly'd stepped into, was about the right number.

"One. And Billy, whoever he is, owns it."

"Then it was stolen."

"Was it?"

"Son, I haven't the foggiest. Me and Mrs. Willingford here have been out California way."

"So call him."

So he rang for Blackwell to hand him the phone, and when it was dialed for him and answered, Blackwell did as ordered—he handed over the phone. Joker asked for Billy. We all waited long enough to grow mold, and then, just before Joker slammed down the receiver in Blackwell's gloved and patiently waiting hands, someone answered. Joker Willingford was told the car was tucked away in its private garage.

Mrs. Willingford said, "Tell him to look."

Mr. Willingford said, "William doesn't do things like look."

"Tell him to tell someone to look."

We all waited some more for whoever had to go look, to look. While we waited Joker eased himself into a chair nearest the telephone, Jane ate another cream puff offered on a silver salver by a maid—in she came, and out she went, no thanks from anyone—Mrs. Willingford noticed her nose, and I wondered if Jane would do as she'd once done: throw up her food. Four cream puffs could do it. If so, the mess would be gone before it spoiled anyone's view.

Joker'd fallen asleep waiting for Billy the Third. The receiver was just about to slip out of his hand when we all heard his voice. It sounded like Oliver Hardy yelling at Stan Laurel. Joker translated. "Car's there. Nice and snug. Now what's all this about?"

I said, "Ask him when's the last time he drove it."

"A month, at least," said Joker, listening to an annoyed spoiled brat. A forty-five-year-old annoyed spoiled brat.

"Ask him who could get to his car."

I got to see another side of Joker when the answer came through. "Now you listen to me, goddammit. You talk to me like that again and I'll have you horsewhipped within an inch of your life." Joker slammed the receiver home and turned to me. "Blamed idiot doesn't know a damned thing. S'far as I can tell, only the folks in his building can get near his cars."

"Where's his building?"

"Right here. He owns the fifth floor."

The good doctor chose that moment to enter a room

filled with Park Avenue sun—morning had showed up around the same time he did. He bent over to whisper into Mrs. Willingford's ear, and then he stood up again, looking grim. Not to mention righteous.

My heart in my mouth, I said, "What's the matter? Is something the matter?"

Mrs. Willingford gave me her widest, most dazzling smile. "Holly is not quite as advertised."

"So?"

"So, Dr. Bloomberg is concerned."

I looked at Bloomberg. "Does your concern mean you're not helping her?"

Mrs. Willingford cut in before the doc had a chance to answer. "Oh, he's helping her. And now he's doing it for free and he's doing it to the utmost of his ability. If not, he'll never see a single one of my friends and neighbors again."

Dr. Bloomberg turned green. His green wasn't a patch on the green of Holly's green eyes.

"Can't wait to see your handiwork, doc," I said to Bloomberg's stiff retreating back.

Mrs. Willingford set down the Bloody Mary which had appeared via Blackwell at some point during Joker's call to Billy. Arched of eye, she looked me over carefully.

"As I think I've already said, you little ol' rascal you."

Mrs. Willingford and I were going to need a talk.

Right after breakfast, Joker Willingford went off somewhere with Woody driving. Mrs. Willingford also disappeared. But since the Willingford place took up the top of the building and the top of the building had a bunch of different layers each at different heights, she could of hailed an air balloon for all I knew and sailed off for the Chrysler

Building. Or she could of been bathing in a tub Joker'd bought at Cleopatra's fire sale. Who knew? The good doctor Bloomberg was off arranging whatever needed arranging to rearrange Holly's face. And, if I knew anything at all about how things worked in the Willingford world, to also remove her mole. So it was just me and Jane and Holly and a covey of hired hands holding down the fort.

Holly was propped up in one of the Willingford's huge beds in one of their huge rooms, the one Joker thought he might or might not die in, a needle in her arm attached to a tube attached to a bottle of something, surrounded by Jane and all the stuff Mrs. Willingford had brought her in that basket. It was some haul. Perfumes, cosmetics, creams and lotions, silk underwear, silk pajamas, silk slippers, silk scarves.

"Sammy dearest," she said, "when you said Lois was A OK, I never dreamed she was this A OK."

"Lois?"

"Isn't that her name? She said it was her name."

"Mrs. Willingford is one surprise after another. Pretty soon, I'll stop being surprised."

"Hush your mouth," said my Holly through wired teeth, "surprise keeps us alive."

"Surprise keeps me unbalanced."

"What a goose you are. Surprise means alive."

"Surprise means we could all be dead any minute."

"Oh, poo. Will you look at this!"

I looked. "What is it?"

"A snood. All I need now is my hair."

"Forget your hair," I said. "Hair grows back. It's time for

that serious talk I said we'd be having." I'd propped myself up against Joker's pillows, next to the ones Holly was propped up against, careful to keep my shoes off the cover. Jane was already lying along her side, her long nose on her crossed paws, her eyes steady on Holly's fractured face. And I wasn't smoking. It didn't take a genius to figure she didn't need breathing in smoke when just breathing was hard enough. The sonofabitch had almost crushed her windpipe when he'd throttled her.

"Do we have to?" She was turning the snood this way and that.

I took it away from her, tucked it back in the basket. "You bet we do. You made it back. I hate to bring this up, but Caitlin didn't."

Holly flinched. I knew she'd rather inspect a pair of silk stockings. I knew she wanted to stretch them between her fingers. I knew she couldn't. My Holly kept each of her fingernails filed to a perfectly tapered end and buffed to a high gloss. Sometimes they were red, sometimes green, sometimes orange or blue. Now they were jagged and broken.

"Hey!" I said to a passing minion, one who came to a dead stop and stared at me like the jerk I was. "Is there a manicurist in the house?"

The dark haired minion would of been a knock-out if her mouth weren't pulled down, her eyes weren't as hard as lead sinkers, and the muscles moving under her skin weren't strong enough to deck me. She said, "I would prefer, sir, if you used my title."

"You got it. What's your title?"

"Mrs. Cora Applegate. As acting head housekeeper, Mrs. Applegate is considered proper . . . sir." This second "sir" came a few beats too late to be the humble end to her sentence.

"Mrs. Applegate it is. Haven't we spoken before?"

"We have. On the telephone."

I said, "I won't forget, Mrs. Applegate."

"Thank you, Mr. Russo. As for a manicurist, Mrs. Willingford uses a very good one. I can have her here in ten minutes."

10

Mrs. Willingford's woman was there in five minutes.

I got told to get off the bed so she could work. Jane was left just as she was.

In a halting voice husked with hurt, Holly had her nails done as she told me and Jane and Mrs. Applegate, plus some manicurist, what happened the night she got into a two-toned high-priced car.

As soon as she climbed into the back, she was offered a glass of something bubbly. As for the car, she still didn't know one end of a Lagonda from the other. All she knew was it was a cinch she'd be earning in one night what she made in a month—judging by the car, the champagne, and the crystal glass vase with its single red rose. It was May. The weather was fine, but the two guys in the front seat wore their hats pulled low. They had thick scarves wound round their necks. She said stuff like that didn't faze her. A lot of tricks weren't eager to be seen. What worried Holly was how she'd started to feel. A girl on the game knows things. They know when they've been drugged. Holly'd been drugged. She'd struggled against it long enough to know the fancy car was headed south, not north or east or west. Caitlin was her last clear memory. The car'd pulled up somewhere. Caitlin was outside looking in. She'd smiled, but her smile faded fast. Caitlin got it. She'd quickly backed up, but was just as quickly seized by the guy in the passenger seat and dragged into the car. Caitlin yelled until he socked her a good one on the chin. At that point, Holly passed out.

She didn't wake up until she heard the sound of tires bumping over ruts in a dirt road.

Caitlin was slumped over beside her. The two men in front were talking but they weren't making a whole lot of sense. Something about the car and honey and flies and how it was a good night's catch. One said he was pleased the Master was pleased.

I leaned forward. "He said 'Master'?"

"Like it began with a capital letter, Sammy."

"Anything distinctive about their voices?"

"They sounded like johns."

I stopped asking her questions. The questions were slowing her down. So I asked myself instead. If she'd heard right, one of 'em said to the other one that the gift pleased the Master. So he was already pleased, already seen Holly and Caitlin, maybe already chosen them? If so, that could mean a lot of things.

By then, Holly had struggled to sit up in the Lagonda's soft leather seat.

They were headed towards a huge house, a house she thought should be in the Deep South somewhere, the kind that was loaded with house slaves and a passel of fine white folk. It had a front door big enough to shove Saint George through along with his fiery steed and a full grown dragon, and just behind, a hallway where you could hold a joust. Holly said she'd seen more than her share of Errol Flynn movies so she knew a jousting hall when she saw one.

"Any idea where?" I asked.

"Where what?"

"The house."

"I haven't the least idea. But there didn't seem to be another house nearby. Not that I could see at the time. All I could see was a steep dirt road winding down through the trees and some sort of tall iron fence with a big iron gate that had some fancy metal letters on it, I think they were an S and maybe a B—the guy on the passenger side had to get out of the car to open the gate and then close it behind us—and then the road ended in gravel where the house was standing in a clearing with a lot of parked cars. There were a lot more of those dark trees. Spooky, really, the woods at night. I could hear water. Maybe a brook or something. The house was lit up like Christmas at Gimbels, windows galore with candles, but no other lights anywhere at all. It was like out of a movie."

"What movie? Which movie?"

"A horror movie, you adorable man."

"And then what?"

Holly was carefully opening a tube of blood red lipstick using her teeth and the hand not being manicured. "Wow," she husked. "This must be what Joan Crawford wears." In seconds, she was tossing the tube back in the basket. "I can't look like Crawford. The woman's embalmed."

This was where Mrs. Willingford came back. For Mrs. Willingford, the entrance was the picture of quiet modesty. She took off a hat she could of worn to star in *Meet Me in Saint Louis*, slipped off her matching gloves, and sat primly in a chair that belonged in a museum.

Mrs. Willingford got a smile from Holly, a hum from Jane, a nervous bow from the manicurist, her hat and gloves put away by Mrs. Applegate, and a quick nod from me. I was working here.

"And then what happened?"

"Well, Sammy dear, Caitlin came to, and we were both taken round the back way by two other guys—not the guys who drove the car. Those guys went in the front way. After a lot of dark hallways and a lot of closed doors, there was this dressing room and in the room was another girl I knew who usually worked the ferries coming in from Manhattan. Chang Chang? Something like that, a double name with two Cs. And, oh my, what a flower. An Oriental orchid. Much prettier than Anna May Wong. Anyway, Chang Chang was extremely nervous. She couldn't keep still, so they held her down.

"Well, of course by now Caitlin and I were really jumpy. Getting drugged and Caitlin getting slugged and now how they were treating Chang Chang. I swear, Sammy, you were right. This is a hard business. I'm buying a gun."

I could feel Mrs. Willingford holding her tongue. Knowing Mrs. W, I knew that cost her plenty. As much as it cost me. Holly going back on the game? Not if I had a say in it.

"So the three of us were told to get dressed in these fabulous dresses. Honestly, they must have cost a bundle once. A long time ago is what I mean, with all those buttons and hooks. But they smelled. You know, like they'd been worn before, all dusty and sweaty. Moldy too. And the shoes, well—talk about the Wizard of Oz! So when we were dressed and with those wigs on our heads, a ton of curls and ribbons and bows, we were led into the middle of a huge room and made to stand on this little round stage behind these dark black velvet curtains. I felt like a piece of stale wedding cake. On the floor there were these three tall gold candle stands, just bristling with lit candles. Any second, we could of gone up in flames. They told us— ”

"Who's they?”

"Servants, I suppose. They were dressed like servants. All in black velvet like the curtain and the drapes. They said we should look as perfect as we could when the curtain was drawn back. And then we had to do this striptease. I said: get out of *these* dresses? They said, just do your best, honey. Jesus skipping rope, what a mess. I would of thought we'd get laughs, the moves we had to make to get at the hooks, but there was only silence. And then, of course, there was lots of sex all over these rather nice red velvet divans. Ouch!”

The manicurist had slipped.

Jane showed an eyetooth at the poor woman. I didn't see Mrs.Willingford's reaction, but I heard Mrs. Applegate's. She coughed to cover a laugh. The laugh didn't sound too happy to me.

"Terribly sorry, Madam.”

"That's OK, sweetheart. I once bit a guy.”

After that crack, the woman kept her hands to herself.

I didn't know how to ask the question I wanted to ask next, but Holly saw it coming a mile off.

"You wanna know what they did when they saw my... um, my... ”

For the first time ever, I watched Holly blush.

"Right. Your um. What did they do?”

"I got applause. And then I was the first girl chosen.”

"Who chose you, Holly? Who was there?”

"The driver of the car chose me. The one they called the Master.”

If I'd been Jane, that last answer would have me panting.

"The driver was the Master?"

"You bet. Someone said the Master got the first choice and up he stepped. He wasn't dressed like he'd been in the car. Now he was like all the others watching us, wearing some really terrific evening clothes with this cunning black hood and this black mask. So attractive. The mask, not the Master. But I recognized him anyway. It wasn't hard. Zorro masks don't hide everything."

I'd got myself in hand, slowed my heart. "Only men?"

"Mostly. Maybe twenty of them, maybe less. I remember a lot of moustaches, all kinds of moustaches. But there were a few women here and there. I could tell they were pretty good looking women, too."

"If you saw him, would you know him? In the Lagonda, he wasn't masked."

"Oh Sam, you know I never look at my johns. If I don't look, I can pretend... oh, who cares now? But yes, I'm sure if I saw him now I'd know him. And the other one too. Because of what came later."

From one word to the next, Holly changed. From light and flippant, she fell into dark and quiet. The dark and the quiet lasted for a long time.

"Tell me, Holly. How can I help you if you don't tell me?"

Holly turned those eyes on me, her beauty still in them, even with her nose bent and the swelling. "Help me? It's already done, and you've already helped me. Lois has already helped me. What else is there to do?"

"What about Chang Chang? And Caitlin? If we know more we can help them."

Holly was a fighter, a survivor. I watched the fight

slipping away. "No one can help them, Sammy, they're dead. I saw them die. They used me and they used them, and then they killed them both—just like that. Their horrid Master stepped up to Chang Chang holding this silver dagger and I thought it was just for show, as if they all thought it was sexy, and lord help me, but so did I—until he stabbed her right in the heart, and then he cradled her as she died. Like he cared for her ever so much, like he loved her. And all those people in their stupid Zorro masks were smiling while he did it. And making the strangest noises, like people at a séance or something like that. And when I saw that and when I heard it, I broke away from the woman who held my arm, boy, was she strong, and I ran away so fast. You wouldn't believe how fast I ran, shoving people out of the way. I called to Caitlin but by then, it was too late. The Master guy who'd killed Chang Chang had her. She was fighting like a wildcat but the other guy in the car, the one who'd grabbed Caitlin off the street, was there to help him. And then more and more. I found a door and then another door, and then I was outside. None of them followed me outside. I thought I'd made it, Sammy, and I ran and I ran. But this other guy just came out of nowhere. He wasn't one of them. Even in the dark and in the woods I could tell. No nice clothes, no mask. I ran harder, and I almost made it, I did, I saw some lights through the trees, and I called out and a light turned on in a window, and I said you're going to make it, Holly, you're going to live. But then I was tumbling down into a brook, I didn't even see the damn thing, and when I was thrashing in the water, there was this explosion in the back of my head. And then—I simply don't remember a thing until the hospital."

Jane knew fear and sorrow and guilt when she heard

it. She crept closer to Holly, humming deep in her white throat.

Me, I took the hand the manicurist no longer held—a manicurist, by the way, who looked as embalmed as Crawford. I figured she was held up by the starch in her uniform.

"I think it was filmed, Sammy. Before I ran, I saw one of those big cameras. I think they were making a movie."

11

I was turning my head, meaning to look at Mrs. Willingford, hoping to find some comfort there, when the open door suddenly opened wider and in came Blackwell, followed by two delivery men and one box. The box was big enough to hold everything I owned, including Jane. Not that I owned Jane.

"Oh god," said Mrs. Willingford, "I forgot." She waved a hand towards the wall facing the foot of Holly's bed. "Have them put it over there, would you, Cora? And Blackwell, if you'd make sure these men are suitably— "

"Already done, Madam."

If Mrs. Willingford didn't mind being anticipated, she sure minded being interrupted, but all that was gone with Holly's reaction.

If Holly still had her hair, it would of stood on end. "Is it... could it really be... ?"

Mrs. Willingford smiled. "Yes, dear. That's where I've been. Mr. Willingford and I don't have one, but now you do. It's your own television set."

Holly made the kind of noise Jane made when I'd come home after being gone too long.

I'd say it misted my eyes, but Bogie didn't get misty eyed. Not so anyone'd notice.

Mrs. Willingford was pacing. As early as it still was, she had a Bloody Mary in one hand and a cigarette in the other.

At her heels, paced Jane.

I hadn't got more than a foot out Holly's door—Holly was watching her television now, an RCA with a built in radio, engrossed in Ted Mack falling asleep on *The Original Amateur Hour*; I hadn't left until I was sure she was OK—when Mrs. Willingford was at me.

"You'll do something, Sam? What are you doing? I can't sit here. I can't eat. Look at Jane. She can't either. We can't do a damn thing but think about your friend."

"Holly."

"Holly. Where are you going? Wherever it is, I'm coming with you. I'd thought... well, I'd imagined... hell, who am I kidding? I *knew* this kind of obscene horror was out there. But with pots of money, and with Joker in tow, and with—oh fuck it all to hell. I thought I would never get close to the life again. But I was as wrong as I could be. I have gotten close, Sam. With this, with... I'm as close as I've always been." She turned her head towards the door Holly and her television were behind. "Those two in Billy's car let her see them because they knew they were going to kill her. We have to do something about that, Sam. We have to do all we can."

It was Kentucky Derby month. It was halfway through May in the year 1949. The Preakness had already run, the Belmont Stakes was coming up. I'd been called Sam Russo since I could remember calling myself anything. My barely grown mother, whatever her name was and wherever she'd come from, had survived the great influenza epidemic the year "Old Bones," aka Exterminator, took the Kentucky Derby—only to die when someone dumped her at the feet of the two great Zawadzkis. It took a lotta tries, but I'd finally escaped from the Zawadzki Staten Island Asylum for Kids back when Bold Venture won the Derby.

It was 1949, dammit. The war'd been officially over for four years.

Point was, I knew a thing or two by now. And one of those things was if Mrs. Willingford was doing something about Holly, she was doing something about Holly. And not just the nursing and the surgery and the silk stockings. I was stuck with her for the duration.

You wanna know the truth? I was relieved. And so was Jane. I knew it. I'd caught her eye when Mrs. Willingford was walking and talking. My grasp of Egyptian was getting better. She'd said: I trust you, kid, but three is better than two.

Hanging around the USA's best racetrack scratching my head over who could be killing jockeys, then getting mixed up in the murderous middle of a Broadway show called *Harvey* with people like Jimmy Stewart and a couple of giant white rabbits, were two things. Wandering off into the wilds of deepest darkest Staten Island where young girls were stolen off the streets, drugged, passed around like canapés among costumed people in black Zorro masks, then filmed as they were killed for the pleasure of all, was another. With Mrs. Willingford along for the ride, I might survive this one. And I might not. But the odds that I would just got a whole lot better.

Plus, I'd have the use of a car, Woody, the handsome comic book reading side of beef to drive it, and a great looking dame with a fast smart mouth to needle me.

Truth was, to search Staten Island I could use a horse. But a car would be better. I didn't want Jane wearing out her feet.

So OK, I was game to let her tag along again. Thinking back, Mrs. Willingford wasn't half bad as a partner. Thinking back honestly, she'd gotten me out of more than one jam.

"The first thing we have to do," I said, "is find out if your neighbor—Billy the Third—was lying to Mr. Willingford. Either he used his Lagonda that night, or someone else borrowed it. So to speak."

Mrs. Willingford threw her Bloody Mary all over the Oriental carpet. She didn't mean to. But what can you expect when you fling out your arm while you're holding a full glass?

Mrs. Applegate was on the mess faster than Lino on free Havana cigars.

"Of course! Billy! We'll grill 'im."

"If someone else took it, it's not so much a question of 'how' as a question of 'why'. How is easy. Knowing where the car was, and knowing how to get it in and out of this building is a piece of cake. Hell, Jane could do it."

"Hell, Russo, so could I."

That stopped me cold. I'd been mostly talking to myself. But with a crack like that, Mrs. Willingford got my attention. "*You* could do it?"

"Sure. What did you think? All I do is buy racehorses?"

"And hats."

"And hats. Since I last saw you, I took lock picking lessons from the same man who taught you, the one who got us into that apartment where Woody saved your life."

"Jane saved my life."

"True. She would have. But Woody got his shot in first. Anyway, Bayonne's not the moon and Mr. Rudy Hiller is very accommodating."

I absorbed that one like a lightweight absorbed an uppercut from Rocky Marciano. Shit. Mrs. Willingford was already pretty good at my game. I didn't need her getting any better. When I could, I continued. "As I said it's the why of the thing. Why use a car like that car? You'd think all parties involved would choose something hard to remember, not something that stuck out like a sore Lagonda."

"You have a point."

"Thank you."

"Come on, Sam. Let's go grill Billy."

Jane had caught her excitement. She had hold of my coat sleeve and was tugging me gently towards the Willingford front door and I was less gently tugging back when I had a terrifying thought. By all the priests in sainted Ireland, I was going to have to tell Mickey Cates and his four fat Irish friends about Caitlin.

Could it wait? Would they know I'd known long before I told them? I had no idea. Mobs always have ways. But I had to risk it. Telling Cates right now could really gum up the works.

"Grab a hat, Lois. Let's go grill Billy."

As Joker said, all by himself William Ransom Cunningham III took up the entire fifth floor of a Park Avenue building that was home to some of New York City's richest, best connected, most powerful citizens—which could only mean Billy was rolling in it. There seemed to be some sort of guard dressed as an elevator operator on every floor. There were also large economy sized elevator operators. No old men, no skinny kids. Every one of 'em looked like your average weight lifter.

If it weren't for Mrs. Willingford—hatless, gloveless, and not one Tiffany bauble in sight: that's how eager she was to get down from her place to Billy's place—I'd be out on my ear along with all the other riffraff.

Jane, on the other hand, would probably find a nice comfy floor to move into. Assuming she'd leave me. All I knew is I wouldn't leave her.

Call me faithful.

Billy's door opening wasn't like the door opening on Room 4-C back in Stapleton. For one thing, Billy himself didn't open it. A liveried manservant opened it, one about to slam it in my face until he caught sight of Mrs. Willingford. Dressed like one of those guys who hang on for dear life to the back of Marie Antoinette's carriage, he wasn't too pleased about Jane, but what could he do? William the Third might own the entire fifth floor but the Willingford's owned all that stuff at the top of the building.

I felt sorry for the guy. Whirlaway raced in silks like his. On Whirlaway, red and black looked terrific. On him, it looked like dead last.

I looked down at my own colors. A trench coat, light brown or maybe tan, not cheap but not pricey either. A dark brown suit, cheap, off the rack. A light brown tie with darker brown slanted stripes, cheap—one of Lino's castoffs. He'd called it a gift. A pair of brown shoes, not too cheap but cheap enough. I couldn't see it, but I knew my hat was brown too. The hat, the usual fedora, was one of my prize possessions. Bogart had worn one just like it in *The Maltese Falcon*.

In situations like this, I'd seen Bogie run his fingers

around the brim of a hat like mine. So I ran my fingers around the brim of my hat and said in a cheap brown voice, "The third Mr. Cunningham at home?"

The sap in the silks eyed Mrs. Willingford, not me. "He's only just been given his morning coffee, Mrs. Willingford. You know how he is before his coffee."

Mrs. Willingford strong armed him. "Scram, Daniels. If Billy'd swallowed rat poison, and nothing stood between him and his coffin but coffee, we'd still see him. I repeat: beat it. And tell him to put on a robe. I never want to see him without one again."

As said, Mrs. Willingford sailed right past him, Jane's toenails ticking along as Jane trotted at her side. I strolled behind, but never letting either of 'em out of my sight. I could get lost in here.

Daniel, Cunningham's version of Blackwell, was off like a rabbit. Not like the Easter Bunny or Harvey the pooka, more like Bugs Bunny.

I was walking the seeming miles to Billy's boudoir acting like Bogart but thinking like Bugs. She'd seen this character without his robe? She didn't care who knew it? It hadn't been a pretty sight? It made me wonder. How did I look? In the raw.

Glancing into side rooms and up short staircases as we went, I saw three busy maids, one narrow guy in a suit, his hair like a tall black shelf on his head, rushing about with a sheaf of papers—a personal secretary would be my guess— and another guy in a white coat and a white hat I figured for a cook or a nurse or for all I knew the house dentist.

I ignored them and they ignored me.

All this was gone with the wind once we'd walked in on

the guy who owned a Lagonda.

12

William Ransom Cunningham III was lying in the biggest bed I'd ever seen. He could of sailed it across the Atlantic if he'd bothered to add a mast. In it, he was small and round and pink and furious.

Seems Bugs Bunny was more than one of those déjà vu moments. I suddenly felt like I'd walked onto the lot at Warner Brothers and into a Loony Tune starring Porky Pig.

I stopped dead in my tracks and gawped. In an entirely baby blue room, the pig was pitching a fit. If I'd known what I'd been missing hanging around up at the Willingfords, I'd of hotfooted it down here a lot sooner.

Daniels was disgusted. A carafe of coffee in one hand, a delicate white cup in the other, the stink of his disgust hung over him like Mrs. Willingford's perfume. Though Billy didn't mean snap to her, Jane's disgust was plastered all over her face. But Daniels' and Jane's disgust was nothing to Mrs. Willingford's.

Mrs. W. strode to the side of that vast ocean going bed, got a good grip on a fat pink ear, and said, "One more fucking screech, Billy, I'll rip this off. You got it?"

The thing in the bed made a mistake. He hadn't got it.

"Daniels! Call the police!"

Daniels, carefully setting down William Ransom Cunningham III's coffee and cup, loped to the closest gold trimmed phone to begin dialing.

What this did was decide Jane. If Mrs. Willingford was

angry at the piggish man in the bed, then Jane was angry with the man in the bed. So, with a single bound—and I mean a single bound, like the cast of *The Whispering Shadow* escaping another of the Shadow's fiendish radio controlled devices—Jane was planted on his pink chest, her red and white face an inch away from his deep pink face, her white teeth bared.

"Jane! Down!"

That was me.

This was Mrs. Willingford: "Daniels, hang up the fucking phone. No one's calling the cops. Jesus, Billy, knock it off. I'm your goddamn friendly fucking neighbor."

"There's a dog on me." said Billy. These were the first words out of his mouth spoken in less than a shriek. "I don't like dogs."

I knew how he felt. I didn't like dogs either. But then, Jane wasn't a dog, not as I'd understood dogs. Dogs were like a certain Bluto I'd met in a Broadway dressing room. Bluto ate. He slept. He farted. He lifted his leg against anything dumb enough not to notice. He drooled. He sniffed assholes. He licked his privates. He was huge and hairy. He shed. He shit. He stank. Especially when wet. Bluto was a real dog.

Mrs. Willingford perched herself on the edge of Billy's bed.

I wasn't Billy's friendly fucking neighbor. He'd never seen me before, but here I was, in his bedroom. My dog was sitting on him. Mrs. W was close to sitting on his head. And me, I was left standing on his blue carpet in trench coat and fedora wondering what to do with myself. The nearest chair was half a block away. Said chair was sited next to a floor-to-ceiling glass door leading to a balcony with one hell of a view of Central Park. Or it would be if you were standing on it looking west. From inside, you mostly saw a bunch of nice windows across 71st Street.

Daniels had it all under control. He fetched me the chair, found two more dainty cups, and we got some more morning coffee. And then, like *My Man Godfrey*, he shimmered away.

A vision of Carole Lombard arose in my head. She was— she should of been—twelve years older than me, born in the year of Stone Street, the slowest Kentucky Derby winner of all time. But who cared how slow the horse was or how old Lombard was? Stone Street won the Derby. And on the screen, Lombard was silver, she was gold, she was forever young and all I'd ever wanted.

When Man o' War passed, I mourned alone in my room. Back in January of '42, when they found what was left of Carole's plane scattered over the side of a snowy Nevada mountain, I wept.

I was called up a week or so later. Holding the draft notice, I didn't care one way or the other. I was twenty-one years old, I was heart broken, and I was more than ready to die for the Selective Service System.

Crazy thing was: Carole's mom went with her. Her mom was afraid to fly. Carole wasn't. So they tossed a coin for it. Heads: train. Tails: plane.

Carole won. Or she lost. I'd never quite worked that out.

The name of the peak that killed Carole Lombard? The fucking thing was called Double or Nothing.

Billy was staring at us over his covers like that cartoon GIs scrawled over goddamn everything. *Kilroy was here.*

Staring back was Jane who hadn't yet budged.

Mrs. Willingford lit up, inhaled, and blew the smoke over Billy's half-bald head. The other half had thin strings of pale brown hair running across it. I thought that was considerate of her. "I'd like to introduce you to Mr. Russo, Billy. Mr. Russo is a private eye."

Billy's eyes widened with surprise. And fear? Had I seen fear? His glance flicked up and away. He'd looked at something. What was there to look at?

"Mr. Russo has some questions he'd like to ask you."

"Questions? Should I have my lawyer present? He's around here somewhere."

Heard at a lower decibel, Billy didn't sound as he looked. He sounded like Betty Boop.

"Forget the lawyer. You know exactly what I'm talking about. Joker just spoke with you. I was there. I heard him."

"Then you'll know the answers."

"These could be different questions."

"Different?"

"You know, Billy, as in... not the same questions. Sam, you want to take over here. You're the one with the license."

Billy got all perky at the word "license." He held out a short fat arm with its short fat hand full of short fat fingers and wiggled all of them at me. "I'd like to see that license, Mr. Russo."

It wasn't often I got asked about a license. But I had one. I even had it on me, folded away in my brown wallet— another present from Holly, real alligator, expensive—in an inside pocket of my trench coat. I was already talking before he was finished reading every word on the paper.

"You a sporting man, Mr. Cunningham?"

"What do you mean?"

"I mean do you follow any sports?"

"You mean like baseball?"

"Right. Like baseball."

"Well, sure. What real man doesn't?"

I could think of plenty of men, real or otherwise, who didn't like sports. Especially golf. But then, golf wasn't a sport. A sport's not a sport if a guy could get fat playing it.

Billy was still reeling off games. "Tennis. Snooker. Croquet. Golf."

"Horse racing?"

"Oh, sure. I'm partial to all the big races. Especially the Kentucky Derby."

"You and me both. So you remember this year's run?"

"How could I forget? Daniels woke me up just in time to hear I'd lost a bundle. As did Rodegap."

"Rodegap?"

"My secretary, Roger Rodegap. You must have seen him as you came in. Tall fellow, too much hair, too thin. Wasn't that other horse supposed to win?"

"You bet the chalk?"

"Certainly. The favorite often wins."

"Or loses. Win or lose, he pays out nothing. So you went to bed late and slept half the next day?"

"How late I sleep is none of your—that late? Mr. Russo, if I had a nickel for every sun I'd seen rise, I'd have—"

"A big bag of nickels. You like the night?"

"I love the—say, what is this? I thought this was about my car."

"And so it is. You told Mr. Willingford you hadn't driven the Lagonda for at least a month."

"I did say that. Because it's true. Maybe more than a month. I have more than one car."

"Who doesn't? But perhaps you've ridden in it."

"What do you mean? I insist you remove your dog."

"Jane. Move. What I mean is, someone else was driving."

Jane moved. But not far. She went from his chest to his pillow, her nose an inch from his pinched ear.

"I— what does *that* mean?"

"Your car, a car like very few other cars, has been seen out and about several times since you say you've driven it. You may not have been driving, but you could of been— "

Billy's fat little mouth had made a fat little O. "I didn't... I never... I'd like to... I tried, but... "

Daniels, who must of lived in the closest closet, was at his side in seconds. "I don't like your color, sir. Remember what your doctor said about your color."

Billy looked at me, at Mrs. Willingford, at Jane, at Daniels. "My color? Of course, my color. I've recently been informed my health is delicate. Thank you for reminding me, Daniels."

Billy Cunningham the Third composed himself. It was a mighty struggle but he won in the end.

"I need some privacy now. I thank you all for coming. I don't get many visitors. Daniels?"

"Here, sir. As always."

Daniels drew back the pale blue silk covers. For a second there, I thought we'd all be treated to a personal view of a man who had now stopped looking like a confused Porky Pig, and begun looking like that sniveling white porker, Squealer. (I did say Holly had elevated me. I'd read all of *Animal Farm*.) Fortunately Billy was wearing drawers. Unfortunately, they were revealing.

Mrs. Willingford threw a dressing gown at him. One of those slinky black things with dragons and flowers sewn all over them.

"Billy, for all our sakes," she said, averting not only her eyes but her whole head, "put this on immediately." Jane never looked away. She had a stronger stomach than we did.

Billy, struggling into the flowery robe, sobbed, "Daniels!"

"Yes sir?"

"I don't care how you do it, but make these people leave. And the dog. Especially the dog."

Daniels turned on Mrs. Willingford with a face full of concern. A decent salary can make a face look like that. "If you could please— "

"Sure. But if I've told you once, I've *told* you, Joker'd hire you in a snap."

"I am aware of the honor, Madam, but when a man commits himself— "

"He finds padded walls."

For that, she got a smile out of Daniels, one he erased from his face faster than a speeding bullet. Me, I wondered why she'd exchange Daniels for Blackwell. Blackwell seemed fine to me. He was English. Weren't the English born to be butlers? Or perhaps she and Joker needed two butlers, one for Manhattan and one for Lexington. Or one for upstairs and one for downstairs.

Mrs. Willingford and I, following Daniels, were at Billy's bedroom door, when I noticed Jane wasn't with us.

I turned. Jane was back on Billy's chest. And the only reason Billy hadn't made this clear was because Jane's whole face was wrinkled into a snarl, one I'd only seen her use a few times before.

Jane didn't like Billy.

Jane didn't like most people. But Billy really got to her. Now why was that?

I had to go back, pick her up, and carry her away.

On our way out, we bumped into Roger Rodegap. Harried wasn't a strong enough word to describe how he looked.

"Sorry about your loss."

That startled him. "My loss?"

"The Kentucky Derby. Wrong horse."

"Oh, that. I always lose."

"Then why bet?"

"Mr. Cunningham insists. Since he always loses, it makes him feel better to share his bad choice."

And with that he was off to what had to be his office. Rodegap's office looked like somewhere Scrooge would of stuck him.

13

We were all back in Holly's room.

Holly'd tried to blow us a kiss but that was a bust what with the new television as well as Dr. Jacob Bloomberg measuring her nose. This time he had an assistant with him. The assistant was built like Jane Russell. I watched the assistant, wondering if the good doc had made her that way.

"I don't like him," I muttered to Mrs. Willingford as I watched her tame doc do his stuff.

"Of course you don't like him. No one likes Bloomberg. But he's the best, so what can you do?"

"I was talking about Billy."

"Join the crowd. No one else likes him either."

"What I mean is, I *really* don't like him. And neither does Jane."

"Jane has good taste. But that doesn't make the little squirt our suspect. Honestly, Sam, can you see fat little Billy the Third involved in something like this?"

"It's a stretch." I squashed an image before it could fully form. "An unnerving stretch."

"What happened to Holly and her friends is evil. It's about the most evil thing I've ever heard of, even after getting to know you. But Billy is merely disgusting. If he has a sex life, which isn't something I ever want to discuss, I'd limit it to newts."

That wasn't my image, but I grabbed it to replace the one that was.

Meanwhile, I'd never taken off my coat. I'd never taken off my hat. I'd been rousted from bed before dawn, I was drowsy and punchy and played out, but I couldn't just find a bed and sleep. And brother, sleep called out to me like one of those Greek sirens on one of those Greek islands called out to passing Greek sailors. Holly was safe. She had a cosmetic doc and a television set with radio. No one was stabbing or shooting Jane. Mrs. Willingford was doing one of those things she did so well: buying some happy endings. Why couldn't I just grab some shut-eye somewhere? There were more than enough beds.

I knew why before I'd asked myself the question. Because Caitlin was dead. Because a girl called Chang Chang was dead. Because the car that had stolen them away from this life was somewhere underneath me.

More than a long nap, I needed to see that car. I'd sleep when all this was over, one way or another.

Mrs. Willingford gave me her key to the underground garage. For once, she didn't want to go with me. She wanted to stay with Holly, keep tabs on the doc. Jane wanted to go with me but after her performance with William Ransom Cunningham III, I thought she could use a break. Or that I could. So I went alone.

The garage was like any other private parking garage on the Upper West Side of New York City. Except for the cars. If I'd cared about cars like my pal Lino Morelli cared about cars, my tongue would be dragging. I didn't give a shit about cars. They got you from one place to another. They worked or they didn't work. I couldn't afford one. Now if this place was full of racing sulkies I might spare the time to have a poke about. It wasn't, so I didn't. I found Billy's Lagonda. Even in the gloom, that part was easy. And so was the next part. Thanks to all those lessons from Rudy Hiller, the reformed burglar now locksmith down in Bayonne—lessons I now knew Mrs. Willingford had also learned—I had the door on the driver's side open in seconds.

The air smelled like gasoline, I could taste it on my tongue. I could taste it halfway down my throat. The silence felt like cotton stuffed in my ears. My stomach growled. A spot on my neck itched. I needed a shave. I could use a drink. I was getting one of my headaches.

But one of my questions was now answered. Why drive around in a car people'd remember? Because any girl would get in a Lagonda. Not only was it a work of art, it reeked of money.

So there I was, leaning over and reaching for something shiny peeking out from under the back seat of a two-toned Lagonda—a silver locket that wasn't shaped like a heart—when I heard the soft sound of shoe leather sneaking over cement, but before I could turn round or roll over or dodge out of the way or even yell for help, my head burst open like a Jap bunker taking a direct hit. And then I was falling into one of those long dark wells Philip Marlowe was always falling into.

Before I felt nothing, I felt like dying. And maybe I was.

Maybe it was great I didn't die. And maybe it wasn't so hot. Because I'm here to tell you nothing hurts more than a hard sap to the back of the noggin.

How long later, I had no idea, but I came back from the bottom of my well with one eye staring at a pebble. A pebble that looked as big as Gibraltar. The other eye was squeezed shut with a deep agonizing pain. For one brief red second I had time to think about Holly and what she'd gone through, but that was lost in the rise and fall and tilt and spin of the inside of my throbbing head. It was lost in the rising bile from the pit of my stomach and a boneless feel to my arms and hands. A long long time ago, when I was still young and my skull was still in one piece, I remembered I'd used the word "unnerving." Now, ashen with sudden age and broken with pain, I was unnerved and unmanned and it took what seemed like three hours just to sit up. When I finally did, when I was upright with my back pressed against the cold flank of a pillar of cement, I knew immediately sitting up was a big mistake.

I had just enough time to lean forward and throw up between my outstretched legs.

Forget movies where some guy gets hit on the head with the butt of a gun—and half a minute later he's wise-cracking away. Is that the bunk, or what?

After the sudden shock and the hideous pain and the drunken spinning came the remembering I'd forgotten. What happened? Before all this, what was I doing? The answer came back to me, slowly, slowly... but it came. I'd been looking into the back seat of Squealer Cunningham's imported Lagonda.

A Lagonda that had been right next to where I was now sitting, the stench of my own puke in my nose—the Lagonda that wasn't there now. And neither was the locket.

Swell.

An hour later, Holly was still in one of Mr. and Mrs. Willingford's beds in one of their bedrooms and I was in another bed in another bedroom. Someone had gotten a pair of somebody's pajamas on me. Pale green, with purple squiggles. Dr. Bloomberg had poked at my head, I'd yowled, Jane had nipped a hole through one of Bloomberg's Argyll socks, his assistant—I still hadn't caught her name but who could miss those bazoomas?—took my temperature, clucking over whatever it was, and Mrs. Applegate, Mrs. Willingford's "acting" housekeeper—whatever that meant—was tying a napkin round my neck so I wouldn't dribble my porridge all over the Willingford's monogrammed sheets.

Not in Mrs. Willingford's league, Mrs. Applegate was still a looker. I hoped she wasn't the one to get my jammies on me.

I was trying to think, which wasn't easy when your head ached like Gallant Fox ran over it driving for the wire.

Holly had been in Billy's Lagonda and that was a dead cert. Billy's Lagonda had been on Staten Island—more than once. What time was it? I'd of turned my head to look if I'd thought there'd be a clock to look at, but I could barely turn my eyes much less my head.

"What time is it?"

"Two," said Mrs. Willingford, all dressed up for standing around in her own apartment and smoking. "In the afternoon."

"How long before you found me?"

"Let's see... " She was looking up at a huge painting of Jokers Wild in a gold leaf frame Joker must of found in a trash can behind the Taj Mahal. The artist got the whole beautiful bay stallion in the picture, half of Joker Willingford's Beeswing Farm spread out around him with mares and foals in rolling green pastures, and most of Joker himself. It all looked idyllic. Joker looked stuffed. "You were gone maybe half an hour before I began to wonder about you. It took at least another half an hour to do something about it. So I'd say when Woody found you, you'd been gone for maybe an hour and a half, maybe a little more than that."

OK. That meant two hours ago, give or take, the Lagonda had also been where Billy said it always was. And now it wasn't. Two hours was more than enough time to get a car as far away as it needs to be. Question was: who needed it to be somewhere else?

"I don't buy somebody just being down there," I said, pushing away another mouthful of Mrs. Applegate's gruel, "at the exact moment I was down there. They had to be waiting for me, or they had to of come for me when someone told 'em I was there."

"True," said Mrs. W.

I suddenly realized something was wrong. "Where's Jane?"

"In the kitchen. Cook's making her something special."

"So who told who? Who'd be watching your place? And why? It had to be someone inside this building. Someone who wouldn't get tossed out. And that means… "

Mrs. Willingford lit up like Coney Island at dusk. "Jesus, Sam. It means Billy's involved."

"Could be. Could be. Even if he only lends out his car. But we never told Billy why we cared about his car. So why would *he* hit me? Or get someone else to hit me?"

"Sam, I'm serious. Billy's involved."

"It was the right car, all right. It was the car Holly said she got into. Just as I got sapped, I saw her locket."

"Where!"

"In the back. On the floor."

"Oh, my god. Billy's involved."

"Could be. Excuse me, I think I'm going to lose my mush."

14

I had to go tell Mickey Cates about Caitlin.

I had to find the big house with the monogrammed gate Holly'd described.

I had to find the Lagonda.

Mrs. Willingford said since Billy lived in her building, who better to watch him than her? I said if he was really involved, she'd better be careful—look what happened to me. People could die from blows to the head. She said not to worry, she had Woody and they'd both be on William Ransom Cunningham III like two ticks on a hound. I said maybe she ought to find out if Woody had a friend or two. Woody alone might not be enough. She said she'd think about it. But if she needed a coupla gunsels, she knew where to find 'em.

When Mrs. Willingford said something like "a coupla gunsels," I got a glimpse of who she might of once been. When she said "ticks on a hound," that long ago Lois took on a backwoodsy tint. Maybe someday I'd see the whole picture. Maybe I'd learn her name. Not sure I wanted to, though. I preferred the woman she'd made of herself: the Park Avenue, Lexington, Kentucky, Saratoga racetrack's Mrs. Willingford with her big hats, her big purse, her big heart and that big mouth.

Joker was off somewhere making money, or spending it. Holly was getting her face fixed at a private hospital a few blocks away. The plan was she'd watch television and recuperate at Mrs. Willingford's. So right now, if I didn't count Woody and Blackwell and Mrs. Applegate and all those other servants, there was only me and Jane and Mrs. Willingford "at home."

Mrs. Willingford had that blue look in her blue eye, her sweet feet out of her Italian shoes, her long slender fingers playing with her hair. She had hair like Bogie's Bacall had hair. I spent a second or two wondering if that was the attraction. Nah. I didn't like Bacall near as much as Bogart did. Mrs. Willingford had her own attraction, as strong as the full moon. She also wrote her own lines.

"So, Sam?"

Back in the good old days, when I said "so" to Flo Zawadzki in any way, shape, or form, she'd say, "Sew buttons on yer underwear."

Damn, I hated when Mrs. Z said that. Not only did it mean "shut up," it also meant I was being raised, if you could call it that, by a moron.

I said, "Yes, Mrs. Willingford?"

"There's just you and me now. Any ideas?"

I reached over and touched the back of my head. It felt like the "seep spot" Citation had the bad luck to step in on some new track called Tanforan out in Northern California. Like that spot on the track, the bone felt spongy and weak. It also hurt like a bastard. My only good thought about the whole experience was at least Jane wasn't there.

If they'd sap me, what would they do to Jane?

"You know how I like your ideas, Mrs. Willingford, but I figure this time I'll have to scratch."

"Poor Sam."

Something in her tone made me study her face. She

wasn't saying I was an idiot for passing up one of our terrific tumbles in bed. What she meant was if I felt bad, she understood, and she felt bad. I could be looking at a crack in Mrs. Willingford's hard-boiled shell—was this good for Sam Russo and did I like it? Or should I run a mile? Even if I could run, the way I felt, I knew I wouldn't run. What all this could mean down the road aways, I decided not to think about.

It was high time for Jane and me to get back to Staten Island. What happened to Holly and to Caitlin and to Chang Chang had happened in my own back yard. It was there I needed to dig.

Then there was this: who knew how many had come before them, and who knew how many might come after.

Sometimes, Mrs. Willingford surprised me. "Get a move on, Sam Russo. Take care of business. Holly's safe here. You have my number. If you need me, just call."

If she'd said: if you need me, just whistle, it couldn't be clearer. Sam Russo was getting to Mrs. Joker Willingford. It might not last. It probably wouldn't last.

Mrs. Willingford had long since gotten to Sam Russo. I'd bask in her sun as long as she'd let me. But I wasn't dopey enough to let her know that.

"Here's seeing you, kid," I said, and then I was out of her door and out of her building.

Jane and I were going home.

Mickey was where he always was. And so was Sal Ploverman.

It was Tuesday. Me and Jane had spent the night in our Stapleton room, her sniffing everything and rolling around in it before settling into our bed to hum one of her hums, me nursing a headache. By now I was used to headaches. Shelling in the war got you used to headaches and terror. But I wasn't too happy about what felt like my brain loosed from its mooring to bob and dip and to keel over hard in a tossing sea.

It was three a.m. before I stopped counting the horses on my walls, only to slip into a dreaming house deep in the woods and the screams of cars who sounded like pigs trapped in its burning rooms.

Anyway, as I said, it was Tuesday, my headache wasn't bad if I left on my hat and moved kinda slow, and Cates was on his usual stool in his usual bar by his usual lonesome.

This time, when we walked in, he dipped his head. I took it as a hearty hello and silently sat on the barstool to his left. Landing in one leap, Jane took the one on his right with her usual grace and agility.

There'd come a day, as it always does, when you take your partner for granted. The good things she did, the not so good things, the bad. If that day was coming for me about Jane, I expected it along about the time a winged horse won the Derby.

Mickey surprised me again. He spoke before I did.

"Ye learn anything?"

"It's not good."

The pause that followed lasted long enough for me to get lost in my own dark thoughts. Like a movie I'd once seen, but was too young to understand, the lonely house deep in the woods played in my mind. Dark figures in dark masks moving together like ghosts through dark halls. As light as they were dark, as bare as they were covered, as open as they were closed, three young girls wove through them, smiling, placating, pleading.

The sound of Cates scattered them all like cinders from stuttering candles.

"I figured. Caitlin hasn't come home."

Nursing a need to catch Cates, a cold blooded killer I knew was a cold blooded killer but couldn't prove, two or so years of blowing on the coals of my outrage, I was surprised at how sorry I felt to give him the news. "She's dead, Cates. Holly saw it all."

Sal slipped me my usual shot and a beer, then, with a born bartender's nice sense of time and place, made himself scarce.

Mickey was silent again, long enough for me to smoke a cigarette, long enough for one of Sal's girls to walk in, ask Sal a question, and walk out. When Cates spoke, I could barely hear him.

"Ye know who did it?"

"I know Holly was drugged as soon as she got in the car. I know whatever they doped her with hadn't put out her lights before she saw them pull up for Caitlin."

"About that car—truth to tell, the boys are lookin' everywhere but not one has found a trace of the thing."

I knocked back my shot, shuddered from the kick of it. "I found it. And I know who owns it."

Only now he turned his face towards mine. The black of his rolling eye was a thing to behold. I tried, but I couldn't help myself pulling back. No more than an inch, but an inch nevertheless.

"The name?" It was like the devil speaking. "Tell me the name."

"Not yet, not until I'm sure he had anything to do with it. He claims it had to be stolen."

Mickey Cates reached over to place his hand on my hand, the one I was using to flip open my Zippo, snap it shut, flip it open, snap it shut again, my nose filled with its gasoline smell. "Ye'll be telling me his name, friend."

It was spoken as softly as a lullaby sung to a newborn babe, but it was more chilling than if he'd shouted.

"I can't— "

"Ye can. And ye will."

What the hell. If Cates could even get in the building— and it was hard seeing how—all he was likely to find was the sight of one of Billy's fits and Daniels glimmering off to call the cops. Besides, maybe Billy did know a thing or two, and I had a feeling he did, maybe Mickey Cates and his four fat friends could shake it loose. Where was the harm?

So I told him the name. And then I said, "Did you find the house?"

"Ah, well, there we've caught a scent on the wind. Would your dog like a drink?"

"What scent? Jane? You thirsty?"

Sal was on us like he had Lucky Luciano in the Garter gunning for Legs Diamond. He placed a bowl of fresh water on the bar for Jane, poured Mickey another beer and me another shot, then was off like a pacer.

Jane lapped her water like the lady she was, all the while watching Cates like the killer he was.

"What scent, Cates?"

"We know. Ye'll know." He was rising from his stool. "Ye'll have to excuse me now. There's arrangements to be made for my poor girl."

I watched him walk as tall as he'd ever walked, away from the bar of the Green Garter, out the door into the soft May sun of a Stapleton afternoon. His back was straight. His head high. His gait steady.

I was watching a broken man.

It was my turn to walk tall, even if I swayed with the pain. Head still hurt. Brain still spun. I expected they would for some time.

"Come on, Jane. We got a bus to catch and a library to bust into."

15

The closest I came to a book at the Staten Island Home for Children was on a winter's day when a North End charity decided to dump off a load of charity for us "poor children."

Us poor kids had maybe a minute of opening boxes in the bitter cold and snatching at stuff before Mr. and Mrs. Zawadzki drove us away, her with a broom, him with a tire iron, claiming later we'd all get a sweater or winter gloves or maybe even a coat, once they'd sorted it all out. We never saw any of it again.

Except for Lino Morelli. Stapleton's future police detective'd got his hands on a wooly hat and was off and running, Mister right behind. The hat ended up in shreds. So did Lino's boyhood butt. For the coupla pennies he could of got for that hat, Mister whipped him raw in front of us all. Not with the tire iron, with his belt. We all knew that was bad enough.

Then there was me. In that one minute, with Mister distracted by Lino and Flo distracted by the rest of us, I'd grabbed the first thing I saw, not a hat or a coat, but a book, and stuffed it down my pants. Turned out to be *The Count of Monte Cristo*. Of all the books I could of snatched, that book was the making of me. First thing I did was hide it in a place only I knew about, way up on the fifth floor. The "home" had once been a hospital. The top floor was where they kept their "failures." In those days, it still smelled of formaldehyde, gangrene and piss. Up on the fifth floor, old wooden filing cabinets were rotting away. I chose the worst looking of the bunch. If anyone else came sniffing around, I figured they were sure to search the best.

To this day, I have that book. I took it with me when I left. Last I looked, it was sitting on a sagging shelf in 4-A between *Murder in the Madhouse* and *The Bride Wore Black*.

I read it over and over. Long hours spent with Edmund Dantès, a wronged man. Like me, Dantès was locked away on an island, without trial and forgotten. Well, that last bit is untrue. The man who named himself the Count of Monte Cristo was never forgotten. Those who did him wrong knew exactly where he was and what they'd done. They just didn't expect to see him again. As for me, I named myself Sam Russo and those who did me wrong were right there with me, doing me more wrongs every day of my miserable life. Anyway, like me, he spent years working to escape his island. But unlike me, he had revenge in his heart. I relished his revenge, followed his every clever move against all who'd taken him down with my nerves lit up and my heart thumping against my ribs. But I guess it wasn't in me to want what Edmund Dantès wanted, even when it was me who delivered the blow that sealed the well deserved fate of the demented Zawadzkis.

Maybe if I'd gotten my hands on a vast and hidden fortune?

Nah. What I wanted I found with my face upturned towards the light of a silver screen. I would be Bogart. I would right wrongs, not revenge them. I would be Sam Russo, Private Investigator.

What a chump.

But a dedicated chump. A chump who could change his

stripes.

This time I was in it for more than righting wrongs. Not to mention paying the rent. This time, I was in it to avenge Holly.

I'd left Holly in the good hands of Bloomberg, Blackwell, Cook, Mrs. Applegate and Lois. I'd left Billy in the interesting hands of Mrs. Willingford and Woody—maybe even in the hands of Cates and his four fat Irish friends and all their Irish friends. But just me and Jane alone were going to find that big house with the big gate, hence the bus along Bay Street.

How hard could it be? Staten Island was exactly that— an island. I'd lived on it all my life, not counting the time I served charging Jap tanks on horseback. There were only a few places like Holly described on the whole heave of rocky dirt, and the most likely place was a secluded ravine called Blood Root Valley. It was also called Black Horse Ravine because of the British who conducted their part of our revolution in it: messengers racing their horses back and forth from the fort on the southern tip to the fort on the northern tip. And vice versa. There was one more name: Valley of Dead Man's Creek. Us kids loved that last one. Long ago, longer than any of us knew, a dead man was found there, lying face down in mud by the brook. No one ever learned who he was or how he got himself dead.

Paul Jarrett used him to scare the little kids silly with tales of what he said was a murdered man rising, white bone showing through rotted flesh, long tangled hair dripping down his broken back with thick black muck, those eyeless sockets and that toothless mouth stuffed with ancient mud— the same mud, said Paul, blood thirsty savages slathered over themselves as they rushed about the island, killing white people, men, women and, best of all, little kids—but the dead man's enormous hands, hands twice the size of normal hands, were white and searching. He'd stumble through the night, feeling with those big hands, looking for the man who killed him. If he couldn't find the man, a little kid would do until he did. And then—he'd scoop out the heart, digging in with his long white fingers.

Who was I kidding? He scared us all silly, me and Lino included.

Anyway, most people called it Blood Root Valley.

Blood Root was surrounded by thickly wooded hills and not too far away was the Vanderbilt Cemetery. I guess once upon a time it was swell to be dead in it, but now it was covered in thickly tangled blackberry bushes, stinging nettles, fallen trees and tipped headstones. Lino had this pet idea that a cemetery, especially a gone-to-seed cemetery, was perfect for dumping bodies. He said, "Not only are they in a real graveyard, but they got a real headstone. You dig up the stiff already there, stick in your own kill, then dump what's left of a Vanderbilt back on top. Then you fill it in again. With a Vanderbilt lying on you—hey presto, you're finally somebody."

I said, "At least, if you ask the Vanderbilts."

He said, "Huh?"

Lino's "huh" was always my cue to change the subject.

The library on Canal and Wright Street looked like Carnegie Hall which, I'm sure I've already said, looked like the box they'd shipped the Staten Island Home for Children to Stapleton in. To me, most buildings looked like shipping crates. Except the Chrysler Building. To me, the Chrysler Building looked like a work of art. One of my unspoken dreams was one day to have an office in it.

What the hell. Dream large. Mrs. Willingford had. Why couldn't I?

As I was saying: going to the library. Whenever Jane and me were going somewhere I thought they'd stop a dog, I learned to take a white cane along. With the library, they thought I was partially sighted (the war you know), and it worked like a whole bracelet of charms.

It took maybe two, two and a half hours, but I found three possible houses. Mansions, really, estates, whatever the rich named the piles they called home. One was maybe five miles past Stapleton's city limits on Victory Boulevard. It was listed as the Bichler House. Place was boarded up now, but once it'd been home to the Bichler family who made their pot of money from legal beer, and then, for a few golden years, from illegal beer, until the cops and anti-German sentiment put 'em out of business.

The other two were in Blood Root Valley. One was at the north end and one was at the south end.

I hoped to see all three.

It was right about then I realized the spot I was in. Rushing back from Manhattan to Stapleton, I'd forgot all about the hole in my sail. I needed a way to get around. I could get to the Bichler house by bus, but that was it. No public transport into Blood Root Valley. Back at Mrs. Willingford's, I'd assumed Woody could drive me where I needed to go. I couldn't call now and ask her to send him over. I wanted Woody exactly where he was, taking care of my girls.

The simple answer? Get my own car. My war was spent on horseback, but I knew how to drive. We were all trained to drive, whichever unit we were in.

How much Willingford money was left after paying the two nurse Bs? Not near enough to buy a car, not even a clunker. How about taking a cab? A cab I could still afford. But I didn't want some cabbie knowing my business.

So, who did I know who had a car, one they'd actually lend me?

Mickey Cates and the friends of Mickey Cates, that's who.

Back at Bay and Victory, Jane rolling around on my Murphy bed and yodeling with joy to be home, I chewed three aspirins, washed 'em down with the last of the whisky, and then I called Mickey Cates. Not at the Green Garter. After what I'd told him, I didn't think he'd be sitting around doing nothing at the Garter. I called the number Mullan had given me, the one he said to call when I needed help.

I'd caught Cates just as he was walking out his door, wherever that was. I was pretty sure it was nearby. We were neighbors. Which said a few things about my neighborhood. And Holly's.

When I asked, I half expected him to say: sure, he'd get me a car, but he'd be in it and driving.

He surprised me.

He said, "In half an hour, look out your window. There'll be a dark green 1946 Plymouth parked on Bay, close as it can get to your place. The keys will be in the ignition."

He hung up before I could say another word.

Half an hour later a dark green 1946 Plymouth was parked on Bay. A Saint Christopher medal hung from the rear view mirror. There was a dead soldier in the glove box. Bushmills, not bad. Chewing gum wrappers were ground into the floor mats, driver and passenger side. The keys were in the ignition.

There was a note on the seat.

Anything at all, I want to hear.

MC

Jane wasn't pleased. With Holly out of our bed and the two Bs out of our room, all Jane wanted to do was lie around and listen to *Martin and Lewis*.

Even if I wasn't hot on the trail, I wasn't listening to Jerry Lewis. Martin was fine, I liked Dean, but Lewis was like a nail in my shoe.

I dragged her out by Holly's Christmas collar, saying, "A man's partner is a man's partner. You wanna listen to some squeaky irritating one note moron, buy your own radio."

Jane wouldn't talk to me until the cross streets ended and Victory Boulevard was on its own.

16

What a place to grow up. On some damn island. One that was close enough to Manhattan to see it, smell it, long for it. But far enough away to be laughed at and snubbed by "real" New Yorkers.

Staten Island, they'd say, isn't that near Jersey somewhere? By Jersey, they meant they wouldn't be caught dead there.

Yet it was also close enough for the rich to build high fenced estates on and hide in them, for the crooked and organized to own whole buildings and use them as their own version of corporate headquarters, for the strange to slink around Stapleton's dingier streets and act even stranger on.

It was also close enough, yet far away enough, for the rest of New York City to dump all their garbage on it. "Real" New Yorkers who'd never set foot on the island called it Fresh Kills Landfill. They also called it "temporary." I'd seen the dump once, during some case of Lino's I'd "helped" him with—a riotous mountain of noxious crap rising up from the once bird-and-fish-filled wetlands like a mountain of noxious crap.

Holding my hat over my face, it didn't seem temporary to me. And if it was, where was it all going next?

One look, and Lino had shrugged. For Lino, stuff like birds and fish were just things to eat or shoot at and stuff like a mountain of garbage was his world.

They also dumped their unwanted kids on the island. A kid like my mother, knocked up and used up and sent off to die in a towered hulk straight out of one of Bram Stoker's better nightmares. Then there was Valley of the Dead Man's Creek which Paul had made into one of my childhood nightmares.

Now I was deep in the dark green heart of the place, parked near a sagging roadhouse at the bottom of a narrow rutted lane leading up to the top of Staten Island's "mountain," a four hundred and something foot rise the Dutch called Todt Hill. In their not so mellifluous tongue, todt meant "dead."

Dead Hill. Swell.

The roadhouse was named, as far as I could tell, nothing. There were two cars parked outside and another in pieces rusting away in a nest of blackberry bushes. It offered home cooked meals and local beer. I could use a home cooked meal, even if "home cooked" was a load of baloney.

And so could Jane.

Jane and I were taking a break. The Bichler House turned out a bust. It wasn't big enough, old enough, or theatrical enough. It also wasn't reached by a steep gravel road and there was no gate. As for woods, there was a house either side of it, both in full sight and both with only two or less trees in the middle of well tended gardens.

Scratch one possibility.

The map I borrowed from the library—when this was all over, and if I survived it, I'd be good and bring the map back—said somewhere around here there were a couple of kettle ponds. After a jockey dying badly in the usual sort of pond near the track at Saratoga Springs, I'd crossed off ponds on my list of must-sees. The map also showed a Roman Catholic seminary at the top of Todt, or near enough. No need to visit a seminary. Mournful guys floating about in dresses muttering in tongues spooked me—which was odd when I thought about Holly. But Holly wasn't a guy. Or mournful. At least not by nature. Also somewhere around here was a two hundred year old, or older, cemetery with a load of deceased Vanderbilts stacked like cordwood in their Vanderbilt Mausoleum.

I wanted to see that, I wanted to see the whole shebang, poke around a bit, and I knew Jane did too—she had her hopeful nose pressed against the Plymouth's side door window, smearing up the glass.

But Holly hadn't mentioned a boneyard. And we weren't fooling around here.

After meatloaf and beer and mashed potatoes—surprisingly good—we were on our way again. Mostly what we saw were trees. It'd been a long time since I'd seen this much green. I liked it and I didn't like it. I figured I had about as much skill in a forest as Mrs. Willingford's downstairs neighbor, William Ransom Cunningham III, did—which was bupkis.

Todt's Hill was closer to the north end of the valley. We were looking for the second big house, the one most promising, the one listed for sale. It'd been on the books for five years before it was sold in '44. The selling price was low, about what they'd ask for the roadhouse. On a cop's wage, Lino Morelli could of bought it. Now you'd have to be a live Vanderbilt to get your hands on it.

So what did that mean? Property values on Staten Island had gone through the roof? Whoever bought it for a song didn't really want to sell it? Or no one could find it?

Personally, after driving up and down a few unmarked roads more like trails than roads, listening to the undergrowth scratch the paint off somebody's '46 Plymouth, I figured they couldn't find it.

And then, from one moment to the next, the Plymouth's nose was headed down a long dirt road between more trees. It kept on that way, twisting and turning and missing fallen logs and potholes until it came to a tall iron fence with an iron gate.

The gate didn't have an S but it did have a B. What Holly had seen was a C and a B.

"Well, Jane," I said, my heart somewhere up near my throat thumping away, "we're here."

Jane, catching my tone, didn't hum and she didn't yodel. What she did was put her front paws up on the dash, stretch her back legs out as far as she could and not fall off the front seat, and from there, strain forward with her red ears perked, staring through the windshield.

Even if we'd wanted to, and I wanted to—something about this whole set-up spooked me more than one of Paul Jarrett's bedtime stories—we couldn't turn round. The best we could do would be to back up on a winding rutted dirt road for at least a mile. There'd been no turn-offs or pull-offs as we'd come down.

So for us, through the gate it was.

Good thing I brought my gun. Not so good it was a snub nosed Colt .38. Where we were, I needed a rifle, something with some range. I could probably also of used a telescopic sight.

I got out of the car. I let Jane out, who raced about inhaling the place north, east, south, west, up, down, and sideways while I checked the gate. It had one hell of a padlock. What else had I expected? After Holly's description of what went on here, would they leave the gate unlocked? Fuck no. I'd prepared for this. I'd gone to the biggest hardware store on Bay Street. The huge sign across the entire store front shouted that inside they had a million things for sale and as far as I could see, they did. Including the bolt cutters I got out of the Plymouth's trunk.

We were inside the gate in about the same time I could of picked the lock. The bolt cutters were in case there wasn't a lock to pick. I always picked locks. This time I used the bolt cutters.

It was probably a mistake. I shook that off like Jane shook off rain.

I put the tool back in the trunk, closed the gate, arranged the padlock. If someone was to come along, and that someone didn't bother looking too close, it would of looked like a padlocked gate with a big C and B on it.

I was counting on no one coming along. Especially as on the lonely road Jane and I had recently traveled, no one "just came along."

In another few minutes, our tires were crunching gravel. A coupla more minutes and there was a carriage house to our right. To our left, the spitting image of Ashley Wilkes's venerable family mansion right out of *Gone With the Wind* gleamed as white as Hollywood teeth. It had a front entrance like the New York Library had a front entrance, but without the lions. Instead there were all these white columns and a wide white veranda. The third floor was a quarter the size of the rest of the house.

It looked like a swell place to lock up the spare mad relative.

After parking the Plymouth, its nose pointing towards

the gate for one of those quick getaways, I stopped myself walking around back to have a look at the slave cabins.

Meanwhile, all around us pressed Henry Wadsworth Longfellow's Forest Primeval. Given time and peace enough, the island's insistent trees would erase the movie set mansion and its movie set carriage house, grow right through them, push away brick and stone and pillars, reduce the wood to mulch, maybe even the redskin would return to take back his land. But for now they were held in check by the graveled drive, the graveled turnaround, and a small patch of mowed lawn. Recently mowed lawn.

No one was here. Or if they were, they had no car, no bicycle, no horse, not even a goat cart. If someone was here, they were on foot.

But just in case, best to act normal, like someone naturally lost and naturally hoping to get found. "Hallo!" I shouted. If I got a hello shouted back, I'd be stuck explaining how I got in. I was counting on no one shouting back.

Jane, sniffing this and inhaling that, began humming. Well, there you go. For the moment, we had the joint to ourselves.

Like the gate had been, the house was locked. Who wouldn't lock their house? It was the American way. Picking the lock was the usual Russo way. Jane and I were inside in about the time it took a good sprinting horse—Pan Zareta, a record breaking mare I wish I'd known, came immediately to mind—to cover five furlongs.

When I bought the bolt cutters, I'd also thought to buy something else. I was sure it would come in handy, even if I never found the house. Every PI worth his salt had a good flashlight.

From inside you couldn't tell if it was night or day outside. All the windows, and there were plenty of 'em, were draped in thick black velvet.

Jane trotted off into darkness, and not even my hissed, "Jane!" stopped her.

I found the light-switch where you'd expect, on the wall to the right of the door. Nothing happened. It was still as dark as a movie theater before the movie starts. The thought gave me pause. From the day Holly was found, my whole life had seemed like a movie. Not a good movie and not a bad movie, just a black and white movie. Great sets, great lighting, a nifty title, but someone else wrote the story. Someone else made up the lines. Who was I? Not even an extra, more like the guy with a mop who stumbles in front of the camera.

I strode to the nearest window and yanked back the drapes. A shaft of light bolted into the room like the guy in 4-C bouncing off walls. Outside the light was dimming.

It'd taken me and Jane all day to talk to Cates, to turn a lot of pages in a lot of library books, to go shopping on Bay Street, to wait on the delivery of a borrowed car, to drive up wooded hill and down wooded dale, to eat a plate of mash and meatloaf, to find this house.

Now it was getting dark.

Fuck.

17

"Jane!"

Her answer came from far away, upstairs somewhere.

"Jane, come back here!"

No sound of clicking toenails. There wouldn't be. No doubt the whole place was as thickly carpeted as the carpet I'd never forget, the one covering the floor in an Upper East Side apartment where six months back I'd come this close to the end of Sam Russo.

Where the hell was Jane?

I was just about to open not just one, but all the drapes in the dimly lit room when the thought occurred: what if someone was watching? They'd know—and then my aching brain woke up. If someone was watching, the jig was already up. A dark green car was parked right in front of the house.

I opened the drapes.

The last of the light over Blood Root Valley was fading fast. Where was that dog?

"Jane!"

This time, all I got for my troubles was an echo.

Not only where the hell was my dog, but where the hell were the stairs?

By flashlight, the staircase at the back of a room as big as Rockefeller's ice skating rink, was like one of those affairs someone like Gloria Swanson once swanned down. At the bottom the handrails were wide and curving. At the top, they ended on a railed balcony that went all along the back

of the first floor room and halfway along either side. Both
sides had doors, lots of doors leading to wherever they led.
On what I guessed was the east side of the house another
staircase rose up to a third floor, not nearly as wide.

Nothing much between where I was standing and the
first staircase but what looked like a blood red carpet and
red velvet, wide-seated, divans set against the flowery pink
papered walls, low tables before each divan, a solid crystal
ashtray and an ornate silver candlestick, a used black candle
in each, on every table.

Over my head was a chandelier. I'd seen chandeliers in
my time, but this one was out to impress. I was impressed.
It also made me nervous. That thing fell, and I'd be in more
pieces than it was.

Between me and Swanson's staircase, was one small
raised dais.

I stared. That was the stage. That was where Holly had
stood along with Chang Chang and Caitlin. That's where
they stripped. The sight chilled me down to the bone. I saw
them clear as I saw my own hand: young, beautiful, duped,
trapped, and doomed. I heard the murmur of anticipation
shudder through the masked guests. I felt the heat of sexual
sickness and smelled the musk of corruption. I was stuck to
the carpet by what I was feeling, the beam from my flashlight
like a single spot on the tiny stage.

Suddenly, from somewhere, Jane, who I'd only once
before heard make a sound louder than a small quick yelp or
a yodel, howled.

It snapped my head round. It nearly shot the top of my
spine out the top of my head. I came *this* close to shitting
myself. Yelling her name, I was up those stairs, three flights

of them, faster than I'd ever done anything, ever.

I found her in a window seat at a big oval window in a fair sized bedroom, her tail uncurled, her nose in the air, her white furry throat with Holly's name tag shining in the gathering gloom. Out of that throat came the most complicated series of yodels and hums and staccato yelps I'd ever heard her use. No time to notice the room, I was with her, looking out the same oval window she was staring out.

Three stories below, parked next to the Plymouth, was a beat-up old pick-up truck. Mid-Thirties model, maybe older. In the bed of the pick-up was a load of stuff looked like groceries, some garden tools, three or four sacks of who knew what, a can of gas. The driver was already out of his seat. Ignoring his supplies, he was all over my borrowed Plymouth. I hadn't locked the doors, hadn't even thought of it. He was inside on the driver's side, checking out the registration in its plastic holder strapped round the steering column. I hadn't even looked at that. I had no idea whose name and address he was reading.

From where we were, all Jane and I had was a good view of the top of his gray hat and the breadth of his shoulders. He wasn't small. And he moved fast.

I felt in my jacket pocket, assuring myself I hadn't done any other dumb thing, like leave my gun in the car. Or the car keys. That gun was the last vital thing I'd thought to take along on a trek into the great unknown of Staten Island's interior along with my trusted sidekick, Jane.

I had the keys. I had my gun. I had a box of spare bullets in another pocket.

The red hair on the back of Jane's neck stood on end. It stood up along the length of her red back. She'd curled back her upper lip so both sharp incisors gleamed in the failing light. My hair and lips stayed where they were, but my nerves sang like a first chair violin.

I'd expected the house to be cared for. But I didn't expect a live-in caretaker. It was for sale, wasn't it? Big mistake. If the broad-shouldered palooka now finished inspecting the Plymouth didn't hang his hat here, I'd eat it.

So here I was, watching him inch up the steps and sidle towards a side door, one I hadn't gone looking for. Note to Sam Russo, Private Eye. Next time, assuming there *is* a next time: check out the whole fucking place before making yourself and your dog at home.

We were still up in that room on the third floor when the unlocked front door opened—another blunder I didn't think Bogie would make. How many now? I should of picked the padlock, not cut it. I should of snapped it shut again behind us. I should of hid the Plymouth, not left it sitting right out in the open. Me and Jane should of walked in from some other direction. I should of relocked the front door.

If there was a Union for Private Eyes, and all this got around, I'd be out on my can in no time.

I had to hand it to the guy. He was some ballsy caretaker. Or as just plain dumb as I was. "Yoohoo," he called out, all the way from down on the dark first floor. "I know you're here, Mr. Colin Dunne."

Colin Dunne? Obviously Colin was the poor sap Cates made lend out his car.

"Might as well get it over with, Colin, and come on out. I'm not such a bad guy and there's a swell supply of top notch hootch in this house. I'd lay short odds you know that. Never say Mitt Coeslak doesn't know how to treat a guest."

From one second to the next, the lights in the house came on. He must of thrown the main switch.

I was tempted to take Mitt Coeslak up on his offer. It was either that or shoot it out with him when he finally found the room we were in. And he'd find it. But then, I'd spent my youth hiding in a house like this. A big dark creepy old house with lots of rooms and lots of hallways and lots of cupboards to hide in. I'd learned how to dodge the Zawadzki's as long as I wanted to. So staying in one room until Coeslak exhausted himself searching through half the others wasn't something I had to do. Houses like this house had to be stuffed with any number of out-of-the-way places. I could keep on the move for ages, even climb out on one of the roofs. Roofs were something I was used to.

But then there was Jane. Jane was a straight for the throat kind of little helper. Two times now, two tough cases, and in both of 'em she'd taken as much abuse as me. Ol' Mitt sounded more than a little nuts. No telling what a nutcase might do. He could come at us blasting away. He could sit in the Plymouth and just wait. He could set the house on fire. He could even have some nutcase brains and do something really sly. Like what? How the hell would I know? That's what made it sly.

I was an idiot. No one knew I was here. I had no back up—except Jane, who was great but was she enough? I'd already made three or four stupid mistakes. What was really on the table here was a schmuck and his clever dog dodging about an unfamiliar house hiding from someone who knew it well. I was also a schmuck with one huge vulnerability: I cared too much about my partner. So what if Jane was a dog. I'd spent the last seven or eight months learning a dog could be a better man than any man I'd ever met.

It seemed to me it came down to only one choice. To get the drop on good old Mitt before he got the drop on me. Then, assuming that went well, finding out if he'd be so kind as to answer a few of my burning questions.

I had one hell of a lot of burning questions.

It was OK risking me. I deserved it. But I couldn't risk Jane. If I locked her in this room, she might not forgive me. I guess that didn't matter if the plug-ugly below shot me dead and called it trespassing, but if I lived it mattered a lot.

Damn it all to hell. I wasn't getting Jane shot or stabbed or burned or buried alive—I'd seen three different kinds of shovels in the back of Mitt's pickup truck—so I was doing this alone.

I was out the door and had it shut, quickly and quietly, before Jane caught on and could make her own move. No sticking around to say I was sorry, I was racing for the second floor before Mitt got up from the first. Whatever was going to happen wasn't happening on Jane's floor, and for sure not near the room she was in.

For the first time in almost a year, I was on my own.

I used to love being on my own. It was who I was. No family, no steady lover, no close friends, just solving puzzles for Lino, and sometimes for a real client. I was a small face watching big faces on a moving picture screen, hearing them talk as if they were speaking only to me. Especially Bogart. Bogie was the only face I understood, the only voice that made any sense.

Now being alone felt strange, wrong—it felt lonely.

"Oh Colin," called Mitt the caretaker, "Come out, come out, wherever you are."

Good. He thought he was funny. He thought we were playing a game. And he was still being thorough down on the first floor. Looking behind drapes, peeking in closets, checking out the room where they dressed the girls for one of his Master's parties, searching the bathrooms and kitchens, whatever was down there.

I had time to plan something of my own. It was crude, but it could work.

One last look to make sure Jane wasn't right behind me—no telling what that dog could do—and I was out of the starting gate and running.

18

The first thing I'd buy if I ever came into dough was a carpet. One as deep as the one I'd just run across.

Mitt Coeslak never heard me. Just as I thought, he'd looked behind every black velvet drape I'd pulled open, so just as I thought, he knew I wasn't behind any of them—especially when I was.

I have to admit something here, something I did I'd never seen a grown man do in or out of the movies, especially not Humphrey Bogart or Jimmy Cagney or Edward G. Robinson. As for John Garfield or George Raft, forget it. Cary Grant would do it. And maybe my old friend Jimmy Stewart could be persuaded. Jerry Lewis would do it without breaking a sweat, but since I loathed Lewis, admitting I did it hurts.

But hell, when a man had to get down some stairs quick and when he's the target of some creep with a gun so he needs to be moving fast, he does what he has to do. He slides down the banister.

So that's what I did. The ends of the banisters widening as well as curving concerned me, but a boyhood of japes and scrapes got me past 'em without too much harm; I used one hand as a brake coming down. Then it was across more carpet and behind the drapes nearest the staircase. Any minute now, Mitt was bound to quit searching the first floor, which meant he'd start on the second floor. That meant he'd be climbing those stairs. And there I'd be, right behind him.

I said it was crude. But it worked. Mitt was walking around like he owned the place, but he wasn't making for the staircase. He headed right for the massive stone mantel above a massive stone fireplace, where he reached up and pushed something. A panel in one of the wooden walls slid open. Of course. A house like this, secret panels leading to secret cubby holes, even whole rooms, was a dead cert.

His back to me, he was choosing which rifle of all the rifles on offer to take upstairs with him. A pistol is good for short range, but he wasn't planning on getting too close to Colin Dunne. He was reaching for a good old lever action .405 Winchester, when I stepped out from behind the soft black velvet.

Nice and quiet, I said, "Forget the rifle. Drop the gun."

He dropped his hand and his gun. The gun, the usual Smith & Wesson Model 10, landed with a soft thud.

"Now turn around."

He turned around.

I was looking at some punk, maybe older than me, maybe younger, hard to tell. About my height, maybe ten or more pounds over my weight. Oiled hair with a part on the right so straight he must of used a ruler.

He had one of those Paul Muni noses, so upturned you got more than you wanted to see of his nostrils. One of those jaws so narrow you wondered how he chewed his food. A raw red scar sloping down from one drooping brown eye to the corner of a drooping red mouth that maybe he got in combat, and maybe he got poking that nose where it wasn't wanted.

I was just opening my mouth to offer him a seat, any red velvet divan would do, when a streak of red and white flew down the stairs, snatched up Mitt's gun where he'd dropped it, and rushed off again. Back where she'd come from was my best guess.

Mitt and I stood there. He had to be pole-axed at what he'd just seen. I knew I was, and with more good reason. It meant Jane knew how to open a fucking door.

If she wasn't my best friend, that dog would make me fucking nervous.

"Sit down. Anywhere will do."

With a snub nosed .38 pointed directly at the middle of his high thin sweaty forehead, he chose to sit down. Even so, it didn't stop him talking.

"You're trespassing. I could call the law."

"Now that," I said, lighting up with one hand, holding the gun steady with the other, "would make life twice as interesting. Considering what goes on here."

I thought that would alarm him, and it did. Over his shoulder, I saw Jane coming back downstairs. No gun. So she'd hid it. One day soon, I expected her to speak perfect English, take up knitting, and use the telephone.

"Nothing goes on here," he said, eyeing my smoke. He wanted to shake one out for himself, but wasn't sure it was a good idea. "Anyone, even a stupid mick can see that."

"A stupid spic, not a mick. Name's Russo. And you're just the caretaker?"

"Yep. That's me."

"The gardener too? Quite a collection of shovels you got out there."

Mitt got a sideways look in his eye. He'd gone far away. Too bad for him, where he'd gone had a dog squinting at him. Jane was doing what Jane did with our suspicious characters:

getting as close as possible as quietly as possible all the while showing all possible teeth.

Mitt's own teeth, too short and too many, were clenched.

"Let's call someone, OK, Mitt? But not the cops. I have a much better idea."

He didn't like it, he didn't like it one damn bit, but what could he do?

The telephone was in a kitchen I'd peg for the St. Regis Hotel.

When I'd hung up and Mitt was tied up and, for good measure, locked in the nearest broom closet, I put my arm around Jane and scratched her neck. It took some doing, but with a lot of that and some roast beef I found in the fridge, she forgave me. But I knew I'd better not try it again. Besides, what good would it do? If she could open a door, she could probably pick a lock—like Mrs. Willingford now could—but without the need of Bayonne's once crooked locksmith, Rudy Hiller, to teach her.

As for Mitt's gun, hell if I knew what Jane did with it.

I expected Mickey Cates to show up. I expected to see the fat man, Mullan. I expected Cates and Mullan to bring along a load of muscle with wild Irish names. I expected Mullan to find a comfy place to rest his bulk, drink the house whisky, smoke the house cigars, and direct operations. I expected the rest to fan out and search every inch of the joint, plus carriage house and grounds—something I would of done if there'd been no Mitt the caretaker or I'd been smarter from the off.

I hadn't expected to see Mrs. Willingford. But there

she was, stepping out of Mickey's neat black Mercury coupe with the red upholstery.

No surprise at what she was wearing. The perfect outfit for a dark night in the deep woods: a slinky black silk dress, a silver fox cubby, green high heels with straps around her slender silken ankles, and a netted green hat sloped down over her face and off to one side. She looked completely out of place, completely at ease, and completely eatable.

I was twice as surprised at how chummy she was with Cates.

I tried to catch it before it careened off my ribs, but there went my heart again. Mrs. Willingford was my friend. I trusted her, I liked her, we made each other laugh, we hurt each other's feelings. She could do what she liked when we weren't doing something I liked. But solid proof didn't feel so hot.

She was in no rush to explain, and I was in no position to ask. So we left it like that and went straight to business. That is, after she gave Jane her due and me a peck on the cheek.

Mullan sent a fella he called Sweet Davy Malloy, the kid eying the stash of guns in the secret hidey hole, to fetch my friend Mitt out from his closet. Sweet Davy Malloy was as pretty as Holly. My guess was he'd die before he wore heels and a skirt.

Mitt came protesting every step of the way. If it was me, I'd shut my mouth. "This is a private residence," he was shouting, "private! When the owners find out— "

Sweet Davy and another of those nice Irish boys slammed him down on a divan. Mitt bounced.

"And who might they be, these owners, Mr. Coeslak?" said Cates.

"A consortium." Mitt spat that one out like he was proud to hear the word formed by his own lips.

"A consortium of what?"

That got him. He could say the word, but he couldn't define it. "Some people who use the place whenever they want to. I'd like a smoke. Could I have a smoke?"

"Ah. And how do they use it?"

"I... well, I don't, I'm not allowed... I'm not here when they come."

"Not here? Where do ye go then?"

Mitt's perfect part was getting mussed. Drool was sliding out one side of his scarred mouth. I've seen men do that. In the war, keeping cover in the dirt behind their dead mount while bullets whizzed over their heads—they'd drool.

Mickey was moving in on him while Mullan sipped his drink and watched, eyes half open with a kind of amused pleasure.

Mrs. Willingford had stepped away, inching closer to me. I had no idea how she and Cates met, or what they'd done since, but it seemed like the Mickey Cates she was already used to wasn't the Mickey Cates she was seeing now.

Jane knew who Cates was. And so did I. Any second now, poor Mitt Coeslak would be getting the idea.

That minute didn't come, not right away.

The front door slammed open, letting in the dark, and a voice called out, "Mickey! Mullan! We've found sumpin' maybe you won't be wantin' to see."

Mullan looked like he'd seen a worm in his whisky. "I think I'll sit this one out, if ye don't mind, Mickey me lad."

Nodding at Sweet Davy to yank Mitt up from his place and bring him along, Mickey walked out the door without another soft word to anyone.

I went with him. And Jane and Mrs. Willingford followed me.

I didn't want to go where I knew we were going, but I had to. Just like Mickey Cates had to.

19

Jane and I got our wish. We'd wanted to have a look at a cemetery and here we were, looking at a graveyard. Not one crammed with defunct Vanderbilts. No white weeping angels, no carved headstones, no grand mausoleum, no winding paths, no sad sayings carved into rocks, not even coffins.

And not by the light of day.

We were off a well-worn path running back of the big white house and then into the big black woods; we were looking at mounds of dirt by flashlights, some old, some not so old, some fresh as new dug mole holes. I was slammed back in time, back to the small woods behind the Staten Island Home for Children.

Backing up a step, my skin clammy and my head aching and my mouth dry, how long could I watch this? I'd played on mounds like these, me and Lino Morelli and Paul Jarrett and a lot of other badly fed, badly clothed, badly treated detainees over the years, shouting out our childhood bravado and nonsense. Without knowing, I'd run across the graves of children—and one of them my own murdered mother.

Mickey slapped Mitt on the side of his head, hard enough to send him sprawling if not for Sweet Davy Malloy holding him up. "Which one? Which one, ye piece of shite."

Mitt Coeslak was doing more than drooling now. His nose was running and his eyes were leaking. He looked bad. There wasn't an ounce of pity in me for him. How many times had he waited, out of sight but probably peeking, while his employers had their fun? How many bodies of murdered young girls had he dragged out into the woods, dug the half-hearted cold-blooded graves for? How many had he dumped in his holes, covering them up just enough to keep them from being dug up again and making more work for him when he had to rebury them?

Did this snub-nosed creep run after Holly? I knew he did. He caught her and he killed her. With all he did to her, he must of thought she was dead. He had to think that. What I couldn't figure was why he hadn't buried her here. Why shove her in a bag? Why take the bag to Stapleton and dump it in Tompkinsville Square? I couldn't take my eyes off him. I had to know.

"Which one what?" he managed to say. As foolish a thing as I've ever heard a man ask.

Mickey grabbed a hank of that slicked back hair with its once perfect part, and pulled hard. I heard the bones crack in his neck. "Ye heard me. Which one?"

Mitt, openly crying now, couldn't answer him. He couldn't even shut his mouth.

Sweet Davy touched Cates' shoulder. "He's after choking, Mickey. He can't be talking if he's choking."

Mickey let go and Mitt's head snapped back. By now, his voice was a croak. Mitt croaked, "There were two last time."

"Then ye'll show us those two."

Like the Ghost of Christmas Past, Mitt raised an arm, pointing with one shaky finger.

Mrs. Willingford gripped my hand. Jane stood on my feet. Mickey walked forward to stand at the side of two fresh mounds.

"Dig 'em up, laddies. Dig 'em both up. We'll be after taking my Caitlin home."

"And the other?" asked one of the wild Irish lads.

"She goes home as well. The poor girl has people too and they're waiting for her whether they know it or not."

I got my moment with Mitt and I grabbed it.

"Why didn't you bury Holly with the others?"

"Who?"

"The girl you chased through the woods, the one who almost got away. You strangled her, you cut her, you beat her face in, you stuffed her in a duffel bag, but instead of throwing her in one of your holes, you took her all the way to Stapleton. Why?"

I didn't expect an answer. Guys like Coeslak usually died claiming they'd never hurt a fly. But he did answer. At first I thought he had an idea he'd hurt me because I cared. Then I thought he knew he was finished so why not one more wound before he went? But it wasn't any of that. He answered because he needed me to know he was proud of what he'd done.

That narrow head came up on that narrow neck. "Because that thing wasn't a girl. It made me sick. Running around naked with a purse. So I took care of it. I do my job here. I won't have a freak like that near the others. You get me?"

I wanted to kill him. I wanted to crush his skull with a rock. All I did was turn away.

It was bad. Two weeks under the ground, Chang Chang and Caitlin were hard to look at, hard to stand close to, hard to gather up, yet Mickey and his boys did it: efficiently, quickly and with tenderness. As if the bodies still held the women once within them, as if they were still young and beautiful—not dead, but sleeping.

Mickey turned to Mrs. Willingford. "Close your eyes, love. Walk away."

I thought he meant from the bodies. He didn't. He meant from Mitt Coeslak. Two of the boys had forced the grave digger, the cleaning man, the caretaker, down to his knees at the edge of the open shallow graves. He was held there as he wet his pants, calling out for mercy. From their God, his God, any damn God would do. The caretaker kept calling until he was silenced by Sweet Davy Malloy putting a .44 slug just above his right ear.

The sharp crack from Davy's gun flew out at the night like a black crow. Like a shot crow, Mitt plummeted straight down—all the way to hell, I hoped. No doubt Cates hoped that too.

When Mitt was down, Cates emptied his own gun into him, then kicked the boneless, headless body into one of the open graves and someone else covered him up with the same dirt meant to hide those two poor girls—forever if the killer's luck held. Judging by the number of mounds, forever didn't seem that far-fetched.

Trouble was, their luck was still holding. I could of got a lot more out of Mitt, or Jane could of. Mitt Coeslak was all we had to learn more about his "consortium," the people who came here and "did whatever they wanted to," leaving Mitt to clean up the mess.

I wanted to ask Mitt questions, a lot of questions. I wanted names, and if not names then aliases. I longed for descriptions, dates, car makes and models, a head count, who he dealt with most, how he'd been hired, how he was paid, telephone numbers if I got real lucky. Now Mitt was gone, I'd lost all that. He may have lied through his tiny teeth, but lies can sometimes tell interesting truths.

I thought of saying all this to Mickey, but gave it up. He wasn't thinking beyond Caitlin now. He wasn't thinking at all. What he was doing was arguing with Mullan. Mickey wanted to burn down the house. Mullan didn't. Mullan said with the house so old and so close to the trees, we could all go with the house before we found our way out of the woods.

I thought that made a lot of sense.

"Sam?" said Mrs. Willingford, cleaving to my side like a Siamese twin.

"Yes?"

"I'm beginning to wonder if I'm a bad judge of character."

I thought of Joker, of Woody, of Jane, even of me. "Nah," I said, "it's just that your brain falls asleep when certain other parts wake up."

"True. Can we go now?"

I didn't know where Mickey, Mullan, Malloy, the bodies and the lads went, but I did know they didn't burn down the house. As for me, I drove Jane and Mrs. Willingford directly to my place in Colin Dunne's Plymouth.

We were back over the line in Stapleton, skimming along Victory Boulevard where it crossed Westervelt Avenue, before Mrs. Willingford opened her mouth again.

Silent for miles, sipping from an engraved silver flask while I picked our way back by nerves alone, she said, "Oh right, I forgot to say. Billy's dead."

"Excuse me?"

"The police were all over the building as we left."

"We? Who's we?"

"And the rumors! It's worse than a men's room."

"What rumors?"

"Billy killed himself. Billy didn't kill himself. He had a lover. The lover killed him. Nobody believes that one. You've seen Billy. He walked in on a burglar. The burglar lost his head and so did poor Billy. For now, the cops like that last one."

"How'd he die?"

"Billy'd never kill himself. With all that money and all that prime cut conceit?"

I tried again. "How'd he die?"

"He fell."

"Billy landed on Park Avenue?"

"Good god, no. Pushed or not pushed, William Ransom Cunningham III had a sense of place. He landed on 71st Street."

"So you think someone killed him?"

"Isn't that the strangest idea? Not even a burglar would bother killing someone like Billy. They'd just conk him on the head, wouldn't you think? If I were a burglar, and I've given it some thought ever since my lock picking lessons— merely for fun, of course; it sounds such an interesting life, snooping about in other people's things, naturally I wouldn't take anything—that's what I would do. Conk him on the head."

"How'd you meet Mickey Cates?"

Mrs. Willingford stared straight out the windshield. It was dark. There wasn't much to see. Even Manhattan seemed subdued on its own island across the water. "He called me. He said you gave him my number— "

"I didn't."

"Well, that's what he said. He told me he was a good friend of yours and that you were in danger. He said we needed to talk. So, of course, I invited him over."

"As anyone would, a nice man you've never met who told you he was my friend."

"How was I to know? You have such... unusual friends."

I gave her that one. "Was Billy still alive at the time?"

"I suppose so. He certainly wasn't making a spectacle of himself on 71st Street."

"And Mickey arrived alone?"

"I thought he did. But when we left, this other young man, so good looking but alas too young, came out of nowhere in one of the hallways and joined us."

"Sweet Davy Malloy."

"Isn't that the most wonderful name?"

"He was a racehorse, the dumb kid I used to be, I'd bet a name like that across the board."

Mrs. Willingford turned towards me and smiled. In it was the closest thing I'd ever seen to a plea for mercy. Maybe Billy weighed less than zero on the Great Scales of Life, but he was still a man, and now he wasn't. And who let the Bogeyman in?

But all I could think was that it was Sam Russo who'd told Mickey who owned the Lagonda, that Mickey had been in Mrs. Willingford's building, and that William III had gone over a balcony.

Killers are generally lonely. But, sometimes, it takes a lot of people to kill one foolish man.

20

Mrs. Willingford spent the night in my Murphy bed.

We didn't eat, we didn't fool around, we didn't do anything but fall down and lie there. Wait. I did do something. She made me change the sheets.

Both of us had a restless night. Somewhere during the struggle to escape into sleep, Jane gave up, jumped off the bed where she'd been squashed between us, and went back to where we'd slept when Holly used the bed.

At the first faint light of dawn, my eyes snapped open. And the first thing they saw was the body of Joker Willingford's wife warm along the length of my own body, bare and lovely and mine for the taking. I got a nasty surprise. I didn't want her, not yet—it was still too close to whatever she'd done with Mickey Cates. I guessed I was going to need time to shake that one out of my system. Waiting for that to happen, I did some thinking which made me see what I should of seen all along. Mickey and Sweet Davy may have tossed Billy off that Park Avenue building, but it wasn't them who sapped me on the back of the bean while I leaned into Billy's rare Lagonda. How could they? They didn't yet know who owned the thing, or where it was. That meant it had to be an inside job. By inside, I meant someone in Mrs. Willingford's building had known I was there, they'd watched me. And then, when I was down in the dim parking garage, off-guard as I bent over staring at the locket Jane and I had given Holly for Christmas, someone hit me with something. My guess was a cane. The only cane that came to mind was Joker's, but I got rid of that idea as soon as it slipped beneath the sheets. Joker told me who owned the Lagonda. If he was involved, he'd keep that to himself. He *did* tell me about the Lagonda? Oh hell. He didn't. Mrs. Willingford told me who owned that car.

A second wave of revelation passed through me, one that curled my toes. If someone in Mrs. & Mr. Willingford's building had watched me, if they could get to the Lagonda without Billy ever being the wiser, then that same someone either lived in the building, worked in the building, or had complete access to the building. They could know Holly was there. Or that she would be as soon as Dr. Bloomberg fixed her up. *If* he was fixing her up.

No one could be more dangerous to the late Mitt Coeslak's employers than a living breathing talking Holly the Singing Hooker.

Fuck! Time to go.

I shook Mrs. Willingford awake, shoved food under Jane's nose, had me clothed and her walked so fast even I was impressed. As for Mrs. Willingford, considering what I'd told her, it was the fourth floor bathroom or nothing.

Mrs. Willingford chose my kitchen sink.

She also called ahead. Doc Bloomberg promised to have Holly in the lobby the minute we ourselves arrived in the lobby.

If we could of used Joker's airplane, we would of used Joker's airplane. A fast cab, a fast ferry, and Woody waiting at the other end to drive us up to Park and 71st was like racing the great Dan Patch against the clock when there were no pacers left to test him. We made record time.

Jane was out of the car and running for the carved marble entrance before we were out of the car.

Mrs. & Mr. Joker Willingford's building had one hell of a lobby. High painted ceilings, fluted marble columns, fancy wall sconces, a bank of slick elevator doors made out of inlaid woods, the marble mosaic floor in some sort of star sign motif, a long snaky granite topped desk for the doorman to sit behind when he wasn't opening and closing doors. Holly was laid out on a fancy gurney, her body wrapped up like a mummy, head and face included—I checked: those open holly green eyes were definitely hers. Doc Bloomberg at her feet, his eye-catching assistant and his assistant's assistant everywhere else, plus me, Jane, Mrs. W., and Woody, the four of us joined by Blackwell and Mrs. Applegate, for now Holly was safe enough. The usual residents dragged around the usual dogs: little snappy yappy ones, on the usual twenty-five buck diamond studded leashes, but they were keeping their distance from Jane which was pretty smart of 'em. Add to this a covey of cops investigating William Ransom Cunningham III's recent demise, it was more like the Marx Brothers at sea than a homecoming.

The man Mrs. Willingford actually called by his full name, Thomas Kunze, was like a director directing a mob scene.

"Sam," she said, "this is Thomas Kunze, senior doorman and the backbone of Park Avenue and 71st. Thomas Kunze, this is Sam Russo, Private Investigator."

I looked at Thomas Kunze and he looked at me. I don't know what Kunze saw, but what I saw was one of those uniformed martinets the war seemed to hatch by the hundreds from soft shelled eggs buried under rocks. A short slim older guy, back as straight as a ramrod, thin eyebrows raised to the thin hairline, any moment I expected him to bark: Get on your blasted horse and bloody charge those blasted Japs.

If Montgomery weren't over in England lording it over his fellow Englishmen, I'd swear he was in Mrs. Willingford's lobby.

We disliked each other instantly.

I liked the feeling just fine. This wasn't the Philippines, he was only a doorman, even if the senior doorman, I was with a Willingford, so to hell with that. I said, "How would a burglar get past you?"

"He wouldn't," said Kunze, "no one gets past me."

"Then Billy— "

"Billy, sir?"

"Mr. Cunningham."

"Mr. Cunningham was the sad result of none of us noticing his call for help."

"From his balcony? Except for maybe a pigeon, anyone would miss that."

For that crack, Kunze gave me a pair of pursed lips, a raised nose, thin and bony, a brown eye, rolling and blood-shot. His face said I may have arrived with a Willingford, but I'd leave as nothing more than a Private Eye. "I refer, naturally, sir, to a cri de coeur."

"His man, Daniels, he didn't hear this cri?"

"I'm afraid Mr. Cunningham chose a moment when Daniels visited his sister. Every Tuesday evening, like clockwork."

"So no one was at home?"

"Of course they were. Mr. Cunningham had a horror of

being alone. His personal secretary, his household staff, all were there. The police have questioned each of them. We've all been questioned. If a burglar wormed his way into *my* building, which I sincerely doubt, no one saw him come and no one saw him go. It seems an open-and-shut case to me. If Mr. Cunningham did not kill himself, then it was a terrible accident. The police are fools."

"How does a fat man accidently fall off a building?"

"He was, perhaps, swatting a fly. Now if you'll excuse me, I have a few tasks to see to."

"I'll bet."

Mrs. Willingford'd come home in the same clothes she'd gone out in. Once Holly was settled in, a hired guard at her door, Cora Applegate was on Lois like a dresser in a fast moving musical. Mrs. W. was out of her black silk dress, green shoes and green hat, and into a pair of cream silk slacks and a cream silk blouse in about one second flat.

Jane went off on a wander. Deep in thought, eating what Cook shoved in my hand, a cream cheese bagel with lox, I followed her upstairs and down, in and out of rooms, out onto the Willingford balcony directly over Cunningham's balcony a lot of floors below.

Jane took a dainty dump in a planter filled with purple petunias. I covered it up. Who would know?

A huge house hidden in the wooded heart of my island, Staten Island, used for a particular kind of party, otherwise empty except for a caretaker doubling as a gravedigger—who owned that house? Who was offering it for sale for enough money to buy the Empire State Building? In the Stapleton courthouse, the house and land was listed in the name of some strange company with a strange sounding name. That name was on the tip of my tongue. I got it. De Kaars en Bloed. Was this Kaars en Bloed, Coeslak's consortium? If Coeslak's consortium didn't own the place, did they rent it? If so, did the owners know what it was being used for? And oh, by the way, did the consortium know Mitt Coeslak was now as dead as their party favors?

Holly said the man in the passenger seat said the "Master" was pleased with the choice of Holly and Caitlin. Did he do the choosing? And Master? What the hell was he master of? What kind of group or club or consortium would have a Master?

Then there was the Lagonda, a car which led directly to the building the Willingfords lived in. The Lagonda was gone, snatched out from under my nose, you could say—along with the locket, proof I'd found the right Lagonda. The cartoon character who owned the car was also now gone—right over the side of the balcony outside his bedroom and splat onto the street five stories down. I didn't have to see the police photos to know that didn't make a pretty picture.

Did Mickey Cates, who'd meant to kill him for what he felt was a good and just reason, do the deed? Mrs. Willingford didn't think so, not Mickey. She didn't think so because by the time Mickey and Davy arrived at her place, Billy was already over the rail. I thought but didn't say: which means they missed their chance. I asked her why the cops wouldn't be all over Cates and Malloy? They weren't your average Park Avenue types. For that, I got another of Mrs. Willingford's looks. Someday I'd learn to stop asking her stupid questions. What cop would bother a guest of the Willingfords?

Back to the car, that hell of a car.

The core, the heart, the answer to the riddle had to be in that car.

21

After dinner, a clutch of Mrs. Willingford's friends came to visit Mrs. Willingford's "broken bird."

Holly's liquid dinner was fed to her, spoonful by spoonful, by Mrs. Applegate. Jane's dinner of the best red meat was cut up, cooked, and served by Cook personally. My dinner was set out on a table me and every kid at the Zawadzki Institution could of used as a raft—if there'd been a lake around, and we'd been allowed to swim.

You'd think after a boyhood like mine, food would get noticed, especially good food. It'd be important. But for me, food was just a necessary interruption to any otherwise interesting day. I'd take a good book any time over good food. I knew enough not to show this to the Willingford cook. I ate my dinner. I complimented her. The Willingford cook was built like a rolling pin. She beamed at me. Beaming back, I thought: don't cooks get fat? Especially ones who cook for the rich?

Like a kid on a church pew, I squirmed to be out of there. What I'd give to drop down to Billy's place and have a talk with Roger Rodegap, that personal secretary. He lived there, he had his own small room next to his own small office—he must of seen something. He also must know something about the Lagonda. For instance, who it got loaned to. How many keys were there? Who had one? Where the spare was kept? I'd love to drop down even farther and go a few rounds with the "senior" doorman, Thomas Kunze. No one could get by him? If that were true, which it wasn't—I'd got by a lot of doormen in my time; it wasn't always a cinch, but I hadn't met a lobby door I couldn't get through—there were a lot of doors in a lot of fancy halls I'd like to knock on.

But as I said, Mrs. Willingford's friends showed up to have a good look at Holly, drink Willingford martinis, and collect all the latest dope on Billy III.

What a bunch. Some lived in the building, some lived in buildings nearby. All of 'em were Park Avenue dames. Most of 'em wore big hats, small dresses, and stretched smiles. Mrs. Applegate and two of the little dark skinned helpers were run off their feet.

A few minutes was all it took to understand Mrs. Willingford's willingness to get the hell out of her own world and into mine.

After Holly was inspected, oohed over, and given gifts, Jane was engulfed.

"Oh, what a poor dear doggie, who cut you?" A dark look my way. "Nice puppy, nice poochie, if you could talk, I'm sure you have a few things to say about *him*." Another dark look, this time with the lift of a scarlet upper lip. "Shot, Lois? This poor thing was shot! And stabbed! How many times? Oh, my dear lord!"

After that, if I'd had a room, I would of been sent to it.

I grabbed a soft and distant chair, a whole bottle of hootch, some brand of single malt whiskey with a hair-raising Scottish price tag still stuck to the bottom, no glass, and eavesdropped while I smoked and drank from the bottle and fumed.

It took a bit of doing, but good old Mrs. Willingford worked them round again. She returned me to my former glory, the man they'd heard her speak of, her PI friend who'd solved all those dreadful crimes. It wasn't my fault Jane was one heroic mutt.

I got myself a glass.

A big redhead named Kay with a taste for small cigars, was having her stogie lit by Mrs. Applegate when it occurred to her to bother looking at Mrs. Applegate. "Excuse me, honey. Don't you work for the Hanley Notters on Park across 71st?"

"Say, that's right," said Gloria, a too tall brunette encased in a zoo of fur leaning forward to have her glass refilled from one hell of a martini pitcher. "Isn't your housekeeper a colored woman, Lois?"

Mrs. Willingford was on that one before Mrs. Applegate got her mouth open. "She's on loan."

"Loan?" This one word came out of every mouth but Jane's. And mine. All I was doing was itching to get my hands on a good book. There wasn't a book, a magazine, not even a newspaper in the Willingford living room. How did they live in it?

I don't know if anyone but me saw Mrs. Willingford make a fist. She longed to deck at least Gloria. I knew the feeling.

She said, as docile as Bluto, this dog we knew: "We've sent Otelie off on the Sip o' Sea. Her annual trip to Trinidad to visit relatives. And Cora here," Mrs. Willingford smiled at Mrs. Applegate who smiled back, "happened to be free to take Otelie's place while the Notters are off in Europe touring fine hotel rooms."

They all exploded at once.

"The Sip o' Sea!"

"Not the Willingford yacht!"

"So much grander than ours. I keep telling Davis we need something bigger."

"Otelie Coleman has it all to herself!"

"You don't mean to say she's alone at sea with that gorgeous captain of yours?"

"Every single year! All the way to Trinidad and back? Doesn't that take forever?"

"Why, you darling you—how generous!"

"Holy Moses, L!"

Kay wagged her cigar in Mrs. Willingford's face, which "L" took well. If I tried that, I'd get kicked. "Oh, sweetie, when do I get to sail on the Sip o' Sea? I hear it's a palace on water."

They'd exhausted the subject. It was time to turn on Billy III.

Gloria started it. Swinging her glass towards Mrs. Applegate—it was filled without a word from either of them—she said, "And now, girls, let's talk about what we came for."

"Billy," said Kay.

"Billy," said Gloria, "is right. What the hell happened? The Billy I know would kill every midget in Oz before he'd kill himself."

"Nicely put," said Mrs. Willingford.

"Was there really a burglar?" asked a sleek seal of a girl, the one who'd eaten every olive but one in a green glass bowl. I'd counted as they went in. There'd been thirty seven of 'em. "Mr. Kunze swore up and down this building was entirely safe, but if— "

A trim little blonde spoke up, one who'd sat keeping

herself to herself throughout. "Has anyone asked Edgar?"

Now I sat up. I'd never heard of this Edgar before.

"Oh BeeBee," breathed a broad who'd seen at least forty long hard years and hated all of them, "Trust you to hit one home. Lois, get Edgar Hubbard up here. If anyone knows, he knows."

"And tell him to bring Larry. I love mixed parties." That was Kay.

Mrs. Willingford snagged the last of the olives and fed it to Jane. "Can't. Didn't you say the Queen of Quotes has a cold?" She was asking BeeBee.

BeeBee sipped her martini. The others had put at least two away each. BeeBee's first glass was down half an inch. "He does. So he's calling in his copy."

Kay said, "But that doesn't mean we can't go down to him."

"If Edgar has even a sniffle," said Gloria, "I pity Larry. He won't be able to write a word, having to wait on Edgar every second of the day and night."

Jane and Mrs. Willingford were nose to nose, humming at each other. "Exactly," said Mrs. W.

By now, I knew who they were talking about. Edgar Hubbard wrote a syndicated column about Broadway, about movie stars who played Broadway, about Broadway stars in the movies. He was also on the radio with his own show. Edgar Hubbard wasn't as famous as Walter Winchell, but he was just as loud and twice as vicious. "Larry" had to be Larry Giuliano who wrote under the name of "Louise Cubbord." Louise wrote romance novels that sold more copies than Zane Grey.

So the rumors were true. Giuliano and Hubbard were

lovers. Gee, what a load of great stuff I was getting here. How handy it was going be in the years ahead. I itched to be out of there, into other halls on other floors, knocking on a whole load of other doors, getting them slammed in my face.

With all the olives gone, the seal girl was working on the cheese. If the sticks stuck through the cheese had been eatable, she would of eaten those.

"So," said BeeBee in her quiet way, "if he can't come to us, we can go to him. My place is right next to theirs."

The hard times broad held up her hand. "I'll second that."

"Go if you want," said Mrs. Willingford, "me, I have a guest in my home."

She didn't mean me, but everyone had forgotten about me. More than a little sloshed myself, I liked that just fine.

"But Lois," said BeeBee, "the girl has Mrs. Applegate— "

"Also a brand new television," added Gloria. "And what about the nurse? Not to mention the bodyguards. She doesn't need you, not all the time, does she?"

"Perhaps not me, Gloria dear, but Billy's place was full of Billy's staff, and look what happened to him."

BeeBee said, "Oh Lois, your staff is so much better."

"Jane?" said Mrs. Willingford, "do you want to go?"

Jane sneezed.

"Can't BeeBee. Jane has a cold too."

"Spoil sport," said BeeBee.

Mrs. Willingford sat straight up in bed. The bed I refer to was not the bed she shared with her husband Joker. Mrs. Willingford did not share a bed with Mr. Willingford. This was her bed, and her bed alone, the one in her room not even on the same floor as his bed in his room. To say I felt strange sleeping with Joker's wife in his own apartment would be putting it mildly.

Jane raised her head before I did.

"Sam," said Joker's wife, "BeeBee was right. We should talk to Edgar."

My head was pounding. Getting woken out of a sound sleep in a strange bed could do that. The earlier hootch didn't help. I touched the back of my head. I said, "Fucking ouch!"

She was already up, already dressing. Jane was already up, already dressed. "Come on, Sam. Put some clothes on."

"It's the middle of the night."

"Not quite. And Edgar never sleeps. What Edgar Hubbard doesn't know about this building isn't worth knowing."

That got me up, fast.

Before we left, I checked on Holly. She was asleep. The guy outside her door was reading. I got a look at the cover. It was called *I, The Jury* by some guy called Mickey Spillane.

I'd have to remember to try that one.

22

"I love dogs. I adore dogs. Come here, doggie."

Larry Giuliano, aka the romance novelist Louise Cubbord, was on his hands and knees in front of Jane. Jane walked right past him to jump up on the couch where Edgar Hubbard was laid out like a slab of fresh salmon.

He flapped a languid hand. "I hate dogs. I loathe dogs. Go away, dog."

Jane made herself at home on the Queen of Quotes' feet, smiling.

It was two in the morning. Mrs. Willingford was wearing a hat. But then so was I. All we'd done was take an elevator from the top of the building down to the third floor, but we'd dressed for Sardi's. Or she had. I was dressed for the Rexall on Bay Street and Victory Boulevard.

Jane was dressed in her usual outfit and a handsome one at that.

Edgar and Larry weren't dressed at all. Why should they be? They were in their own home minding their own business and Edgar had a cold. Or so he said. If he did, it wasn't much. A few coughs into a spotless white hanky, a bottle of cough syrup on the table beside him, a spoon for the syrup. The spoon looked clean to me.

Speaking of clean. Larry and Edgar's apartment looked hosed down. If there'd been scuppers in the floor, I wouldn't be surprised. The joint was sleek and modern and what they called minimal. It was clean enough to lick. I hated it.

I chose a chair that looked like Edgar's cough syrup spoon and tried to sit in it. Not sliding off was the tough part. I got a grip and held on. Mrs. Willingford leaned on some sort of gleaming black room-divider with a planter on top. She was using the planter full of clean plants as an ashtray.

I'd been introduced to them. They'd been introduced to me. They'd both got a huge taste of Jane. Now we were just sitting there. Or leaning.

I was fast wondering why we'd bothered.

I'd met a few homos in my time; some of 'em I liked, some I didn't. Some I liked a lot because some were Cole Porter. Porter was a real gent. And some were Holly. Not that Holly was a homo. I didn't know what Holly was, but she did. Holly knew she was a lady.

I wasn't all that taken with these two. Larry Giuliano was prissy and silly and sly. He wrote sly little books under a pen name that were pretty good. I'd read exactly one of them. The publisher called his books "romances," but I thought they were clever little digs at the rich and the famous. You could get enough of 'em, or I could, and I did. But I didn't slight the guy. He could write. Larry Giuliano was also scared. I'd say he was scared of Hubbard. If I were Giuliano, I'd be scared of Hubbard too. The Queen of Quotes was mean. Where I grew up, we'd get one like little Edgar Hubbard in every new batch. He'd be the snitch, the whiner, the hoarder, the practical joker, the conniver, the liar, the coward, the thief. His head would wind up in an unflushed toilet.

We learned it only made a creep creepier, and sneakier.

It looked to me like Hubbard had parlayed all these qualities into a New York City newspaper gossip column. And then into a syndicated radio show called *You Can Quote*

Me. I'd heard it a few times. I didn't like Winchell, but sometimes I listened. The first squawk out of Hubbard, I turned the dial.

Years of gathering the dirt on everyone he knew, and Edgar Hubbard was now a scary guy—if you had something to hide, and who didn't? Even I did, not that I knew what it was, but looking at Hubbard looking at me, I knew whatever it was, he'd find it. And, if he needed to, use it.

I remembered why we were here. If there was something about Billy that got him killed, Edgar would know it.

Into this vacuum, Mrs. Willingford dropped one of her small bombs.

"Fuck this."

"Shall I quote you, Lois?"

"Here's a quote. Let's stop pussy-footing around. Holy mackerel, girls. Sam is a PI. He's working a case on Staten Island. It led him here. You're a gossip, Edgar. And Larry, you know what Edgar knows. Billy didn't kill himself and he wasn't burgled. You two are in hiding. What gives?"

Larry's hand flew to his mouth. "Oh!" he said.

Edgar's hands stayed right where they were, folded like the pale white hands of angels on headstones. "I have a cold, maybe even the dreaded flu. You know, the one that's catching."

"Tell me another. What's scaring you?"

"Tell them, Edgar," said Larry, "please. This whole thing is driving me crazy."

"Now now, Miss Cubbord."

I said, "What whole thing?"

"We know who borrowed William's car." Larry was ticking with nerves. What he'd said came out as a blurt.

Edgar sat straight up and yelled, "Louise! Shut up!"
Then fell back with a whump. It was the worst imitation of
exhaustion I'd ever seen. Jane hadn't moved a hair. Neither
had Mrs. Willingford. But "Louise" had run from the room,
crying.

"Now look what you've done," said an exhausted Queen
of Quotes. "She won't be back for hours."

"We didn't come for Larry. We came for you."

"How cruel you are, Lois, how horribly cruel."

"You don't know the half of it," said my Mrs. W.

Edgar sat up as fast as he'd flopped down. "I don't?"

"You bet your sweet flabby fanny you don't. I'll tell you
what. You give me a little. I'll give you a little."

Edgar Hubbard thought his life was in danger. He thought
his lover's life was in danger. But here he was, endangering
both for more gossip. He was going to make that deal, I was
sure of it.

"You first," he said.

If my chair had let me, I'd have sat up too.

"Fine. When I was four, my drunken father beat my
drunken mother to death. I was under the kitchen table. I
saw it all."

The silence that followed was profound. I stared at Mrs.
Willingford. OK, right, I was already pretty sure she'd
dragged herself out of some sad and terrible hole somewhere.
I was damn sure that all on her own she'd made herself into a
classy upscale dame. But this? This was worse than anything
I'd heard from the kids at "home," and I'd heard and seen a
lot. She hadn't said much, but what she'd said made the sad
little story of my own life sound like *Rebecca of Sunnybrook
Farm*. I hadn't seen what happened to my mother, I'd only

played on her shallow unmarked grave.

Much more of Mrs. Willingford, and I was in more danger than Giuliano and Hubbard. I could be falling in love.

On the other hand, she could be lying.

I looked at Jane and she looked at me. I couldn't even count on Jane. Jane liked Mrs. Willingford.

When Edgar finally spoke, I knew I didn't just dislike him; I hated him more than I hated his taste in interior decoration.

"I can't use that. My listeners wouldn't dislike you. They'd dislike me."

"I know, darling. That's why I chose it. Now spill. Who borrowed Billy's car?"

All the way back up in the elevator, the three of us checking on Holly, checking on the bodyguard sitting on his chair outside her room, getting into bed, Mrs. Willingford hadn't said another word.

Now she was sleeping like a three year old kid. Lying next to her, I was like the guy playing the corpse in a whodunit. Wide awake, moving only my eyes, I knew every shadow on her ceiling, every fold in her drapes, every twitch of Jane's ears, every sound from down on Park Avenue. There wasn't much happening. It was raining, but not much.

Jane hated rain. I loved rain. It was the only thing we argued about.

Inside my head, everything was happening at once. First, it took everything I had to keep the image of little Lois out of my mind—if that was really her name back when. Lois Lane was Clark Kent's secret passion. Superman was Lois

Lane's. I couldn't believe Mrs. Willingford had chosen the name. Lois? Nah. Lois Lane was as swift as Lou Costello. There must be some other reason for the choice—unless it was her real name.

If I didn't ask, I wasn't going to know. And I wasn't going to ask. I wasn't going to ask her about any of it. Maybe one day she'd tell me. But I wouldn't bet on it.

Just before she fell asleep, Mrs. Willingford finally spoke. What she said was: "What a load of hooey."

"What's a load of hooey?"

"Those names Edgar gave us."

"Sounds possible to me."

"Sounds like purest crap to me."

"What? That people close to the Rosenberg crowd are not only traitors and communists, but sexual deviants and murderers?"

"Exactly."

I thought about that. "Well," I said after the longest time, long enough to wake her up, "rotten apples are usually rotten all the way through."

"I'll tell you about apples, Sam Russo. In a basket of them, most are just fine. Some are bruised and will eventually rot. A few are well on their way. But only one is really rotten. And it's that one apple that causes the rot in the first place."

"What makes you an expert on apples?"

"Trust me," she said, "I'm a world authority on rotten apples. I repeat: what a load of hooey. Now shut up."

And then she fell asleep again.

Some time later, I kicked off the covers. Bogart wouldn't lie here thinking about Lois Lane and Superman. And he wouldn't think about rotten apples—he'd be up and doing something. I had a trail to follow. The names Hubbard gave us were hooey to Mrs. Willingford, but not to me. The way so many Americans felt after the war—like the poem would say: *People, people everywhere, and who knew what to think?*—the country was a nervous wreck. So Truman got stuck with the Loyalty Oath demanded by scaremongers like the House Un-American Activities Committee chaired by J. Parnell Thomas. Or maybe Truman was in on it. How would I know?

A year back, just before my case of the three dead jockeys up in Saratoga Springs, which was before Jane and I were an item and before I got close to Holly, I'd been up to my usual evening pass-time: alone and reading books. Or alone and listening to the radio—I never missed Jack Benny. This time I was alone except for the usual bottle and skimming Drew Pearson's newspaper column.

Suddenly, with nobody listening but me, I was off the bed and yelling as I raced round my own room. "Wow. Wow. There's a God after all!"

What Pearson had written was that J. Parnell Thomas, the same asshole who'd pledged to "ferret out" all those who sought to destroy the American "way of life," the same exact guy who sent down a bunch of Hollywood writers, had got himself caught for fraud. The man who'd thrown screenwriters in jail for citing the Fifth Amendment went down citing the Fifth Amendment.

Sad thing was, the Loyalty Oath stood. If you didn't swear you were loyal, then you weren't. Makes good sense, right? But if you weren't loyal, who the hell would admit it? So, loyal or not, people signed. I was lucky. I didn't work for anybody but myself so I'd never been handed a pen and told to sign an oath or else. But I did wonder: loyal to what? I'd spent a lot of hours on that one and none of the answers made me proud of the new American "way of life."

I thought about Bogart. He and a bunch of his Hollywood pals cooked up a committee against the un-American committee. They marched on Washington. But a year or so back, Bogie said he'd been "duped." He said he hated commies as much as the next guy.

I didn't hate commies. I didn't hate Bogart for hating 'em. Most of all, I didn't know what a Communist was. I knew a couple who said they were members of something or other, but they seemed regular working joes to me. Bottom line, the whole subject interested me about as much as needlepoint.

What I *did* think was I ought to have a closer look.

Playing his sleazy game of gossip and dirt, Edgar knew everyone and everyone knew Edgar. From top to bottom, he had something on all of 'em. I got his thinking. It went like this: why wouldn't a traitor to his country also be a traitor across the board? He'd also think I'd be stupid not to check. And he'd be right.

I also had to go back to Mickey and Mullan. They didn't get to gun down Billy. Or cut his fat throat. Or hoist him over his own bedroom balcony onto 71st Street. Someone else got there first—which was a lucky break for such a nice bunch of Irish Catholics lads. Porky was probably just some fat schmuck stuck in the middle. If I'd never met him, I might muster up some pity. I shook myself. I did pity him. As much as I could. William Ransom Cunningham III was probably only guilty of being William Ransom Cunningham III. Not bad enough to justify knocking him off. Besides, the Irish mob would want the two creeps Edgar Hubbard fingered more than they'd ever wanted Billy.

But this time, I'd get to them first.

I pulled up the covers. I was asleep in seconds.

23

"Jesus, Lois. Not again. Give me a break."

Mrs. Willingford was kissing my face, my eyes, my mouth. I pushed her away. She was back, wetter than before.

"No!"

When my eyes snapped open, I was staring straight into Jane's.

Gah. Not getting kissed, but licked.

"Get off dammit! Stop it, Jane."

Nothing woke Mrs. Willingford, but me, I was fending off Jane and her long Egyptian tongue.

She was talking. I even knew what she was saying. She was saying: Wake up. Get up. Follow me. Come quick.

She won. I did all the above.

Jane running flat out—it was all I could do to keep up— suddenly let out a yodel Heidi would envy. And then she changed gears and disappeared, right towards the door to Holly's room.

The only thing on the chair meant for her bodyguard's butt was I, The Jury. The book was splayed open face down.

Jane and I were in that room faster than I've ever been in any room.

Under all those bandages, Holly was fighting to breathe. Her hands were raised, her fingers scrabbling at her throat. Tied tight around her neck was her intravenous line.

No time for knots. I snatched up the surgical scissors off Holly's table and cut the line, a line that should of just hung there, innocently connected to her bottle. Instead it'd been choking the life out of her.

Once it was cut, whatever drug Doc Bloomberg had given her conked her right back out.

I stood there, catching my own breath, looking down at her. My poor Baby Shauer, my prickly funny pretty Holly, the girl in the room next to mine, the one who walked the streets dreaming of Hollywood. Twice now, someone tried to kill her. Before the old bruise had faded, there was a thin new bruise circling her slender neck. I leaned over and kissed her forehead.

"Sam's here, Baby. Jane's here. You sleep."

Behind me, I heard her guard rushing into the room. Coming to a skidding halt, his face was white with professional shock.

"A piss! I swear I only took a piss."

"Shut up. Where's the emergency call button?"

He pointed. I rang the damn thing. Holly needed a doctor and she needed one right the fuck now. I left the guard dying on his feet until I was certain one was on his way.

That done, he had my full attention. "How long?"

The man was gonna cry. Not for Holly. He didn't know Holly. All he knew was the hall outside her room. He must of felt like crap. He knew he could lose a plum job with the Willingfords. Add that to getting canned from his agency, he had a lot to cry about. I didn't give a damn how he felt.

"A minute, maybe two. But no more than that. I used the servant's toilet. It's right across the hall. See?"

He strode back to the door and pointed. Jane and I followed and looked left, right, straight ahead, up, even down. Holly's paid guard really could of been gone maybe a minute, maybe two. But a minute could be one hell of a long time for someone waiting to take advantage of him pissing. They'd of had to wait for hours somewhere real close to get this one perfect chance. But there wasn't anywhere nearby. Not to hide and wait in. And not to go unnoticed in.

The guard was hopping from one foot to the other. "It had to be an accident. She had a bad dream. Something like that."

With a head full of Edgar's treasonous spies and Truman and loyalty oaths, it followed as a closer follows a sprinter that I was wondering if brought in as a bodyguard, maybe Joker's hired help was actually a double-whatever. In other words, an assassin. J. Parnell Thomas said America was overrun with 'em, we had a commie assassin spy a block.

An accident, my ass. Tubes don't accidently tie themselves.

Jane was sniffing the guy's shoes, the cuffs of his pants, his hand, the floor beneath him, the floor just inside Holly's door.

"What's your name?"

"Howard."

"How long you been on duty, Howard?"

"Four hours and seventeen minutes of a six hour shift."

"Who's been in her room?"

The guy used his fingers. "Let's see. Who hasn't been in her room? The doc. The doc's assistant, who is, by the way, va-va-voom— "

"Forget that."

"It's forgot. Mrs. Applegate. Blackwell. Two maids cleaning things. The cook. Cook was in and out a lot, stayed talking when the girl was awake. Uh. Mr. Willingford."

"Joker? When was he here?"

"Four hours ago. Give or take."

If Joker tied Holly's tube—so easy, even an old fart could do it in seconds—two things would now be true. Holly would be long since dead. Somebody coming along after Joker would notice she was dead. Scratch Joker.

"Who was the last person to go in?"

"A maid. I think. Yep, pretty sure it was a maid."

"The usual maid?"

"How would I know? This place is loaded with wall-to-wall help."

Howard was right. The Willingford's staff could of kept the Queen Mary running. A chill ran from the top of my head right out through my toes. I knew all along someone would need Holly dead. Holly was a night's entertainment—after that, all she was supposed to do was die. Like Caitlin and Chang Chang. But Holly didn't die. Holly still hadn't died.

Alive, she was a danger to all of 'em, a fatal danger.

Holly wasn't safe. Not at my place. Not in a hospital. Not in the Willingford's Park Avenue joint at the top of an exclusive well guarded building. Not even with extra security laid on.

The only reason Holly wasn't dead now was because of Jane. She'd heard it or sensed it or whatever the hell she did, but Jane saved Holly.

How many times would that happen?

Fuck.

"Jane?"

Jane practically stood at attention. What am I saying? She did stand at attention.

"Stay here, Jane. Guard Holly. Don't eat a thing anyone offers you, not even if it's Cook. Don't let anyone touch you. Above all, except for the doc don't let anyone near Holly. Got that?"

She got it. By now, I could tell. I was learning her language.

Howard had watched, open mouthed. "You always talk to dogs?"

"Sure. Especially dogs three times smarter than you."

Howard got pink, then red. He wanted to say something, but what could he say? The girl almost died on his watch.

I said, "Sit the fuck down and don't let anyone but the doc in this room. Not a maid or Cook or Mrs. Applegate. Not even Joker. Unless I say so."

"But— "

"You want to keep this job?"

He nodded. Oh yes. He wanted the job.

"You move, you're dead. Holly is worth ten of you. I'm serious. Mrs. Willingford will be down in a few minutes to back me up."

"OK."

Howard sat down.

I was up the stairs as fast as I'd come down them. Trouble was, I got lost. Where the hell was Mrs. Willingford? Where was I? How could anyone live in a place they could get lost in?

I needed to be out running down the two names Hubbard gave us. I needed coffee. I needed to know who tried to kill Holly—again. Most of all, I needed to keep her safe. But for the moment I needed a map.

I ran smack into Mrs. Applegate.

Didn't she ever sleep? Didn't I?

"May I help you, Mr. Russo?"

A quandary. Did I admit I was looking for Mrs. Willingford's bedroom in her own house with her own husband around somewhere? Or did I pretend I had a room of my own and get directed somewhere I'd never been and then what?

Mrs. Applegate took pity. "Allow me to assist you."

Trim from behind with a nice walk on her, the borrowed housekeeper led me down a few halls and up a few stairs, and there it was, the door to Mrs. Willingford's room—which was really a suite of rooms.

I thanked her.

She didn't smile. She didn't speak. She just left me there. If not for the danger Holly was in, I'd of been abashed. I didn't even know what abashed meant, but I was sure that's how I felt.

It was the work of mere moments to get Mrs. Willingford up, dressed, and downstairs calling for Blackwell.

The man wasn't exactly as magical as Billy Cunningham's Daniels, but he'd do. Perfect aside from his untied shoes, he'd appeared from somewhere, alert as Jane. "Yes, Mrs. Willingford?"

"Assemble everyone in the joint. I want to see every man jack of you in Cook's kitchen in five minutes. Not a second less."

"Yes, Mrs. Willingford," he said, and was gone.

Left to ourselves, I said, "Why the kitchen?"

"Where else? Aren't you starving? I am."

I saw her point.

"Where's Jane?"

"Guarding Holly."

"Ah, good. No one will try again with Jane there."

"And Howard."

"Who's Howard?"

"Never mind."

24

Ten minutes later, the yawning Willingford staff was standing in the Willingford kitchen—and what a kitchen, not that it mattered. What mattered was how many there were. When Christie assembled her suspects at the end of a book, she kept the number to a manageable level.

My suspects were legion.

This was 1949. We were in Manhattan. There'd been a world war a few years back. People were hurting for money. Who had staff? This was ridiculous.

There was Cook, upset at the use of her kitchen, a young man who must be her main assistant, and a set of matching colored helpers. Only in my own kitchen to boil water or heat a can of soup, I wouldn't know what helpers helped her do except clean up the mess she'd made cooking. There was Mrs. Applegate, the housekeeper-on-loan from the neighboring Notters. There was Blackwell the butler, who doubled as Joker's valet, the one Mrs. Willingford would like to replace with Billy's man, Daniels. A thought. With Billy a goner, maybe Daniels needed a job? Blackwell wasn't going to like that. There was Woody the chauffeur who'd once saved my life while Jane was also busy saving it. Woody, built like a boxer, and about as smart, was a magnet. Maids, like iron filings, clung to him. If Woody noticed, you couldn't prove it by me. He was smoking a long brown cigarette and idly playing with Cook's hanging pots. Cook quickly and quietly got him to stop it. Mr. Willingford also had a driver since he and the Mrs. often went in opposite directions.

No one clung to him. A small man with a small brown moustache, man and moustache as compact as a suitcase, he kept to himself in one far corner. As for Cook's helpers and all those maids, I was having trouble counting heads. Twelve in all? Thirteen?

"Mrs. Creez," said Mrs. Willingford, "I need coffee. Mr. Russo needs coffee. I expect everyone needs coffee. Make a big pot of the stuff and keep it coming. We might be here awhile."

Aha. That was Cook's name: Mrs. Creez. Mrs. Creez hopped to it.

I loved watching Mrs. Willingford do her stuff. In the muck at racetracks, up to her hips in Hudson River mud, driving too fast on narrow wooded back roads, breaking and entering, navigating hats through doorways, a bed here, a bed there—the woman was better than most of the movies I'd seen.

A man didn't know where he stood. OK by me. I wasn't standing anywhere.

Her cup balanced in one hand, a cigarette in the other, one robed hip holding her steady against a huge chopping block, she said: "Not more than an hour ago, someone tried to kill a guest in my house."

Up rose the expected gasps of surprise, horror and innocence.

Trying to catch every face at once—impossible—I missed Jane like I'd miss an arm. Jane could smell guilt as easily as dinner, or fear.

As for me, over my own cup of coffee, staring at a lot of frightened faces, I got it. Not in Stapleton, and not in Ashley Wilke's house hidden away in the middle of the wilds of

Staten Island, and maybe not in this kitchen, maybe not even in this apartment, but somewhere in this building lurked the answer to what had happened to Holly. It was suddenly as obvious as the moustache on the upper lip of Joker's driver. Before Mickey and his friends executed Mitt Coeslak, Mitt said he worked for a consortium. A consortium was nothing more than a clot of people with a common interest. Killing young women for fun couldn't be all that common, but that was about the size of it.

The rare car Holly and then Caitlin got into came from Park Avenue and 71st Street. The man who owned the car that took Caitlin and Holly and Chang Chang away was murdered at Park Avenue and 71st Street. Someone had tried to kill Holly, and came this close to getting away with it. And where? In a classy apartment in a Park Avenue building with a round-the-clock doorman and a guard outside her bedroom door.

A load of rich people lived at 71st and Park, enough to form more than one consortium and rich enough to buy a big isolated house on Staten Island. I'd lay down good money that not one of them was called either of the two names Edgar Hubbard gave us. Mrs. Willingford had that one down cold. It was a load of hooey.

Mrs. Willingford was still scaring her staff. With a head full of martinis and moustaches, I'd listened with only half an ear.

"Isn't that right, Sam?"

"What?"

"What I just said. Aren't you listening?"

"No. Is there a dumb waiter in here?"

"No. Unless you mean you."

"Snappy. Answer me, kid. Is there one?"

"No."

"Just a thought. Isn't what right?"

"Honestly, Sam. I asked who else could have got to our Holly except someone in my apartment?"

I looked at a load of black and white faces who were staring back. They all looked guilty. They all looked innocent. I said, "Looks like it."

"*Looks* like it? Who else could it be?"

"Dumb waiters. Balconies. Secret passageways. Hidden doors. Extra keys. An innocent visitor not so innocent. An employee with other ideas."

I watched for a reaction to each word I said. People like Blackwell and Mrs. Applegate were trained not to react, not even when the people who employed them were halfwits, thieves, sons-of-bitches, murderers, or pointing fingers. People like Woody were too dumb to catch on. People like Mrs. Creez lived in the kitchen and for the kitchen. The rest of 'em needed the job. Every face in the room was stony.

"It could even be an accident."

That lightened a few brows.

"But, believe me, it wasn't."

They all went dark again. Stony, but dark.

Mrs. Willingford was staring at me like I'd escaped solitary at Bedlam. "No dumb waiter. No secret doors or passageways. Who could get from one balcony to another? An ape maybe?"

"I've read that. Poe, right?"

Turning back to her trapped staff, Mrs. Willingford was closing like Whirlaway. "Anyone let anyone in last night?"

A lot of shuffling, a lot of turned down faces, some

more of Woody playing with Cook's stuff, this time the knife rack.

"Is that a no? A yes? For crying out loud, answer me!"

Mrs. Applegate stood forth like the trouper she was. "The staff is my responsibility, Mrs. Willingford. Just as it's Blackwell's responsibility. Let us question them each individually. Why don't you see to your guest? Cook will make you and Mr. Russo breakfast. We'll have answers for you as soon as possible."

The lord of the manor chose that moment to limp into his own kitchen, what little hair he had standing straight up, every year he'd lived and then some carved into his face like the rocks of Mr. Rushmore.

He lifted his cane. "There you are, Blackwell!"

"Indeed I am, sir."

"Where the hell is my coffee? And today's paper?" He stopped, finally took a good look round, and almost dropped his dentures. "What in blazes is going on here!"

Mrs. Creez slipped coffee into his hand, Blackwell slipped a chair under his rump, his wife steadied him as he sat in it. She said, "There's been an incident during the night."

"An incident? Where? What kind of incident? Someone been at the horses?"

"Here, darling. New York City. The horses are fine. It was Holly, the young woman in your special room."

"What about her?"

Time I said something. Who was Bogart here and who wasn't? I said, "Someone tried to kill her. Strangled her with her intravenous tube."

Joker choked on his coffee, tried to stand up, fell back instead, spilled the rest of his cup in his lap, and coughed.

The coughing was, in a word, spectacular. Why it didn't kill him on the spot, I couldn't say. It would of killed me.

Everyone tried to help him at once, until one voice rose high above the hubbub. Mrs. Willingford's, of course. "Blackwell, call his doctor. Now!"

"He's already here, Madam. He's with your guest."

Fifteen minutes later, we had two invalids and one doctor rushing back and forth between them. The doc was the Willingford doc and I knew him well. Dr. R. T. Budge also knew me well, as well as he knew Jane and my luxurious room over in Stapleton. He'd gotten stuck with us—well me; Jane had her own doc who liked her—after I'd been shot three times and she'd been stabbed eleven times up in Saratoga Springs.

For two months, just for me, Doc Budge had been stashed away in a local hotel on the Willingford dime.

I didn't like it much. He was ill with fury.

Old Doc Budge made a point of not saying hi. I made a point of not only saying hi, but following him around, asking him questions, second guessing him, and just generally getting him to like me even more. Jane, sticking to her guns, wasn't budging from Holly's side. I'd had to hold her back so Budge could do his job.

Turned out both patients would live. Joker had his own bottle and tube now and his faithful wife forking over the scrambled eggs and soothing his troubled brow. If Joker hadn't done the deed, someone had—in his home, his private domain, his castle. Joker Willingford, fourth generation owner of Joker's Special Blend, distiller of great booze, and fourth generation owner of the venerable Beeswing Farm, breeder of fine horseflesh, was steamed.

Holly was hooked back up to her own new bottle. With me doing the spooning, Holly got Cream of Wheat. As for the soothing brow thing, Jane was doing that by lying next to our Holly and humming a catchy tune.

Around about then, with the Willingford apartment thrumming with nerves from top to bottom, I noticed something I hadn't noticed before. I got up and walked over to it. On the wall was an ornate frame. On every damn wall wherever you looked, there were ornate frames framing all sorts of stuff: some of which I liked, some I'd wrap fish in. But this frame was different. It wasn't just a frame with a nice painting of Fleeting Fancy in it. Frame plus picture was a hinged door. Like a cabinet door. It'd been left open a crack which is why I noticed it now when I hadn't noticed it before. Behind the frame plus painting wasn't a cabinet but the back of another painting. The backs of paintings are obvious. They're made out of canvas and they give a little. I pushed the second painting, also hinged.

It swung open into the room next door. And who occupied the room next door? A big room, nicely done, with en suite bath and a small kitchen.

Blackwell the butler and valet, that's who.

I imagined my little gray cells were loop-de-looping.

25

Seven years back, the Kentucky Derby was cancelled because of the war. But Colonel Matt Winn, the final word at Churchill Downs, stood his ground. The old man'd said, "The Derby's always run through every war. It'll run through this one. It'll go on even if only two horses run, and only two people watch."

The race was on.

With gas rationed, Winn discouraged out-of-towners and told the locals they couldn't show up in a car. If they were coming, they'd have to get to the track any other way they could. Sixty thousand flocked to the first wartime Derby and all sixty thousand came on foot, on horseback or in horse-drawn streetcars.

The Kentucky Derby of 1942 was called the "Streetcar Derby" and I wish I'd been there for all sorts of reasons. One of 'em meant I'd be missing my part of the war. Another was to see all those people on horses again. And another was to see Count Fleet win—and, if I got lucky, to see him act up.

The Count's worst ever finish was third thanks to a filly called Askmenow. Askmenow wasn't asking, but the Count was offering. Askmenow was running their race in heat. The Count's jockey, Johnny Longden, said, "He came up, got a whiff, practically propped all four feet to slow himself down, and then just galloped along beside her. I couldn't budge him."

At the end of the race, Longden had to jump off, and

haul Count Fleet off the track.

I mention all this because of what happened next.

The kitchen was full of Mrs. Applegate drilling the staff. But out in the living room it was three in the afternoon and the joint was stuffed with women. The last clutch came back, every one of 'em: BeeBee, Kay, Gloria, whoever and whoever, and more besides. Most of 'em had a dead animal flung round her neck. Beady black eyes were everywhere.

A fluffy young blonde stood over Holly. Next to her, a sleek brunette, older but still a doll. The place was stuffed with Willingford friends; these two were Holly's friends. Once they'd been friends of Caitlin and Chang Chang. Together, they worked the ferry or Tompkinsville Square.

One look from Mrs. Willingford and "her" friends had nothing but smiles for Holly's friends.

I knew them both and they knew me. The youngest was Kitty Anne. If she was sixteen, I was fifty. The older one called herself Ruby. The Willingford joint made 'em nervous but they'd come bearing Holly's favorite flowers, peonies.

Only one face surprised me. The head doorman showed up as an extra added attraction.

It was Kunze got me thinking about Count Fleet's Streetcar Derby which made me think of Count Fleet's worst finish. I figured Kunze was here following his nose. Turned out Mrs. Willingford and friends had demanded his presence. He was supposed to be their building's first and last line of defense. They had some questions for him.

I was glad to see him. I had a few questions of my own.

Even better luck, lost behind a pillar, lurked the late William Ransom Cunningham III's private secretary, the one Billy said was too thin and had too much hair on his head.

Billy, fat and balding, was right. Roger Rodegap could of passed for a palm tree.

Rodegap was another character of interest. He had to know some things I'd like to know myself.

That cute couple down on the third floor were invited too. Hubbard and Giuliano sent a boy along with a scented note. It said: Thanks but no thanks.

I'd miss 'em. But I planned to corner one without the other. First, Larry. Pick on the weak. It works.

I'd make a try for a whole lot more of 'em as soon as the time was ripe.

Meanwhile, there was the little matter of getting into Blackwell's room without anyone seeing me. I had a little plan, one that needed Jane.

Jane was free. Holly didn't need her for the moment.

Joker's "death bed" had wheels. Mrs. Applegate, with Woody's help, steered Holly out into the middle of the enormous living room as the guest of honor. In the center of a clatter of oohing and aahing dames, she was having a hell of a time. She couldn't sing, she still couldn't talk in that funny husky voice of hers, she sure couldn't dance, *and* she was wrapped up as the Mummy's Daughter, but somehow, she was managing a show.

As the center of attention, Holly was at home again, her friends at her side, but I needed more of a distraction than Baby Shauer. I needed a show stopper, something that would focus every eye on something, anything, that wasn't me.

I had Jane in a corner, just about to set her in motion, when the doorbell rang. It took a couple more long hard rings before Blackwell heard it over the racket of everyone talking at once, but when he did, he scurried off to answer.

Wouldn't you know—Mrs. Willingford had thought of everyone. Mickey Cates and Sweet Davy Malloy stood there, hats off for a change, reasonably dressed with white carnations in their wide lapels and their shoes shined. The guns were probably in their socks.

Mrs. Willingford's friends were thrilled. If they didn't think they were meeting real life *Guys & Dolls*, I don't know what they thought. Speaking of which, one of my deepest regrets was never meeting Damon Runyon when he was still walking around, writing his stories and running his great little string of horses, at the same time betting all he had on some nose or other.

All we needed now was Sal Ploverman and the party was made.

Fuck. I made myself sick thinking this was a party and the guests just guests. I forgot what was real here and what was pure sick crap. Holly was lured off the streets to a party supposed to end in her death—the big finale. Holly lived. But Caitlin died. Chang Chang died. Two young women were thrown in a hole behind a hidden house and covered over in dirt. They'd be there now with all the others if it weren't for a man I'd hated for years—a man who killed people for a living. I took a real good look around me. Mickey Cates and Sweet Davy Malloy were what they were. No pretense, no apologies. Mrs. Willingford was also the real deal. I had no gripe with Lois Willingford, the little girl who hid under a table watching her father kill her mother, hearing every brutal blow, smelling the blood and the bone and the madness of it. For the first few years of her life she lived with drunken fumbling love and drunken vicious hatred, sick and sour and deadly.

She was once a little girl who couldn't save her mommy.

And then again, maybe not. Who really knew? She could of made all that up on the spot for Edgar Hubbard, the *You Can Quote Me* creep.

Either way, Mrs. Willingford was a woman who'd invented herself just as Holly had invented herself.

Sam Russo, hardboiled Private Eye, stood there filled with love for two brave inventions.

I snapped out of it when Kay shrieked, "Jeez Louise, Lois, you know the most cunning people!"

Getting fed something delicate on the end of a fork held out by the solid little blonde, BeeBee, Holly tried to smile.

Beside me, Jane sighed. With a fingertip, I followed the long curve of one of her scars, the slice that came closest to killing her.

"Jane?"

I got her full attention. Looking Jane square in the eye was all I needed to know someone was in there. As if I needed more proof.

"I never thought I'd say this, but all I want is to go home. I want you and me and Holly back in Stapleton, me reading books, Holly singing in the tub, you humming along."

Jane closed her eyes and hummed. For that one long moment I hummed along and was happy.

That is, until I looked up and they were all still there, all the rest of 'em, Mrs. Willingford's shrill painted pampered "friends," and the numberless people who tended to their needs, quietly, efficiently, moving through each and every day nursing whatever needed nursing. You name it. Someone was nursing it.

Looked like I didn't need a diversion. Staff was either being given the third degree in the kitchen, or out tending to the guests. The guests were either cooing over Holly or oohing over Mickey and Sweet Davy. No one would try for Holly in the midst of this mess and for sure not with the Irish about. I'd had a few short words with Mickey. He got it before I was finished telling it. Either Cates or Malloy would be no more than two feet from Holly for the duration.

I'd checked on Blackwell. Joker's butler was sticking close to Joker after his dressing down for the lack of morning coffee and morning paper.

This was my moment. Jane and I took it.

Blackwell was not a minimal man. If anything, he was Victorian. If there was a spare inch going for one more trinket, statue, framed photo, lamp, fringed tablecloth, ashtray, candy dish, candlestick, table lighter, doily, shell, vase, or throw pillow, you couldn't prove it by me. Jane saw the doll collection before I did. Blackwell had enough dolls for a doll museum. I'd think about what that meant later. Right now I was making a beeline straight for a framed picture on hinges that matched the framed picture on hinges in Joker's special room—the room Holly lived in until I could get her out of it.

On Blackwell's side the frame had a small brass latch. In other words, while Joker had no way of keeping his own picture with frame where it belonged, which was flat on the wall, Blackwell could latch his.

I opened and shut his picture a few times, opened and shut the picture behind it. Open, it gave whoever was looking a perfect view of Joker's bed. Or, in this case, Holly's bed.

I'd wondered where someone could wait unseen for

Howard the bodyguard to leave his post. Howard was bound to leave. No man could sit on a chair for that long without needing a piss. Or something. Well, here was the answer.

The paintings that were also doors didn't bother me. If Joker's special room was set up for him to die in, then it followed he'd need checking on from time to time without a lot of fuss and bother.

What bothered me was Blackwell. Whoever waited for Howard's move, had to use this room. But so did Blackwell. It was his. He bathed in it, slept in it, kept all those dolls in it. If it wasn't Blackwell who'd dashed in and out of Holly's room as soon as he saw his chance, then who did? If it wasn't Blackwell, where'd he spend last night and did he spend it there knowing someone was in his room when he wasn't?

"May I help you, sir?"

I spun round. Joker's butler and valet had not only opened his door, he'd closed it behind him, without Jane noticing.

I called that slick.

Jane, her head buried deep in the pile of dolls, noticed now. She was up and fast heading his way. I caught her collar just before her leap.

"Help me? You bet. Where were you last night?"

With Jane poised for action, with me holding her back, in the face of my question, Blackwell kept perfectly still. Except for the left corner of his mouth. It twitched. He said, "A gentleman doesn't tell."

"Oh, he does," I said, "he tells everything he knows, or his employers will finally call the cops and cops are such snoops, doncha think?"

"I have nothing to fear from the police. Mr. Cunningham's

death was ruled an accident."

"I'm not talking about the fat man."

"I repeat, sir, I have nothing to fear from the police."

"Righty-ho. I'll go tell the Willingfords that."

I'd dragged Jane to the door, was just turning the crystal knob, when Blackwell spoke. "With Mrs. Applegate, sir. I'd hate to have you ask my friend to verify this, but if you must."

"Your friend?"

Blackwell had the grace to blush. "Well, I, she— "

"I get it. You're saying you weren't in your room at all last night? You were in Mrs. Applegate's room?"

"That, indeed, is what I'm saying. Although we call them quarters, not rooms, sir."

"Quarters. I'll remember that. But OK. We'll stick with your story for now. Where's Applegate's quarters?"

"Next to Mrs. Willingford's, sir."

That meant while I was lying there counting wolves, household hanky panky was going on in the next room. For shame.

"Bit risky, eh what?"

"If you say so, sir."

His accent was catching. I heard myself say, "Don't be cheeky, Blackwell. Look around. Any signs of someone else spending last night in your quarters?"

If Blackwell was lying, he was close to the best liar on my list of all time great liars. He looked about with interest, noted my fiddling with his picture frame door, clucked his tongue over his dolls—Jane never slobbers, her nose was never wet, but she'd dug deep into the dollies which tumbled them every which way—checked his bed was as he'd left it, his sink, his bureau drawers, his closet, his collections. He was so thorough, my left bicep fell asleep. That particular bicep was a legacy of my last big case, the one where I got hit with a rolling pin.

"Yes. I'd say someone was here."

"Why?"

"The cushions." He was pointing at a rocker. "One is facing the wrong way. Unless you, sir— "

"Didn't touch it."

"In that case, someone else did. So yes, someone has been in my quarters. Aside from you and your dog, of course."

My dog was back messing with his doll collection.

"Will that be all, sir?"

"Jane! We're leaving. Knock it off."

Jane's red and white head rose from under the dolls. Held neatly between her perfect white teeth, dangled a black mask.

Blackwell and I did the same double take at the same time, but only I said, "Fuck me."

26

If it was Blackwell's mask, you couldn't prove it by me. Or Blackwell. The butler hadn't turned colors. He hadn't proclaimed his innocence. All he'd done was looked confused as he stared down at the gift Jane had brought me. He said, "What's that? None of my dolls wears a mask. And none is sizeable enough to wear this mask. How did it get here?"

The question I would of asked him; he'd saved me the trouble. So I asked him another.

"Ever hear of De Kaars en Bloed?"

If the man was lying, he got even more impressive. Not a fidget out of him, not the twitch of an eyelash. "Never, sir."

"Neither had I, until I did. Give it here, Jane."

Jane dropped the mask into my outstretched hand. I slipped it into a pocket.

OK. So someone had spent the night in Blackwell's room. Someone had slipped out his door when Howard made a break for the nearest can. They'd slipped into Holly's door, tied the tube the doc had stuck in her around her neck, and slipped out again. That someone badly wanted her dead. And what other reason could there be for that other than needing her mouth closed, forever? Did that someone, for some reason, leave the mask on one of the dolls? Or stuffed down between them? And were all those someones Blackwell?

In other words, did the butler do it?

I felt faint. Not as faint as getting sapped leaning into a

Lagonda, but faint enough. Bordering on dizzy. Bloody hell, as Blackwell would say, Bogie wouldn't sit still for a Christie plot for all the dope in China. Wait. There was that moment in *The Maltese Falcon* where he was the only good guy in the room—if you didn't count the dame, and turned out, you shouldn't. The world got steadier. Not as steady as it was before Holly disappeared but steady enough.

Jane and Blackwell and me were out of his quarters as slick as Blackwell'd got in.

Back in the fray, I pulled Mrs. Willingford away from the hats and mouths and beady black eyes and into a corner. Jane didn't come with us. She was off sleuthing on her own, taking a whiff of everyone there. If there were awards for Best PI of the Year, Jane would win before me.

Mickey Cates, not a man to miss a trick, left Sweet Davy Malloy to stand near Holly and was off and sliding our way. What the hell. Before my chat with Blackwell, Mickey knew as much as I did. Now I knew more. No reason he shouldn't too.

So, under the leaves of some sort of huge plant, I told the both of 'em about Blackwell's quarters, about Blackwell himself. I showed 'em the mask.

Mrs. Willingford wouldn't touch it, but Cates crushed it in his fist. If there'd been a face behind it, he'd of gouged out an eye or two with his bare fingers. I got the mask back off him before he could do more than rumple it.

Both of them looked for and found Blackwell. He was back to hovering over Joker. I looked for Mrs. Applegate. I didn't find her. But she was around somewhere. She had to be. It was her job.

"Is it Blackwell, Sam," said Mrs. Willingford, "is he part

of the consortium? The Bloed people? Dammit, Mickey. If you hadn't been so hasty, we could have learned so much from that loathsome gravedigger."

"I'd do it again," said Mickey. "No man deserved it more. For no more than a wage, he went about a terrible business. The others do what they do out of a dark sickness in the blood."

Mickey did what he did for a wage. I passed on saying so. Instead I said, "Or they're nuts."

"Or wicked," said Mrs. Willingford, "as wicked as Hitler. Or Dracula."

Mickey smiled. I'd never seen him smile.

"Blood!" hissed Mrs. Willingford, "I forgot. A friend who speaks Dutch, told me De Kaars en Bloed is Dutch. It means Candle and Blood. Or close enough."

Well, whaddaya know? That explained the C and the B on the gate I stupidly opened with bolt cutters. The house in Blood Root Valley housed a club. Nice. The Candle and Blood Club.

As expected, Mrs. Applegate was back, working the crowd. I was keeping an eye on the borrowed housekeeper, hoping to see her keeping an eye on Blackwell, when Mrs. Willingford suddenly said, "I have an idea!" Then galloped off.

Mickey and I admired her exit.

"Now there's a woman."

"You said it. And one likely to gum up the works."

"Possibly, boyo. But watching her do it is after being a pleasure. You're a lucky man."

"Um," I said.

"Now answer me this, Sam Russo. Ye've seen the house,

ye've seen the filthy graves and what was in 'em, ye've seen the car and the locket, ye know just as I know the fat man was a killin' not an accident, ye've heard what our Holly has to say, and ye know the lass's life is in danger, even here, on this street of streets. What do ye and your dog make of it?"

Mickey's accent was getting thicker by the second. I put it down to us becoming pals even if only for now. I was no pal of Mickey Cates, but though I fought against it, manfully I might add, my righteousness was fading away.

"That the consortium is right here in this room. Or at least some of them."

"And why would ye be thinking that?"

"Because the problem has never been getting into Holly's room. It's been getting into the building. Which can only mean it's already in the building. That means whoever killed the fat man and is trying to kill Holly is in this building or can get in whenever they like."

Mickey's second smile was wider than his first. Only a few days back, I wouldn't of believed it—it was charming. He gave me a small salute. "I'll leave ye to it then."

Mickey was off to watch Mrs. Willingford. Jane had settled on Mrs. Applegate. I settled on Kunze the head doorman.

Kunze—just Kunze, if he had a first name I didn't care if I knew it—was all he'd been the first time I'd seen him: Field Marshall Montgomery in a doorman's uniform. He was as close to the punch bowl as he could get without hopping in. He had a weenie on a stick in one gloved hand and a martini glass in the other. There was a smear of mustard on his chin.

"Remember me?"

Kunze looked me up. He looked me down. He stopped looking at me at all. "The gumshoe with the mutt."

"Nice. You live in the building?"

"Who wants to know?"

"That would be me."

I watched Kunze thinking. It was painful. He was thinking that either one of the Willingfords could get him the sack. He was thinking I might have enough muscle with the Missus to make that happen. If he was thinking anything else—and he was, his jaw was working and a blood vessel had popped out on his forehead—I wasn't yet privy to it, though I hoped to be.

"I got a place here, yeah."

"In the basement?"

"Fuck you."

"No thanks. You must know everyone, and I mean everyone."

"Sure."

"You check their guests?"

"Natch."

"You don't talk like this to them, right?"

"Talk like what?"

"Like a poor man's Dead End kid."

"Fuck you."

"Ask all you want, I'm spoken for."

"Huh?"

"If I recall, and I do, you claim no one gets into this building without you knowing."

"That's right."

"How many entrances?"

"Plenty and they're all covered round-the-clock."

"That's what I thought. Makes it look bad."

That remark got his attention, all there was of it.

"What the hell does that mean, bub?"

"Oh, nothing."

I floated off.

I found Roger Rodegap in the library sitting in a wing-backed chair near the fireplace. It was May. There was no fire but there were plenty of books. Everyone else was half a block away talking or posing or drinking. Roger was hunkered down and reading. A reader myself, I checked the title. *Leave Her to Heaven.*

I thought I might take that advice.

I sat in the chair next to his. Mine was also a wingback, but I liked my fabric better.

"Good book?"

It was like he was shot. Rodegap's head jerked back, taking all that hair with it, his eyes rolled around until they found me, and there they stayed. "Book?"

"You're reading a book. I'm great at spotting these things. Is it good?"

"Not bad. They're on a beach."

"Good for them. You work for William Ransom Cunningham III, right?"

"I did. Poor man."

"I met Mr. Cunningham. Gotta ask. What did he need a private secretary for?"

Rodegap smiled. At least I think he smiled. Maybe he'd eaten something.

"He was writing his memoirs."

"He had some?"

"Not really. But as do most people, he liked to think

so."

"He get far?"

"If you call age five far, I guess so."

"That accident, what a way to go—a fat man falls over a chest high wall. Not something you read about everyday. Where was Daniels?"

Roger Rodegap's gaze lifted off and came to rest far away, somewhere across the long tall-windowed room.

"It was Tuesday evening. Daniels' night off. He said he was going to his sister's."

"Been back since?"

"Now that's a curious thing. With Mr. Cunningham's staff finding new jobs, or like me, helping the estate with his affairs, such as they are, you'd think Daniels would be Johnny-on-the-spot. All our wages are paid until the end of the month. But no one's seen him since he walked out the door."

"And Bil... sorry, Mr. Cunningham, was still alive?"

"Well, yes. Alone in his bedroom. He was usually alone in his bedroom. He virtually lived in that bed. I heard Daniels say he was off—excuse me. I simply must ask. I've told all this to the police, why am I telling— ?"

"Because I think Billy was murdered."

If Rodegap could of, he would of jumped out of his skin.

"But I... but they... but... you *do*?"

"Do you?"

"Why, yes. I think I do. I heard something that night. After Daniels had left, perhaps an hour later, I thought I heard the front door open again. With a key. Only the staff had keys. With the exception of Daniels, who had left, everyone was in their room. I'm damned sure of that."

Puzzle pieces were falling together in my head, a large and messy puzzle. "You have a look?"

Rodegap's eyes were back on *Leave Her to Heaven*, his long pointed fingers caressed its cover. I knew the feeling. He longed to be back in its pages. "No. Well, yes. But only a peek. I confess I'm not a brave man. If it were a prowler, what would I do? I have a phone in my room but I had no real reason to call the police, just a feeling."

"How'd the peek go?"

"I didn't see anyone. But Mr. Cunningham's door was just closing."

"You didn't wait 'til it opened again? Try for a look at who went in coming back out?"

"No. I didn't think it *would* open again. I merely thought William—I was allowed to call him William—had peeked out just as I had. I thought we'd both been mistaken. But then a few minutes later I thought I heard the front open and close once more."

"You tell the cops this part?"

"I tried. I don't think they were listening. The head doorman was always nearby, Kunze. He was loudly and continuously proclaiming no one ever got past him, and certainly not on Tuesday night. He was also adamant that once Daniels strolled away, as he did every Tuesday night, he did not return. So I left well enough alone. After all, Mr. Cunningham was gone, and he wasn't coming back."

"One more question and I'll leave you to your book."

"Why, thank you."

"You're welcome. The car, that Lagonda of Billy's, how many keys were there?"

"Two. One on Mr. Cunningham's keychain. It was there when the police came."

"And the second?"

"Daniels was charged with it. For safe keeping. I don't know where he kept it."

That tore it. I took the mask out of my pocket, showed it to Rodegap.

"Ever see one of these before?"

"A black mask? Yes I have. Once."

"Where?"

"On Blackwell, the Willingfords' butler, he said he was attending a costume party."

27

Holly was back in her room, exhausted from her day's efforts—if anyone was born for stardom, it was Viola's baby boy, little Baby Shauer, come to earth in Tottenville, south of Nowhere, Staten Island—Sweet Davy Malloy had replaced Howard, not outside her door but inside where they both watched television. They made a cute couple, or would of if Holly were still cute.

I caught myself. No matter what, Holly was one cute kid.

The painting frame doors between her room and Blackwell's room had been nailed shut, I assumed Blackwell was in there rearranging his dolls, and Mrs. Willingford and I were on her balcony, looking out at the lights of Manhattan. From the Willingford balcony we could see the short block to Central Park. 59th Street and Fifth Avenue was blocked by apartment buildings like the Willingford building, but across Central Park the West Side looked like the necklace I'd priced for Holly's birthday. I'd worked out the cost. Three years of my time, and nothing left for dog food. She got the pink silk purse from Macy's, the one she'd carried the night of the Candle and Blood party. The one she'd somehow held on to.

Jane was lying on a cushioned bench, her dazzling white front paws crossed, her black nose on her paws, her eyes gold by the light of candles.

Mickey Cates was seated in a huge whicker chair, a

brandy in one hand, a Havana cigar in the other.

I'd told them about Roger Rodegap, about Daniels, about Kunze, about where Rodegap had seen a black mask before. After I'd wound down, we'd all gone silent.

Mrs. Willingford was the first to break it.

"The way I see it's like this. My entire building is infested with dangerous pests and you, Sam, are the pest remover for which you will be paid a handsome fee."

I could use the money. So could Holly. But cash wasn't even in the gate. I said, "The way I see it's like this. Your building is infested like mine has cockroaches. Holly has to get out of here."

"Pests can swarm," said Mickey. "She's safer here than your place."

"I wasn't thinking of my place. You must know somewhere."

"I do indeed. But not for the likes of her."

I bristled. "What's that mean?"

"That means, she's too fine a lass to get stuck with the likes of me and mine." He slugged down Joker's brandy, made by Joker's distillery, and poured himself some more. "So was my darlin' girl, my Caitlin. I was after havin' dreams of the both of us going back to Belfast, maybe buying a pub. If a man's dreams make the man, then what am I now? My dreams have been stolen away."

I couldn't answer that one. All my dreams were borrowed from images playing across what they called the silver screen. When the picture wasn't playing, all I saw was white. Mickey's dreams were set on an Irish girl, a lass who walked the streets. Jane's dreams were full of humming and paw twitching. People always assumed cats were chasing mice, dogs were chasing cats. I assumed Jane was chasing crooks.

Mrs. Willingford, who never lost a chance to pursue a dream, broke it up. "If Holly stays here, then you and Sweet Davy stay here, Mickey."

Mickey drained his glass. "Done," said he, "but I'll be needin' another man."

"As many as you want," said Mrs. Willingford.

My stomach sank but my spirits rose.

"Just the one, Missus. Davy and me and the other, we'll take it in shifts. I'll be wantin' the closest empty room."

Mickey Cates winked at me. So he knew. He knew and he was giving me a gift. I didn't wink back. How much more before I liked this guy?

Jane and I were alone on the Willingford roof. It'd been some time since we'd been on our own, just us and the starry sky over Manhattan.

"Jane," I said.

"Hummmmm," she said.

"We don't know who killed Billy. We don't know if Billy was mixed up in all this or just some useless rich mug with a great car to take whenever needed. You heard Edgar's pet, the lovely Larry. He said they knew who borrowed the Lagonda. I don't think he was lying, but I think Edgar was lying. Traitors and spies. That was him slinging hash to cover for Larry telling us a truth. They're scared. We know that much, right? What else do they know? We don't know who tried to kill Holly. We don't know who hit me over the head and took the Lagonda away. Was it Blackwell? I'll tell you what I know. One crummy little creep or a lotta crummy creeps, they're part of Mitt's consortium, the Candle and Blood Club. We know they own the house in the middle of Staten Island's deepest woods. We know they've owned it long enough to monogram the gates which means they've held a lotta parties there. We know Blackwell is a member. If you think about it, so is Mrs. Applegate, that is, she's a member if she confirms she spent the night with Blackwell. I'm willing to bet if I asked her, she'd say she had. And I'd say: in a pig's eye. The Applegate dame wouldn't give Blackwell the butler the time of day. But she'd cover for him. Which is why I don't need to ask her. Call it a hunch."

Jane agreed. I could tell by the pitch of her hum. It went up.

"Let's call that two of 'em. If we add Daniels, there's three. Either Daniels came back and let someone into Billy's place, or someone else has a key. That someone makes four. Or three if Daniels is out of it. None of 'em could be the guys who drove Billy's Lagonda, or Holly would of noticed and said so. So those two guys are two more. Either they used Billy's spare key with Billy none the wiser, or they used Billy's key because Billy was one of 'em. Holly said there were at least twenty in that house. She wasn't counting the servants. You remember what Holly said?"

"Ooooooh."

"You said it. She said the one in the passenger seat called the one driving: 'Master.' He said he was pleased the Master was pleased with their catch. Their catch was Holly and Caitlin. Someone else delivered up Chang Chang."

I lay back and counted the stars. With the glow from a sleepless city, there weren't many to count. I could name a few I learned from a kid trapped with the rest of us at the

Home for Those who Hadn't Run Fast Enough.

Jane hopped from her seat to mine. I held her, nuzzling her ears, scratching her scarred chest, pointed out the one star shining through New York City's own starlight. "Sirius, Jane. Brightest star in the sky."

Mrs. Willingford had her dreams. I had mine. I still wanted to be Bogart. Maybe I'd always want to be Bogart. But for now what I wanted most of all was to be Sam Russo and nail the sick sonofabitch a sick bunch of ugly people called Master.

It was a safe bet Jane was happy being just Jane. Who wouldn't be? She was swell. Right now she was humming up at the brightest star in the sky. For all I knew, she was communing with the beings that lived there.

Once upon a time my favorite beings down here on Earth were horses. They still were, with the exception of Jane. But you couldn't run around New York with a horse. You couldn't let a horse sleep in your Murphy bed. And, so far, I hadn't met a horse who could talk. I'd seen a talking mule but that was in the movies.

For some reason Sir Barton entered my head. Sir Barton won the first Triple Crown of horse racing, not that they called it that then.

Sir Barton was a throwback to the miserable Boston. Like Boston, sire of the great Lexington, he was surly. Sir Barton bit. He kicked. He hated humans and didn't much care for animals. His feet hurt. He was lucky the day of the 1919 Kentucky Derby. The track was muddy and it soothed his aching feet. He was called the Great Hophead. Sir Barton spent his races stoned on cocaine.

I wasn't doing anything but wandering around in my

head. I'd like to call it thinking, but without Hercule Poirot's "little gray cells" it wasn't getting me anywhere. I gave over some of my gray cells to the idea of cocaine. Cocaine could get me thinking, or at least running around and babbling. Forget cocaine.

But the whole idea of running around mindlessly babbling gave me an idea.

I'd get round to the two charmers on the third floor, the liars who hadn't lied about knowing who drove the car, but first there was Mrs. Willingford's friends, the rich dames who gathered in her idea of a parlor, putting away pitchers of martinis and yakking a mile a minute. And the first liquored up babbler who came to mind was the cigar smoking Kay.

I wanted to know about Mrs. Applegate without asking Mrs. Applegate. I didn't want to ask Mrs. Willingford's staff about her either. If Blackwell wasn't on the up and up, then who else wasn't? Anyone in the whole fucking building could be a member of the Candle and Blood Club. But I could ask Kay. I could be wrong, but Kay seemed the type who'd tell anyone's secrets—except her own. I could be wrong again, but I didn't think Kay was the type to wear a mask and go oooooh! when a man called Master slit a girl's throat.

No asking twice for information and addresses. Mrs. W. had it all in my hand faster than she could run.

Redheaded Kay was a pauper compared to the Willingfords. She was poor compared to the late William Ransom Cunningham III. She was Midas compared to me. The cost of her dye job was probably more than a week's rent on Room 4-A.

Kay Kershaw lived in a building next to the Willingford

building. Not the one on Park, the one on 71st Street. It was closer to New York City's grandest park but farther from Park Avenue. It was smaller, shorter, newer, and the doorman's desk was wood not marble. That must of hurt.

Kay was widowed once, divorced three times, childless, seemingly without family and certainly without any obvious skills if she ever needed a job which I doubt she ever would. She was also a cigar smoking lush. It was ten thirty in the morning. If she didn't slide off her couch by noon, I was John Barrymore.

The woman was dogless, birdless, fishless, and legless— as the Brits would say—but not catless.

A feline the color of old pewter walked into the room. It had a face as fat as Billy's had been, but it wore nicer fur and had smarter eyes.

Jane was on her feet instantly. I was on my guard. I wasn't getting anywhere if Jane ate Kay's cat.

"I don't believe in giving an animal a silly name," said Kay, scooping up her pewter cat. "This is Frank Sinatra. Named after my favorite singer. It was either Frank Sinatra or Mel Tormé. I did toy with Bing Crosby, but Frank Sinatra it was."

Nothing silly about that.

I said, my hand inching nearer to Jane's collar because the rest of Jane was inching nearer Kay's cat, "Frank's a good looking cat."

"Not Frank, Mr. Russo, Frank Sinatra." She nuzzled Frank Sinatra who looked, frankly, bored. "Now how can I help you, honey? On the phone, you said I might be of some assistance."

She held out one of her cigars for me to light and I lit it

with my Zippo. There was one of those huge table lighters right out there in the open, as obvious as the economy sized bottle of Joker's Special Blend, but we both ignored it. I was the only one of the two of us who ignored the booze. I'd already decided a woman like Kay required a clear head. Also it was too early even for me.

"What do you know about Mrs. Applegate, the woman you said worked for the Hanley Notters currently infesting Europe?"

"Oh. Her." Kay looked disappointed and who could blame her? A man who I'm told resembled Robert Mitchum sits in her best chair, lights her cigar and he wants to talk about another woman? The other way round, I'd be disappointed if she looked like Lombard. Hell, if she looked like Lombard, I'd be devastated.

"Yep, that's the one. In your opinion, which I imagine is as sound as a dollar—"

Kay perked up a little at that, fed Frank Sinatra something out of a bowl on the table and gave herself more in her glass.

"—can you see Mrs. Applegate sleeping with Blackwell, the Willingford's butler?"

Kay spat Joker's Special Blend all over her red negligee. I'd noticed she hadn't bothered dressing up to greet me. Or perhaps she had. I also noticed she was alone. No butler, no maid. Just Kay and her cat.

"Sleeping with—you can't mean?"

"I do."

"But Blackwell? Who'd sleep with Blackwell? Unless he was rich as Rockefeller, who'd even use the same toilet? I mean, she's only a housekeeper, but—the very idea. Excuse me, but I need a drink for that one."

Of course she did. Frank Sinatra got a chance to make his escape, and took it. Unfortunately, so did Jane.

"Sit down, Sam," said Kay as I stood to give chase. "Frank Sinatra's come out on top with bigger dogs than yours."

Shit. Was I going to have to shoot Frank Sinatra?

The rest of my time with Kay was spent trying to listen to her, to me, and to the distant sound of a cat shredding my dog.

I left when Jane came trotting back, unscathed and humming.

I wondered if Frank Sinatra was crooning the same tune.

28

To sum up, what I got out of the redheaded lush was that Blackwell was lying. He hadn't spent the night with Mrs. Applegate. But if he had, the two of 'em hadn't done more than play a few hands of cribbage.

Jane and I paid our next call on Gloria Bentworth.

Gloria was taller than me, her hair was darker, her voice was lower—to my ears, anyway, and she was an office supply heiress. Not like Doris Duke was an heiress (tobacco money), or poor old Barbara Hutton was an heiress (Five & Dime store money), but however much she'd been left, she was having a great time spending it.

Gloria lived in the building on the other side of the Willingford building, the one facing Park Avenue. She did not smoke, she'd never been married though she was constantly asked—seems pots of money will drive any man to the altar—had never been widowed, but made it into the society pages at least once a week. She had no cat. What she did have was a foul tongue. To say our conversation was spicy wouldn't be spicy enough.

"Applegate fuck Blackwell? I've seen things in the zoo that woman would hump sooner than Blackwell."

"You know Mrs. Applegate?"

"Well sure." Gloria paused. She had to think about that. Does a person with a certain social status "know" the housekeeper of a matching set of persons with their own social status? "I mean I don't actually know her, you understand, Biblically or any other way, but I've seen her at the Nutter's place doing whatever she does, and then there she was at the Willingford's. It surprised me."

"You get any feeling about her?"

"You could fucking say so, buster. I get chilled. She's cold as fish piss."

Cold as fish piss? I'd remember that, use it myself.

I said, "So... unlikely to be anyone's lover?"

"Oh, I don't know about that."

"Which means?"

"Unlikely to fuck men is more what I meant to say. Your dog there, the bitch on my Aubusson, might see some action, but not you." Gloria, the paper clip heiress leered at me. "You wanna dance? I got one hell of a record collection. Hold on. I'll put a record on."

"No... wait... I... shit."

Frank Sinatra. Who could of guessed? *I Don't Stand a Ghost of a Chance With You* drowned out whatever she was saying over by her record player. I wasn't sure I cared. I lied. I knew exactly how I felt. I didn't care.

Gloria danced by herself. Jane and I watched with a jaundiced eye. I don't know what Jane saw, but I saw a contortionist's act.

Gloria suddenly whipped the needle off. It didn't do the record any good; worse than that, I discovered I needed a dentist. As Gloria would say: fucking ouch.

"OK," she said, "so you're a cold fish too. What the fucking hell d'joo fucking wanna hear? Hurry up. I gotta see a man about a shave."

"What about Blackwell?"

"What about him? He's a butler."

It was hopeless. Mrs. Willingford's fabulous friends paid no attention to the "lower classes." They were there merely to hand out the goodies and keep their traps shut.

I gave it one last shot.

"How about Billy?"

"Who?"

"William Ransom— "

"Oh him! We called the fat little bug Tick, as in mattress ticking. I never saw Tick out of bed. Of course, I seldom saw him at all. Who'd want to? Lois didn't tell you that? She didn't tell you we called him Tick?"

"'Fraid not."

"Fuck. Why should she? He didn't really exist until somebody killed him. But why they bothered, for the fucking life of me, I couldn't fucking say."

BeeBee Nash occupied an apartment on the third floor in the Willingford's building. The rest of 'em would call it small. I liked it. I liked it a lot. BeeBee Nash's walls were slathered in oil paintings I understood. There were trees in 'em, and farmhouses, and some horses. Her chairs and couches were leather, soft and old. She had a real fireplace with real logs. There were flowers in tall vases and none of 'em roses. Big yellow flowers. Hell if I knew what they were but they made me smile.

One whole wall was full of books. I was glad she kept me and Jane waiting. I could look at her books.

"Whaddaya think, Jane? Think we could get to like this room?"

"Hummmm."

"Tell you what, we ever get any money, I'll get us a place

like this. Not on Park Avenue. Even if I hadda lotta dough, Park Avenue isn't for us. I'll tell you something, the whole place gives me the heebie jeebies. I'm asking you, would Bogie hobnob with this bunch?"

"Oooooh."

"You said it. The Village, that's the place. Look at this. This dame's got *Raintree County* too. Funny the guy goes and kills himself with four kids and his book selling. No telling about people, is there?"

"Hummmmm."

"What's this?"

I'd pulled *Raintree County* off the shelf, up high and off to one side, but not too high and not too far to one side. I was looking at the dedication—Miss Nash'd got it signed by the author—when I noticed something tucked behind the books shelved on its left. I was telling myself I shouldn't snoop when I remembered who the hell I was here. Someone once called me a "peeper." I hated it, but if it didn't fit, what did? I peeped.

What I was looking at was what you'd call a "dirty book." No image on the cover, no author's name, no publisher. The cover itself was rough blue paper. Inside, the printing was third-rate, but you can take my word for it: it was legible. Behind this one, was another dirty book bound in plain paper. Still no author, no publisher. And behind that, another one. I flipped through some pages. A couple had pictures inside.

I was no prude. I loved doing interesting things with Mrs. Willingford. I loved her doing interesting things to me. But these nasty little books turned my stomach. They weren't just books talking about sex the way I'd heard Henry Miller, the banned book guy, talked about sex, and they weren't just about sex between a man and a woman. The way I understood sex, they weren't about sex at all. I guess you could say they were about making people feel small. They were about hurting them.

I pulled out a few more. All in all, there must of been a dozen or more of the things.

"Woooooo," said Jane.

I could tell from the rising pitch, she was telling me to put the books back and step away from the wall.

Not a moment too soon. BeeBee Nash was in the room. She wasn't smiling. She wasn't not smiling. Had she seen me shove *Raintree County* back? Had I been caught stepping away from the books too fast?

I didn't know. Did I care?

The BeeBee I'd met at Mrs. Willingford's wasn't the BeeBee I was faced with now. Mrs. Willingford's BeeBee was quiet and mild and helpful. This BeeBee had her feet planted on her carpet like Count Fleet's were once he got a strong whiff of the filly Askmenow.

"Yes, Mr. Russo," she said, "my maid said you wanted to see me?"

The questions I'd thought to ask her now had dried on my tongue and I'd swallowed them. I was chewing on new questions, questions I couldn't ask because if I was right, she'd lie—so what'd that get me? Lies.

Good old Jane. With me standing there looking as guilty as hell of something, Jane took a sudden leap at BeeBee Nash. Not an attack, it was one of those things some dogs do that everybody hates.

Even so, even I was surprised. Jane never jumped up on people. Not only was she too refined for such crap, she didn't need them to like her. Since most of the time she didn't like them, why should she care if they didn't like her?

I realized I'd just seen why I was never going to get to the bottom of Jane Russo, Sam Russo's best friend. She'd covered for me, taken BeeBee's mind off what I might or might not be doing while I waited for her.

"Get your dog off me, Mr. Russo. Make her sit!"

"Jane, for pete's sake, sit."

When I told her to get off Billy, she didn't. When I told her to get off BeeBee, she did. She dropped to the floor as if nothing had happened, and sat there, cleaning her front feet. Like a cat.

I was back to facing Miss BeeBee Nash: not married, not divorced, not widowed, not somebody's mistress, not an heiress, yet rich. She made her money decorating other people's apartments.

Looking down into her rough blue eyes—Nash was short, the top of her small blonde head reached about as high as my small red bullet holes—I answered my own question. Did I care what she knew or thought she knew? As Gloria would say: fuck no. I didn't need to ask what BeeBee surmised or didn't surmise about Mrs. Applegate or Blackwell the Willingford butler. The only thing I cared about was those hidden books. So what if she'd seen me with them, or if she noticed later sometime they weren't like she'd left them?

What I wanted to know was who was BeeBee Nash. Why own books like those books? I didn't have to ask why she'd hide them. Who wouldn't?

A picture was forming in my mind. Blurred edges, no center, but a picture nevertheless. The only problem was how did I frame it?

"Well, Mr. Russo? You're here. I'm here. What's this all about? Did Lois send you?"

Time to scare somebody. I was betting that scaring BeeBee would scare somebody else and that somebody would scare somebody else, and pretty soon there'd be some scared people. They were already scared. Why else did they try and silence Holly? But Mickey Cates was with her, and so was Sweet Davy Malloy, as well as some other nice Irish lad over from Érie, so if she wasn't safe now, she never would be.

I didn't like the sound of that thought so I took it off the turntable.

It seemed to me that whichever creep was "master" of the Candle and Blood Club needed a new target and that might as well be me.

"No, Miss Nash. Mrs. Willingford doesn't know I'm here."

BeeBee was getting jumpy. I liked it. The jumpier she was, the less jumpy I was. Goes without saying that the less I was, the less Jane was. It was a nice situation.

"So what are you doing here?"

"Something wrong with paying a call?"

"Yes, if you don't know the person you're calling on. And they don't know you."

"There you're half wrong. I'm getting to know you."

"Excuse me?"

"OK."

"I'd like you to leave, Mr. Russo."

"I'd like that too."

"Then why don't you go?"

"You want me gone, answer one question."

"What question?"

"Why were you so eager to get Mrs. Willingford and me out of her apartment?"

"What are you talking about?"

"I'm talking about the day before yesterday. I'm talking about you suggesting we all leave the Willingfords."

"And where, might I ask, is the harm in that?"

"It left Holly on her own."

"You know as well as I do she wasn't on her own. She had the Willingford staff. She had a guard."

"And yet someone got to her anyway. Speaking of staff, how well do you know the Willingford's butler?"

"I don't make a habit of knowing butlers. And that's more than one question."

"How well do you know Mrs. Applegate?"

"Who?"

"You know exactly who I mean."

Jane and I were told to leave. We were told nicely. There was no sense of rush or panic.

BeeBee Nash had lied to us three times. She'd denied she cared one way or the other if either of us ever left the Willingford apartment again. She'd denied she knew Blackwell at all. By not answering, she denied she knew Mrs. Applegate.

If I'd asked her about the books, she'd of lied about them. She'd say: What books? Maybe even: Oh my God, where did those come from?

Jane and I went on our way up from the third floor to the top floors of what I thought of as the Willingford Building. We were humming a tune she'd made up.

29

Holly was sparring with Sweet Davy Malloy. She had him on the ropes and she knew it.

Swaddled and bandaged and half bald, she was still Holly and she still had what it took.

It was her eyes. It was the way she had with words. Mostly it was Holly. There wasn't anyone like her, no one as funny, as open, as unexpected—except maybe Lombard. I had no higher praise.

"Jane! Sam!" she said when Jane and I walked into her room. "Come give us a kiss. Here I am, learnin' a bit o' the Irish."

Her voice was still husked. I would of loved the sound of it if she hadn't got it the hard way, the hardest way.

I nodded at Sweet Davy Malloy, who nodded back, then sat on the chair I'd already spent hours on. Jane hopped into my lap. From there she was on a level with Holly's sight line. I couldn't see it, but I knew she was making Jane faces. I couldn't see Holly's smile, but I knew it was there.

"Davy," I said, "Could you be fetching Mickey and Mrs. Willingford? Time we had us a talk."

Davy wasn't out the door before Holly laughed. "Well, now, Mr. Russo. Ye said ye didn't know how to speak other than English. Ye lied."

"I never lie," I lied. "I love you, Holly."

"I love you too, Sam Russo."

Jane and me and Holly waited for the little talk I planned

and all the while I held the hand Holly'd stretched out to me. Holly's nails were growing. From delicate thumb to delicate pinky, they glowed with lizard green polish.

Bogart didn't cry. Sam Russo did. But only a tear or two.

Mrs. Willingford, Mickey Cates, Sweet Davy Malloy, Jane, me, we all sat around Holly's bed.

The third man, Matthew, stood at her door, making sure no was "just passing by."

Speaking low—just in case—I'd told them everything I knew, everything I suspected, everything I thought we should do. I told them I didn't have proof, no point in alerting the local cops. We could point out the graves, let 'em know what'd been going on, but knowing Police Detective Lino Morelli, he'd go straight to the *Staten Island Advance* so he could get his mug on the front page. I could see the headline now. SEX AND DEATH HOUSE ON STATEN ISLAND. I could see the photos. Lino pointing at the house. Lino pointing at the graves. Lino pointing at himself.

Once the Candle and Blood Club read the paper, they'd buy another house somewhere like the Great Swamp of New Jersey, and that would be that.

So, considering which cops we'd get, no cops.

I told Mickey I needed his help. I needed Sweet Davy's help. Mickey said I'd get help from every Irishman he knew.

I'd counted on that.

Then I told them how hard it was going to be.

They, meaning "them," the bad guys and gals, knew we knew about the house. They had to know. Holly had told us. But did they know I'd found it? Unlikely. I was counting on that too.

They had to know their man, Mitt Coeslak, was gone. Did they know he was dead, buried in one of their graves in the woods behind the house? Or did they think he'd run off? No reason for him to leave. No reason for him not to. But since I could think of a lot of reasons a man would leave a job like Mitt's, maybe they could too. They'd think: a plaything had survived. Bound to rattle more than a few nerves.

How long had they been holding their little Candle and Blood parties? Long enough to dig more than a few dozen holes in the ground, long enough to fill them. They had a taste for it.

I said I'd bet even money they'd be planning their next party. Mrs. Willingford said by now whoever they all called "Master" must have engraved the invitations. The rest would be mending their hoods.

I said: they might of settled on a date, they might not of. But as soon as they did, we had to know when it was, we had to be there for it.

I looked around. "Any ideas about that?"

Mrs. Willingford said, "I'll get myself invited."

I said, "And how the hell will you do that?"

"I'm *the* Mrs. Joker Willingford. I'm invited to everything."

For three weeks, while Joker rested up in his own rooms in his own world, taking calls, shouting orders, and signing things, Mrs. Willingford paced around the Willingford joint, receiving invitations. On her silver salver got dropped engraved invites to the Mayor's Ball, to some sort of fireman's charity event, to a dinner for the preservation of Manhattan's remaining small parks, to a dog show (Mrs. Willingford went to that one; she took Jane who maybe would of won something just for being Jane if we'd entered her), to a horse show, a bunch of book launches, one new magazine launch, to private dinners, private showings, private previews of new plays and new musicals, private concerts by new composers, new songwriters, new singers. She got an invite a day for debutante parties.

New York was one hell of a new and private town.

It was turning out nothing was more private and exclusive than the Candle and Blood Club. In her own building, from lobby to roof garden, Mrs. Willingford tried to look interested without looking interested. She couldn't ask; she wasn't supposed to know anything. Since I only knew three names for sure, neither of us were sure the right one to ask anyway.

If she could, she would of sacked Blackwell. That would be a dead giveaway. So far as he knew, we hoped, both his employers believed him about the night Holly was attacked. He got a lecture. In the future, could he do what he had to do in his own quarters? Her guest wasn't completely safe if the room next to hers was empty. Blackwell was grateful. He said he was honored catering to the likes of Mr. and Mrs. Joker Willingford.

Mrs. Applegate was a loaner. She wouldn't expect to be spoken to. So she wasn't. She didn't have to be. Blackwell would tell her.

I went out and found some books. The backroom joint I found 'em in made my skin crawl. My few fellow customers made the hair on Jane's back rise. We were in and out fast.

Back at the Willingford's I showered, a maid bathed Jane. It was partly the neighborhood, a lot to do with the bookstore, some to do with the proprietor—glad I wasn't a little kid in a lonely alley when I met that guy—but mostly the so-called "books."

Mrs. Willingford flipped through only one, wrinkled her nose, then left that one lying around—not too obviously but obviously enough. When it'd been there long enough, she whipped it away. She dropped comments near Mrs. Applegate, or near Blackwell, supposedly not meant to be heard.

She threw her own party, invited the whole building as well as the occupants of the buildings either side of her—clever Mrs. Willingford also invited their help to help her help. She and I staged a loud public spat. The fight was the point of the party. Everyone had to see I was out of the picture, that Lois was on her own.

The idea was I could stay because of Holly. With a choice between a small unused maid's room behind the kitchen, or the couch in Holly's room, I slept on the couch. Jane slept on me.

Mrs. Willingford worked her friends, any and all of 'em. She made slanted comments, mostly to Kay and to Gloria but BeeBee got the lion's share. If staff was about, so much the better.

I didn't trust anyone anymore. Not even Cook. Every meal she made for Holly, Jane and I watched her. Which is why we were with Cook when Mickey showed up. He'd come to tell us something. It didn't look like he was bearing presents.

"We'd best be off, Russo."

"Off? Who's we?"

"Me and Sweet Davy Malloy. Matthew is stayin'. Mullan says Matthew is here until ye say so."

"Holly stills needs watching," I said, "We need more than Matthew." I was having trouble here. Where did Mickey have to go, except back to The Green Garter?

Mickey thought about lighting up, caught Cook's stern eye, and changed his mind. "Davy has a job, Russo. And a commitment."

"And you have?"

"I do what I do. It's time I got back to it."

The soft spot for Mickey got hard. He did what he did? It's what he did I'd been chasing for so long. But with Caitlin and Holly, I'd forgotten. And now he was forgetting Holly.

I took a step forward. Mickey didn't move.

"Beat it then. Get out. Someone tried to kill Holly, the same someone who killed Caitlin, but you have to do what you have to do. So go on, get back to it."

He rubbed Jane's fur but now I didn't like Mickey, she didn't like Mickey. She lifted her lip. She growled low in her white throat. As for me, I got nothing but a shrug. Ten minutes later, Mickey Cates and Sweet Davy Malloy were gone.

As the last bit of 'em disappeared out Cook's door, it felt like the day on Luzon we lost half our men and half our horses. I felt exposed. I wasn't telling anyone, not even Jane, but I felt lost.

What I felt was that I wasn't up to cracking this case. It was too big, it shifted around too much, too many people were hiding too many secrets. I was only a man and his dog.

Maybe Jane could figure it out, but not Sam Russo. I wasn't Bogart. I wasn't Marlowe. I wasn't much.

But I wasn't leaving Holly—and that made me more of a man than Mickey Cates.

Fuck him.

As for Matthew, he was the strong silent type. He knew six words. Food. Fag, as in cigarette. Whiskey. Jax, as in toilet. And feck off, as in scram with emphasis.

Woody was there every moment he wasn't taking Mrs. Willingford somewhere. Since she barely left the building, no matter how private the occasion was, Woody was with me and Matthew a lot. Woody knew more words than Matthew but after hearing his entire collection over the course of half an hour, I was glad to leave him to his comics.

Holly never went anywhere in the Willingford joint without one of us. She was never left with any of the staff, not even the newest maid—by the look of her, a mere kid. She never went outside at all, not even onto a balcony.

The only way Mrs. W. could talk to me was to give Woody notes. I kept most of 'em. I told myself something could be in one or two that would prove important. By the end of the second week, I had a lotta notes. I couldn't leave 'em lying around. I couldn't carry a brown paper bag everywhere I went. I sure as hell couldn't carry a purse. That left me slitting open one of Holly's sofa pillows and stuffing them there.

My last note to Lois said: *Any more notes, I'm stealing your pencil.*

Her response? *Feck off.*

Holly got nothing but better and brighter. She started writing her own notes: to me, to Mrs. Willingford, to Woody, to Jane. Holly'd taken a shine to Woody. What he felt, I couldn't tell, but I kept a close eye. One false move from the man who'd saved my life, I'd plug 'im.

Holly was up and about, doctor's orders. She needed moving. If not, she was sitting over a fancy card table playing cards with Matthew. Maybe he didn't talk but he played a mean game of rummy.

Dr. Bloomberg showed up one morning, trailed by that assistant.

I crowded his left side, Woody crowded his right, Matthew blocked any sudden move for the door. Jane stood up from her place on Holly's bed and displayed an eyetooth.

Anyone could be a Candle and Blood member. We never forgot that.

"We" included that man of few words and card player, Matthew. I was glad to see it.

"How can I work like this?" snapped Bloomberg, using his elbows.

Woody used his own elbows. "You'll figure a way."

Doc Bloomberg couldn't look Holly in the eye, but his assistant could. She said, "Today's the day, sweetie."

"What day, darlin'?" said Holly.

Suddenly Holly got it. Her eyes looked scared. I bet mine did too. Doc Bloomberg had his hand out, expecting something. "Now would be a good time, Miss Crane."

Miss Crane slapped a pair of scissors on his open palm.

"Oh fudge," said Holly.

If her heart was doing what my heart was doing, we both needed to keep our mouths shut. Who knew how good Bloomberg was? Who knew what Holly would look like now?

Bloomberg was talking more to Jane than to Holly. Both of 'em were listening for all they were worth. "I don't want you to judge things by how he'll... she'll look now. There's still some swelling. Some discoloration."

Miss Crane leaned in close and Woody had hold of her wrist, fast. It stopped her short, leaving those "bazoomas" heaving. "Say, what's this?"

"Not too close," he said.

"Gee. I just wanted to tell her she's gonna look real swell after. Why, I seen the doc here make downright ugly people look like Rita Hayworth. In fact— "

"Shut up, Miss Crane," said Bloomberg.

Miss Crane shut up.

We all smiled when the bandages came off. We all said she looked great. We all made jokes.

She didn't look great. No one really felt like smiling.

Holly cried.

Bloomberg was adamant. Give it more time, he said. He said it was the best work he'd ever done.

On their way out of Holly's room, Miss Crane crooked a finger and I followed her into the hall. "Listen, mister," she said, "Doctor Bloomberg is a fat-head but he's no quack. That guy might even look almost as good as me."

"Holly is a woman."

"Sure. Whatever you say."

30

On Saturday, May 7th, the day after Caitlin, Chang Chang and Holly's deadly invitation to a Candle and Blood "party," Ponder, coming from dead last, had taken the Kentucky Derby. But only barely. The sprinter Capot hung on for second. I'd expected to hear that race with Holly and Jane, but it'd been only me and Jane hanging on the announcer's every call. On Monday the 9th of May, Holly'd been found by a bum in Tompkinsville Square. She'd been strangled, beaten, stabbed, and stuffed in a duffel bag to die slowly and alone for two nights and a day. On Friday, May 14th, Capot, a speed horse as well as Kentucky Derby long shot, took the shorter tight cornered Preakness Stakes, leaving Ponder no room for his closing run. By the running of the Preakness, Holly was well enough to listen to the race with me and Jane in Room 4-A.

On Saturday the 11th of June both Capot and Ponder were entered in the third leg of the Triple Crown. No matter who won the Belmont Stakes, neither would take home the Crown, but if Capot got to the wire first, I'd collect. That didn't happen too often. I needed some new shoes. Jane could use her own copy of *Lad: a Dog.*

Today was June 10th. For three weeks, Mrs. Willingford'd dangled herself like a lure on the end of a fly fishing line. She hadn't got a bite. Judging from her latest note, she was somewhere in her huge Park Avenue spread still luring.

The only place I was supposed to be was with Holly.

Suited me. It didn't suit Jane. But Jane hadn't been dumped. She came and went as she pleased, everybody's doggy.

Friday evening on Park Avenue and 71st Street, William Ransom Cunningham III'd been washed off the sidewalks of New York, his Lagonda hadn't returned to its place in the garage, a coven of other Cunninghams had flapped in like crows and picked his place clean, the joint itself was on the market for the price of the Hope Diamond, and Holly and Jane were watching *Talent Scouts*. I was trying not to watch *Talent Scouts*. I'd made a discovery about television. No matter how bad the show was, you'd find your eyes straying to the small gray screen.

"Holly, this is crap. Arthur Godfrey hasn't got talent."

"True. But he discovers it, darling."

I knew what she meant the moment she said it. It meant it kept her from feeling like Frankenstein. At the Willingfords, Holly either wore a pink satin negligee with a huge collar of pink feathers, another gift from her friend Lois, along with matching pink satin slippers—I always knew where she'd been by her trail of pink feathers—or loose long sleeved silk pajamas. I'd still catch glimpses of the stitched wounds on her arms and her body. They looked as bad as Jane's. Holly's voice was gone and maybe never coming back. I didn't want to think the lovely face I'd known was gone forever too. And neither did she.

Baby Shauer still dreamed of being discovered on *Talent Scouts*.

I held Jane, whose small body was scarred as Holly's might be scarred. No getting round it, Holly was gonna be scarred.

I shut my mouth and watched.

Holly was laughing at some guy called Wally Cox. Cox looked like a peanut. Anything that made Holly laugh was jake with me.

The thought occurred. What if the Belmont wasn't just broadcast on the radio, what if they showed it on television?

It might happen. It could happen. But it wasn't happening this year.

Holly and Woody, Matthew and me and Jane, we'd all agreed to sit around Holly's new radio and listen to it. Mrs. Willingford was providing the bookie. He'd be around in the morning to take our bets. I was putting all I had on Capot. All I had was twenty bucks. Jane chose Capot too. Bankrolled by Mrs. Willingford, Jane was putting up a hundred across the board.

Mrs. Willingford shook me awake at ten minutes after eleven. We'd dozed off early, Holly and me. I'd been dreaming I had a pair of new shoes. Now I was blinking up at Mrs. Willingford. She had her hand over my mouth.

"It's come," she said.

I said, "Huh?"

"The party, stupid."

I was awake faster than Man o' War.

"You were invited?"

"You could say that. Come on. Matthew's staying with Holly. He won't be more than a foot away, not for a minute, and he's got not one, but two loaded guns. And a knife. I saw it."

I finally got my eyes open and what wits I owned were working. Jane was already out the door, fully awake and fully ready to get herself messed up in another of my adventures. So far, they'd cost her as much as they'd cost me. Knife wounds, bullet holes, terror, confusion and sorrow.

I'd made a few bucks. She got regular dogfood and me.

A bargain.

I looked at Mrs. Willingford. She was all in black, but not the black Holly'd described as Candle and Blood party clothes. No black velvet mask, no velvet hood. Whatever it was, it was one piece and it fitted over that body like her own skin. As for the hat, it was some close fitting thing Clara Bow used to wear, one of those flapper hats. Except it had straps. Second thought, it was like something Amelia Earhart disappeared in.

She was in her sneaking-around-in ensemble.

 I was in my striped cotton pajamas.

Jane and Mrs. Willingford were halfway to the manned elevator before I came hopping along behind stuffing my gun into a new shoulder holster and trying to tie my down-at-the-heel shoes.

Woody, fully suited up as a rich woman's driver, had us to the Staten Island ferry in nothing flat. We just caught a sailing, mostly because Woody threatened the man at the barrier.

"OK," I said, "we're dressed in black, we're in the car, the car's on the ferry, we've got guns or at least I have— "

"I got two matching Colts," said Woody, who turned around to show us.

"—and so does Woody. You use one of those last year?"

"Yep."

"Good guns. OK, Lois, I figure now's the time to fill us in. Spill. Don't leave anything out."

"I was going to bed."

"So far, so good."

"And my private telephone rang."

"The one that doesn't have an extension."

"Exactly."

"And then?"

"I answered it."

"Now we're cooking with gas. Who was it?"

"A man."

"You recognize his voice?"

"Yes, but before I tell you who, I'll tell you what he said."

"What'd he say?"

"He said the lights were going on in the house, that cars were starting to arrive."

"How would he know that?"

"Because he's watching the house."

I stopped myself smacking my own face. What a moron. I meant me, of course. Mrs. Willingford hired someone to watch the house. Simple. Brilliant. I never thought of it.

"How long?"

"How long what?"

"How long ago did you hire him? And why didn't you tell me?"

"I didn't hire him. And I didn't tell you because I didn't know."

That felt better.

She said, "I should have thought of that. *You* should have thought of that. One of us should have thought of that. I'll bet you anything Jane thought of that."

Jane, sitting on Mrs. Willingford's lap, hummed.

"If she did, I blame her. She should speak fluent Yank by now. She's watched enough of Holly's television. Anything else?"

"He said the people arriving were dressed as Holly described them. Evening clothes, hoods, black masks. No doubt about it, it's party night."

"Step on it, Woody."

"Gotta wait 'til we're off the ferry, Mr. Russo. I'll step on it then."

"Of course. That's what I meant." I turned back to Mrs. Willingford. "Anything else?"

"Yes."

"Well, what?"

"The name of the man who called."

"I'm all ears."

"Mickey Cates."

"Cates!"

"Mickey and Sweet Davy Malloy and a whole gang of Irishmen have been camping back in the woods since Mickey and Davy left here. There's not a thing happened in that house they don't know about."

If I had a badge, I'd of eaten it.

31

The year I met Lino Morelli, Flying Ebony, black as tar but born for mud, won in the brown slop of his year's Kentucky Derby. Flying Ebony, owned by a New York carpet maker, was great for two reasons. First, the magnificent Earl Sande rode him. Second, his half brother was Zev, one of the greatest of all the great race horses.

Flying Ebony was three years old. I was five. Lino was pushing seven.

That was the year I first noticed this skinny kid climbing out a window on the fifth floor of the Staten Island Clink for Bad Little Boys & Sad Little Girls. To me he was a grown up. By then I'd learned grown ups yelled and hit and locked little kids like me in closets. In a closet a kid went without light and without food, and if it lasted long enough, without hope. It lasted long enough a lot.

So when I saw some other kid in the same spot I was in, but with the moxie to be going out a window, I ran to watch. Opening my own window and sticking my head out, the drop made my stomach leap up my throat.

In that moment, I was smitten with Lino Morelli, daredevil.

Maybe a day, maybe two days later, I was climbing out windows too.

By then, love was also out the window. It hadn't taken long to figure out my hero was a bully, a snitch and only brave when it came to high windows, in other words, I learned he was a born cop.

Lino met Paul Jarrett through me. I was already friends with Jarrett because Jarrett had the bed wedged next to mine. Paul was eight but he'd let me tag along behind him. He liked me admiring him from close up.

Jarrett and Morelli hit it off like a house on fire. Paul was funny and daring, so Lino liked him just fine. Lino wasn't funny and he wasn't half as daring, so Paul liked him just fine. The both of 'em tolerated me, Sam Russo, the pushy little snot they couldn't scrape off.

In time, Lino Morelli survived the Zawadzkis—not all of us did—and somehow wrangled his way in with the local coppers. That one made me think. Even with the best of us, plus me, sent off east and west to fight a world war, it was hard to see Lino in the job, much less rising all the way to detective.

But he did and he had. I couldn't claim, even if I wanted to which I didn't, that he'd *never* cracked a case when I wasn't around. But I don't think he did. OK, so I was gone for five years. In five years he might of solved a few things on his own.

But I doubted it. And I wasn't blowing my own horn. What I was saying was Lino Morelli couldn't find a lit match in the dark.

Then again, maybe nothing much happened on the Isle of Staten since so much was happening everywhere else.

Anyway, I'd been stateside four years. My old friend Lino gave it a few months and he was back too. Not stateside since as a cop, not to mention yellow, he'd never been called up. What I meant was, he found out where I'd taken a room and there he was, back to knocking on my door. Back to asking me to just come have a little look. Back to getting me up to my ears in his messes just so long as no one saw. Back to shoving me aside when a reporter showed up.

On second thought, about Lino being yellow. I was right, he was, but who wasn't? A man walks into that kind of hell and he isn't scared? Then he's either lying... or dumb as a bullet.

I should of called Lino from Mrs. Willingford's. I should of agreed to meet him and his men in Stapleton on our way through. As soon as I knew about the Candle and Blood Club I should of told him. I should of filled him in on the hidden house and caretaker Mitt and the graves and Billy getting pulped and the ideas I'd had since, the ones that were starting to make some kind of surprising sense. If Lino did nothing else, all along he should of been on the lookout for the Lagonda.

The entire might of Stapleton's police force should be racing behind us and in front of us, making noise, getting in the way, and armed to the teeth.

I'd never had the slightest intention of talking to Lino. I didn't call. If all went as it should, Police Detective Lino Morelli wasn't ever going to know a thing. Fuck him and his men. None of 'em gave a damn about Holly when she was found. The most they did was haul her broken body to the hospital, a few blocks away from where she was dumped like garbage. To them, their case ended there. After that, Lino never knocked on my door, not when Holly was in the critical ward, not when she was doing her best to mend at my place. He never asked me to help with the girls who'd gone missing. Why should he? He probably didn't know they'd gone missing. Hell, they were nothing but streetwalkers. In

Lino's world, streetwalkers took their chances. If they got hurt, even killed, they were asking for it.

His way of seeing things made me figure why should he care we found a happy little sex and murder club in the woods of Staten Island?

Lino and cops like Lino were why the Candle and Blood Club could hold their little parties. If it weren't for Holly making it out the back door when she did, if she hadn't gotten too far from the house so she fell into the hands of Mitt Coeslak instead of the "Master" or one of his minions, if Mitt hadn't done his best to kill her his way, then stick what was left in a duffel bag so he could drive her all the way to Tompkinsville Square and dump her where the cops wouldn't think twice about her being there, well then, Lino and the boys would never connect her to anything but a john gone badly wrong.

Mitt was right. They didn't. They didn't care either. Just another hooker getting what she deserved. They'd said so. I heard 'em.

I was doing this for Holly. That's all I'd been doing the whole time.

And the best men, woman and dog were on the case with me.

The way I felt about Lino added up to this: when Woody sped out of the Staten Island Ferry parking lot headed towards the center of Stapleton and taking the corner of the Richmond Terrace and Bank Street on squealing wheels, I didn't so much as glance at the Stapleton Police Station.

Past world famous Stapleton, lampposts were scarce, houses were scarcer, things got dark. All we could see was a narrow curving road and trees huddled like beggars either side. Me and Jane hadn't been here before. I didn't know an inch of it.

We couldn't use the easier faster route I'd taken the first time. The Master's guests would be using Victory Boulevard and then probably Manor Road. If any of 'em recognized any one of us, the jig was up.

Somewhere past the flat and silent Silver Lake, Woody'd turned off Victory onto a windier narrower road. We also needed a way to come at the house from the back.

Woody pulled over the first place he could, a small scoop in the trees. No lights coming either way. There hadn't been any lights since he'd chosen this road. When he snapped open the glove box, I saw it was full of maps. The one he unfolded on the passenger's seat looked like a dandy of Staten Island.

Cupping my face in my hands to light a Lucky off a match, a match I'd lit with my thumbnail—another year or so and I'd be as good as Cagney—I slid my glance over Mrs. Willingford.

"You keep a map of this island?"

"A girl should know her exits," she said.

"We're behind this hospital here," said Woody, jabbing at the middle of the map, "the one for lungers."

Jesus. He meant we were maybe fifty yards from Sea View Hospital.

One winter, every kid at the Home came down with the flu, a bad one. We got told if we kept coughing the house down, which we were, we'd get locked up in Sea View permanent. I remember thinking: how could some old hospital where you could see the sea be worse than where we already were? We could see the sea too, but only by risking our lives on the rooftops.

Lino spent the rest of his flu hiding. Coughing and hiding.

The Zawadzkis never sent for a doctor. They said we'd get over it if we'd just shut up and stop coughing.

They were right. That time, most of us did.

Behind Sea View Hospital, the road was dirt, it was potholed, it was narrow, by now if the trees weren't a tunnel over our heads, the starless moonless sky was. This back road led deep into Blood Root Valley. It was perfect.

Like the Irish fella who owned the Plymouth Cates'd lent me, Joker was going to need his shiny car repainted. Or buy a new one.

I said, "Mickey say anything about a house where they're camped?"

"He said they were by a brook— "

"Holly saw a house. She was headed for it."

"As I was saying, Russo, before you interrupted me— "

"Sorry."

"—they're camped by a brook which is near that house, but there's a way round. Woody took the details. We'll be hiding the car and walking in."

"Oh good."

Half a bumpy hour later, Woody pulled Joker's car into what looked no more than a black hole in the dark. Beyond that, the hole widened into a space big enough for ten cars. There were eight cars there before us.

We parked between "my" Plymouth and a pale four-door De Soto sedan.

I barely got our door open before Jane was off, haring into the darkness without a sound.

Mickey was right. The house next door couldn't see us

and we couldn't see them, but there was a curl of chimney smoke just over the tops of the dark shape of the trees. Jane had disappeared in the other direction.

Out of the gloom came a whispered voice. "Welcome to our wee home, yez. I won't be takin' yer coats."

No mistaking it. Sweet Davy Malloy was here to guide us into the dark woods behind a darker house.

32

Holly was a torch singer. Torch songs were what she sang at the Garter. But she knew other songs, some in French, some in German, two or three in Italian, an endless supply of ditties in a tongue I couldn't pin down, and some were hill songs, miner's songs, backwoods songs, songs she'd had to live to know.

Holly sang them all in the bathtub. Or she did until King Kong's cousin moved into 4-C.

After that she'd sung them to Jane and me on nights when she wasn't walking the streets. I always asked for *Stewball*. *...and way out yonder, ahead of them all, came a-prancin' and a-dancin', my darling Stewball.* Jane preferred *Old Dog Blue*. But Holly's favorite was the one she called *The Raggle Taggle Gypsy-O.* Her song began as soon as I saw Mickey's camp.

What care I for my house and my land and what care I for my money-o? Tonight I lie in the strong dark arms of my raggle taggle gypsy-o.

Standing at the camp's edge with its fire banked low and its small tents of canvas with dark figures moving through the shadows, an image rose up of Mrs. Willingford and Mickey Cates and for that one moment my heart shut like a box.

"Russo!"

The hiss was low but it was near and I heard it clear as day. I turned and there was Mickey Cates, an M1 carbine rifle under one arm, a handgun in a shoulder holster, his face unshaven, his eyes red from soot and from sorrow. I remembered who he'd lost and how he'd lost her. I let go my boxed heart.

Gypsies are loud, colorful, and messy. The camp was a colorful mess—we'd make that kind of mess on Luzon and we'd be doing pushups for days—but it wasn't loud. Men crept about like Apaches. How many men, I couldn't say. Or women. There were women with 'em and they weren't there to cook and put out for the lads. One look said they were soldiers, zealots like their men, and armed to the teeth.

They were all hooligans. But for the moment, at least, they were *our* hooligans.

Mrs. Willingford slipped her black gloved hand into a tight black pocket, pulled out a slender silver flask, and said, "Let's drink to something, Sam Russo. You too, Woody."

Woody said, "I'm all for that."

I said, "Like what?"

"Like getting out of this alive."

I drank to the Raggle Taggle Gypsys-o.

Where the hell was Jane? What if she'd streaked straight through the heart of the damn camp and made for the house? She knew exactly where we were.

Sam Russo, Private Eye, did not pray. That sort of thing fled on faraway battlefields. But I came close to it now. If Jane burst in on the Candle and Blood Club, she'd not only blow what Lino and his cops would call "the sneak," she'd get herself killed.

I spent a good five minutes looking, but it was Woody and Mrs. Willingford found her.

Jane was as close to the house as she could get and still be in the woods. She was leaning into Holly's Christmas collar, choking herself. If not for Mullan holding on for all he was worth, Jane would of crashed the party.

"Jane!"

Jane's left ear flipped back, her right drooped, and down she sat on her red rump. Licking my hand, she stopped doing everything except stare at the house none of us could see through the dark mass of shrub and tree. She was smelling it, no doubt knew who and what was showing up.

It made her quiver with rage.

Mickey stood with us and watched her.

"They've been after coming for hours. One car at a time."

"The Lagonda?"

"The lad on watch says not."

"It'll show. With special guests."

"And aren't we waiting for exactly that?"

Mrs. Willingford curled herself into a crouch on the ground next to Jane. From down there, she said, "When do we go in?"

"We?" That was me. It came out before I could stop it.

Her head snapped back. I was standing behind her and she wanted a good long look. "Those women are going, I'm going. Don't try and stop me, Sam. Don't even dare to try."

If I'd been trying, I stopped. I asked Mickey: "How many are we?"

Mickey answered Mrs. Willingford. "Counting the lasses, we're twelve. A fine fat number."

"How many of them?"

"From what your one says, twenty, thirty, maybe more."

"But not armed. Except for their master."

Mickey shrugged. "No telling what's up their sleeves."

I was suddenly struck numb. The thought I should of been thinking the whole ride here slammed into my brain and shoved out all the oxygen. I took another closer look around. It was just us waiting for the Candle and Blood Club. With no cops, there'd be no arrests. No cops, no trials. No cops, no trials—then what were we doing?

Triple fuck.

What was the plan here? For my guys to rush in aiming Irish guns, shouting Irish mouthfuls, creating Irish mayhem, as they slaughtered the Candle and Blood Club?

Was I going to be part of that? Was Jane? Worst of all, was Mrs. Willingford? She said she was. She as good as told me to back off, it wasn't any of my business.

Jane was always getting hurt. I'd sworn the last time that'd be the last time. What if it wasn't? As Sweet Davy would say: Sure Jaysus, and what if Mrs. W got hurt too?

With Lois needling me, I felt like Bogie. With her at my side, I always felt like Bogie. The world was my oyster when we wrestled in bed. But now, facing this, with Mrs. Willingford willing to face it too, I felt like a heel.

I knew what Mickey and Mullan and Sweet Davy Malloy were doing here. The bunch of them were here to right the terrible wrong done to Caitlin. They were mixing it up for Holly and Chang Chang. They were getting some of the pain out of their hearts. Doing all that, they'd be saving the lives of the next guests invited to the party. But at what cost?

Sam Russo wasn't Custer. Hold on. Custer wasn't a name to chew on when planning a massacre. So OK, Sam Russo wasn't Al Capone. I was a Private Investigator. I took cases, I solved crimes. I didn't commit them or avenge them or become a victim of them. Not if I could help it. As a PI, you can't always help it. But if you're still standing around thinking about it, you got options. I could walk away. I could make Jane walk away. We could walk all the way home and go to bed in Room 4-A.

But I couldn't make Mrs. Willingford walk away.

If I was ever in a jam, this was it.

"Jane."

Good dog Jane dropped back until she stood leaning against my leg. I put my hand on her small hard clever skull.

"Stay near."

Jane looked up at me. By firelight, the look in her eyes said OK. But if Mickey and his wild Irish friends were to attack the house, would it still be OK? When Jane got sore, all bets were off.

When no one was looking at me or at Jane, I dropped to my knees and crawled towards a house I knew well. Jane dropped to her belly and crawled beside me.

In June the meadows and woods of Staten Island were crammed with brambles and wildflowers. We crushed hundreds of them pushing our way through the undergrowth.

Jane and I crept out the other side. We were on the south side of the house, away from the front door—but we could see part of the veranda and all of the drive. I made her sit there with me. No lunging across the wide strip of mowed grass as one car at a time parked on the gravel drive we'd once parked on. After five minutes or so, candles began to be lit in the windows, every window, all floors. If I didn't know what they were there for, I would of found them worth looking at. Where I grew up, we lived by the light of dim bulbs. When they blew out—and they always blew out, like some of the kids who lived by them—it took Mister days to replace them. "Light bulbs cost money," he said. "What d'joo need light for after it's gone dark? You up to something?"

A candle in every window was like Fifth Avenue at Christmas. Only this wasn't Fifth Avenue and it wasn't December.

There was nothing for it but to sit and hold Jane and watch the Candle and Blood Club gather for one of their parties.

I was facing the worst choice of my life. I could sit quietly by while Mickey and his gang of Irish hooligans cleaned up for Caitlin and Holly. I did that, I'd lose Mrs. Willingford. She was going in. If I didn't go in too, we were finished. So it was walking in with my nice new friends and filling every sick punk I saw, male and female, with lead.

The last time I did something like that, they were the enemy hunkered in bunkers. It didn't feel good then. Now, it'd feel a million times worse.

And then I remembered who they were. The war was a war. Like all wars, it was stupid and useless, it was fought by the guileless young for the sake of the greedy old, but it was still a war. This was only a party. It wasn't just too loud, too gay, and as much fun as watching a cock fight. This was a rare and secret party, members only: a gathering of the ugly and the sick. Most'd be going home with some terrible hole in their dry hearts filled—but only for an hour, a day, maybe a month.

A few wouldn't be going home at all.

I felt Jane tremble under my hand. My head snapped up. There it was, pulling into the driveway, as foreign and sleek and priceless as the last time I saw it—the late William Ransom Cunningham III's Lagonda.

It was met by a man in a mask holding a candelabra. By candlelight, Billy's car looked like an enormous bug brought back from the head of the Nile. The guy in the mask looked too small for a candelabra.

The driver's side door opened. Too dark to make out who it was. A man, a woman? I couldn't tell. The passenger's door opened. A woman for sure. Familiar, but who?

Whoever the woman was, she opened the back door and out tumbled their "special guests."

I knew all three of 'em.

A bottle blonde called Kitty Anne, as coy as her name. Ruby, as hard as hers. Both young, both pretty enough. Kitty Anne was too young. And then, more like Carmen Miranda than ever, Tompkinsville Square's saddest, sappiest, and oldest doxie, Big Ivy.

It hurt to see Big Ivy's small flashing eyes and large flashing teeth. She thought she'd died and gone to Heaven.

Which she had. The first part anyway. How dumb could some dames be? I'd told her about the two-toned car.

I guessed she didn't believe me.

33

Deep inside Jane, a rumble started. If it got much louder, we'd get noticed.

"Knock it off, Jane," I said.

Jane knocked it off—for less than a second. Then she was up, on all four white feet and running straight for the house.

Jane! My good dog Jane!

More than one party goer would know who she was. They'd know she wasn't alone. But before they did whatever they'd do about us, they'd kill her.

"Damn, Russo, what'll we do now?"

Mrs. Willingford's sudden voice in my ear stopped my heart.

I turned all the way round. Only Mrs. Willingford. No one else. I was grateful for that at least.

I should of known Jane wouldn't just charge the Lagonda. Jane had never been slow on the uptake. Why would she be slow now? What she'd done was streak across the open space between the trees and the house, head, tail, neck and belly low, then dropped down into some big flowering bush under a set of tall windows.

I knew those windows. The room Caitlin and Chang Chang died in was on the other side of them.

I had no choice. Jane had just made it for me. I couldn't let her do what she was doing alone, I had to go with her.

I was rising to do just as Jane did, head and belly low in more ways than one, but Mrs. Willingford's hand on my arm stopped me.

"Wait for Mickey," she said.

I turned on Mrs. Joker Willingford. In my time I'd yelled at her. I'd insulted her. I'd ignored her. I'd thought ill of her. But I'd never been as damned angry with her as I was now. "Wait for Mickey to do what? Go in with all guns blasting?" My anger felt bad. It felt foolish. It made me feel like I often feel but don't talk about. You hear Bogie whining? You hear Bogie taking it out on someone else, especially a class act like Mrs. Willingford? I couldn't shut my stupid mouth. I had to keep talking. "You and me and Mickey and Sweet Davy Malloy, the whole itchy fingered gang, we'll walk right in and slaughter 'em all? And in the hell we make of the place—with all that blood splattered around and us stepping in gore and the screaming ringing off the walls since most of 'em'll beg us to stop even if they deserve it—we'll get lucky and miss Big Ivy and the other two who don't know what the fuck is going on? You think Mickey'll do that, that he'll stop once he gets started? You think you and me, once we're in the middle of it, we'll stop? What if some of 'em have guns and shoot back? We couldn't stop then. We'd be in it up to our necks. And when it was all over with just the smell of blood and gunpowder in the air, then what? Those left standing will walk away, that we'll leave behind an unholy mess, get back in our cars, share a coupla jokes, pop a cork, scatter back to our cozy beds?"

The look that slowly changed Mrs. Willingford's face as she listened, the one I saw by the distant light of candles in windows and arriving headlights, was like the look that must of crossed my own face when I suddenly got it. Hers had to be worse. No one was slapping me around but me. But right now I was slapping her around. I was doing it on the quiet, in the dark. I was doing it like it was a bad dream, one I couldn't wake up from. I was sorry about it. I knew I'd be a lot sorrier if and when we got out of this in one piece. For now, I was just sorry.

I knew it. I'd always known it. Sam Russo, Private Investigator, sure knew how to dish it out. He was one hell of a guy.

But she got it. No cops, no arrests, just angry Irishmen with guns. And us. Oh yeah, she got it. We were either going in with 'em or we weren't going in with 'em.

Either way, it was a deadly mess.

"Oh Sam," she said, "I didn't think… "

Mrs. Willingford was never weak. She wasn't weak now. But she was confused and frightened. The both of us had just figured out we were in what I guess was called a moral dilemma. It wasn't new to me. I'd spent five years getting my morals kicked around. It looked like she was taking her first punch.

I put my hand round the back of her neck and pulled her face towards mine. I kissed her. I said, "We got ourselves into this. I guess it's time for us to get ourselves out."

For the second time, I was up, and crouching, I made for that bush, the one I hadn't taken my eyes off ever since Jane disappeared into it. I didn't look round, but I knew Mrs. Willingford was right behind.

We made noise, but our noise was nothing compared to the rumble of car engines, car doors slamming, shoe leather squeaking and high heels clicking on the wide wooden stairs and across the wide wooden veranda, people talking, dangerous people who felt safe chatting away out here in the middle of nowhere, surrounded by a lot of dense Staten Island woods full of what they were sure was nothing but deer, a few coons, the nests of sleeping birds, maybe a stray goat, a couple of distant inbred natives.

None of their noise paused for a second. No one had noticed us just as they hadn't noticed Jane.

Jane hummed a low hum in greeting. Tucked away in our bush, barely breathing, the three of us had a great view of the party's three special guests being led round to the back of the house, of a Cadillac arriving, of the two well dressed gents getting out, already in masks and hoods, crunching across the gravel. We heard a snatch of what they were saying. "...got lucky the last time. He assures us it won't..."

They were up the stairs and into the house before we could hear what "he" assured them. My bet was the "Master" said things would go better than last time, the time the little whore got away. I also bet the Master made sure everyone here tonight knew about Holly, where she was, how she was doing, what she knew, what she didn't know, and what he was doing about it.

We counted cars. Twelve. Plus the Lagonda. Twelve cars could of brought at least two party goers each. From Holly's tally, that sounded about right.

With Mrs. Willingford practically sitting in my lap, and Jane backed close up against us, I whispered, "We have to stop all this. Not just the party, we have to stop Mickey and his friends."

"Jesus, Sam, how?"

"I wish I knew."

"Oh, swell. You don't know."

"Nope. All I know is two things. Even if we called the cops we'd be calling Lino Morelli which is worse than not calling. Second, I know who we'll find in there."

"Here's what I know. What I know is I have an idea."

An *idea*. Mrs. Willingford's ideas gave me goosebumps. "Shoot."

I listened with growing respect. Her idea had flair. It took nerve. It needed my gun which was good since I had it on me. It might work. It filled my head with moments from my favorite movies. There was me as Bogie, or Bogie as me, standing in front of one of the black velvet curtains, rubbing a finger over his lip. I knew what he would do. And what he would do, I could do.

The best part was, we might not get killed.

Deep in a bush smelling of jasmine or honeysuckle or deadly nightshade, Jane listening to every word, we quickly made our plans. We had to act fast. Any minute now, Mickey would be putting his own plan into action. A plan that would work in its way, one that made a kind of cockeyed moral sense, but one neither of us could be part of.

But with our plan also in play, his was sure to get us shot to pieces.

What the hell. All our plan needed now was for the cars to stop showing up, and for Mickey not to rush the place for a good five minutes after that.

It also needed guts. Jane and Mrs. Willingford had all the guts we needed.

The cars stopped showing up. The front door stopped opening and shutting. The sound of a phonograph started up. It took a second to place the music. I got there before

Mrs. Willingford.

It was Billie Holiday singing *Strange Fruit*.

The lanky guy in the Aloha shirt, the one who'd taken the missing Mitt Coeslak's place, the one who because of the shirt must of seen action in the Pacific, left the front of the house. Mrs. Willingford looked at me and I looked at Mrs. Willingford. We knew where the guy in a shirt as flowery as our bush was headed. Out back to wait in the carriage house with his shovel until it was time for him to clean up.

"Well, Lois," I said, "ready?"

"How's my make-up?"

I looked her over by the light that shone down on us in our bush, the glow of a single white candle.

"You never looked lovelier."

She smiled. "Then I'm ready."

34

The last car was parked. The last guest arrived. Inside the big house standing alone in the middle of the woods, the black masked, black hooded guests awaited their special entertainment. Behind the room they waited in, a room draped in black velvet with a small stage for their evening's "show," Big Ivy, Kitty Anne and Ruby were being prepared as Holly, Chang Chang and Caitlin had been prepared before them. And before Holly, dozens more.

"Jane."

Jane looked up with eyes as intelligent as any I'd ever looked into. More intelligent than some.

"You'll walk in front of us. You hear me? In *front* to guide us. No running, no biting, no ideas of your own. You got that straight?"

Jane got that straight. It didn't mean she'd do what I told her, but I knew she'd heard me.

"It's now or never, Mrs. Willingford. Shall we go?"

As silent as Mary Pickford—excuse, make that Theda Bara, Jane slipped out of the bush, Mrs. Willingford and I following. We snuck round back, making sure the caretaker was in the carriage house, biding his time. I'd worried he'd be curious about his new job, that he'd be doing some sneaking about on his own, but this one wasn't the curious type. We could see the top of his hatted head through a cracked and greasy pane in the carriage house window. He raised an arm a few times, lowered it again. Smoking, drinking, and listening to the radio would be my guess. Maybe a game of solitaire on top of a wooden box. The usual pastimes of a patient gravedigger.

If things weren't so damned serious, I'd of spent a moment or two lamenting the Belmont Stakes. The way things were going, I was sure to miss it—and that was a damned shame. I wanted to hear Capot come roaring home. I knew he would.

He'd better. I'd staked all I had on his nose.

I was in black. Mrs. Willingford was in black. Jane was in red and white, the white so white anyone looking could of spotted her a mile away. Seemed no one was looking.

The back porch was half the size of the front veranda but the back door was just as big and probably just as locked. Jane crept across the porch, followed by me, then Lois, each of us gently pushing aside a mass of brambles, brushing off bits of web, testing for loose boards.

I was right. The door was shut tight. But there, glaring at me, was the usual lock. I got to my pick before Mrs. Willingford got to hers.

I was gracious. My elbow and her ribs merely kissed. I said, "Allow me."

I'd of loved to shut Jane out. If Mrs. Willingford was willing to risk her gorgeous skin, that was her choice. If I wanted to risk my manly hide, fine by me. But Jane risking hers wasn't fine by me. Trouble was, I couldn't shut Jane out. As I said, she probably had her own set of picks.

It was dark in the back and it didn't get much lighter as we crept along looking for the party. Kitchen to our right, dark. Pantry to our left, dark. A choice of halls. One to the left, one to the right, one going straight ahead. All three dark. If it weren't for Jane, we might of stumbled about until we fell down the cellar stairs. Jane knew exactly where we were and where we ought to be going. We followed Jane, ducking into some sort of recess just in time to miss the "servants" leading Big Ivy, Ruby and Kitty Anne from a makeshift dressing room. They had to be headed for the big front room where the party must be in full swing and they were the main course.

Holly was right. They looked like stale wedding cakes.

From somewhere ahead, it sounded like the Marx Brothers smashing dishes.

"*Night on Bald Mountain*," whispered Mrs. Willingford.

"What?"

"On the Victrola. They're playing *Night on Bald Mountain*. Where's their imagination? What an obvious choice."

I had no idea what she was talking about. The music, I supposed—a terrible racket which only got louder as we got nearer. I knew where Jane was—her white parts: legs, chest, neck, tip of her curled tail, glowed in the dark—until they didn't. She was suddenly gone. Right in front of me one second, so close I'd almost tripped over her more than once, and then the next second, vanished.

"She's gone."

"Shush. We're right behind one of the doors. Who's gone?"

"Jane."

"Where?"

"How the hell would I know? Don't you?"

"If I knew, would I ask you?"

That was enough of that. What we were doing called for, at the least, silence, and the most, deadly seriousness.

Months back, I'd discovered Mrs. Willingford and I had trouble with both of these qualities. It wasn't funny. It could cost us our lives.

But where was Jane? It made me sick not knowing. It ruined my concentration. I needed my concentration just as much as I needed my gun. Next time I saw her, and there'd better be a next time, we'd be having a little chat about leashes.

One more door and Mrs. Willingford and me, we'd be attending a party: uninvited, unwelcome, and unmasked.

Worried about Jane, I opened the door to find it draped on their side. As Mickey might say, the thick black velvet was a thing of joy. We had time to breathe, shake off nerves, gather our wits. Or Mrs. Willingford did. Fucking Jane. Thanks to her my wits were scattered—but the hell of it was the living breathing Lois was at my side. I knew she was terrified. I knew she wouldn't back down.

I was already in over my head. I wasn't backing down either.

If it was the last thing I ever did, I was here for my partner. Bogie didn't love his. I loved mine.

"Ready, Mrs. Willingford?"

"Ready, Mr. Russo."

A gun in my hand, a flashlight in hers, we stepped through the curtain.

It must of been the year the gelded Clyde Van Dusen won one of the slowest Derbies ever. That meant I was nine. Or maybe a little younger. I got called into Mister's "office."

Mister's office was the basement and if the basement to a kid wasn't a House of Horrors, I don't know what was. What did I do? Who the hell knew. With Mister you didn't have to do anything. Some days he just needed some kid to beat the crap out of. That day was my day.

They had to call in Doc Hickman. The Zawadzki's hated spending money, especially on us, so it had to be bad. Some things it doesn't pay to remember.

But I doubt it was as bad as Jane gone missing and me and Mrs. Willingford making our grand entrance into a gathering of the Candle and Blood Club.

We got spotted right out of the gate. Whatever hellish music was on the turntable was stopped with a tooth aching scrape of the needle. The three half naked doxies on the small round stage froze in place. But everyone else, masked, hooded, and caught in the middle of a communal howl, turned as one—like they were all working with one brain. I think eerie about summed it up. Their howl also stopped on cue.

It creeped the shit out of me. If it didn't creep the shit out of Mrs. Willingford, there was something wrong with Mrs. Willingford.

I was back in the room as big as an ice skating rink. I was looking at the flared staircase leading up to the second floor where it ended in a railed balcony along the full width of the first floor room and halfway along either side. There were all those doors again; there was the smaller staircase climbing up to a third floor, there was the chandelier. And who could forget the wall paper with flowers you could just about smell and the dainty red velvet wide-seated divans, the crystal ashtrays, silver candlesticks and the flickering black candles?

Up on the balcony was a professional motion picture camera. Maybe the guy manning it was a professional and maybe he wasn't, but Holly was right: they filmed their parties.

So there I was with Mrs. Willingford, a loaded gun, and a handful of extra bullets.

I said, "You fucks take the biscuit."

Maybe one second passed, maybe two, but one of the fucks finally moved. He took one step towards us.

If I wasn't looking at their Master, I was—hell, of course I was looking at their Master. In a hard dark voice, a voice that told me and all his minions that he was the better man, the Master said, "So, Superman, which one will you shoot?"

I'd seen this scene in a movie, or maybe more than one movie. The idea was simple: our hero has the drop on the bad guys, but since there's three or four or twelve bad guys, he could only shoot one or two before the rest shot him—if he was lucky. What's the hero to do? What the hero always did was point his gat at their fearless leader and say: I can shoot one for sure, and that's you, pard. And then the leader broke out in a sweat and ordered his gang to holster their gats.

Did this bunch have guns along with their candles? I couldn't answer that. I remembered the gun case. For all I knew, the black velvet room could be stuffed with armed freaks. So I went for broke. I didn't say a damn thing. All I did was shoot the guy with the big mouth. I'd aimed for his ear, and got it. Lucky for us both. I already said I don't kill people.

Remembering how Billy screeched, it wasn't a patch on

the noise this guy was making.

"Mrs. Willingford?"

"Yes, Sam?"

"Have a look under the mask. See who the screaming asshole is."

Nobody pulled out a gun. Nobody pulled out a knife. As Lois walked over, what the rest of the brave bunch did was part like the Black Sea. Mrs. Joker Willingford reached out, got a good grip, and ripped off the Master's bloody mask. Jesus. Getting an ear shot off won't kill you, but it makes a real mess.

I knew it. I got it right. In the car on the way over, I'd told Mrs. Willingford who the master was. I was right and here he was to prove it. Sam Russo had solved something. It felt great.

And then Big Ivy had to pipe up, which made me notice she had a swell body to go with her funny face. "Hell's bells! Why'd you have to go and do that for? You just ruined everything. We was gonna get paid good dough for this. Now look what you done. Say! You're that friend of Holly's, aren't cha?"

Mrs. Willingford turned on her. Her voice was as cold as a severed hand in the snow. "What you were going to get was dead. So say thank you and shut up."

Big Ivy's mouth popped open like a drowning fish. Whatever she wanted to say didn't come out, she couldn't make it come out, so she took a swing at the nearest masked party goer. She missed, but she made the guy step back and tread on the guy behind him. They both fell over.

"There's my thank you," said Big Ivy, "now who's driving us home?"

At which point things got confusing. Ruby and Kitty Anne leapt off the "stage" to claw, bite, kick and punch their way towards the door.

The "Master" made a break for it. He wasn't headed for the front door. He was going for the back. That would be my choice too. No doubt the guy was going while the going was good. The rest of his flock could do as they liked. He'd never have a left ear again, but losing an ear was nothing compared to what else could happen.

Right then, someone jumped me from behind. I knew who it was without looking. It was the Master's lover. I could of whipped the poor brave romantic fool with both arms tied behind my back. Trouble was, in the tussle, my gun got knocked out of my hands. The thing went skittering off under the feet of a few dozen sickos. As soon as they saw that, everyone got moving at once. I tossed the lover into the flowery wall, and, like Kitty Anne and Ruby, pushed shoved and slammed my way through the melee, ripping off masks and moustaches as I went, looking for my gun before someone else found it, all the while yelling for Mrs. Willingford to follow the Master.

Mrs. Willingford was off like Citation. I'd never get used to how fast that woman could run.

What a fucking hell hole. It was worse than charging Japs on horseback. OK, so it wasn't worse than that, but it was bad, especially when the lover found my gun before I did and waved it at me.

I was standing there, in the middle of the floor. All around me unmasked assholes were climbing over each other to get to the front door. I knew half of 'em which meant I really had nailed this case. Nailed or unnailed, any second now someone would get the door open and out would spray Candles and Blood like bugs in a sneeze. And I couldn't do a thing about it because my own gun was pointing at me.

The lover holding it said, "You shot him! My God, my God, how could you shoot him?"

"Easy. You pull the trigger and a bullet comes out." That's what I said, but what I was thinking was: how do I get my gun back? Any minute now this idiot could shoot me.

That's when I felt cold steel being pressed into my hand. I looked down without looking like I was looking down. I should of guessed. I should of known as soon as Jane disappeared. Jane didn't run from things; she ran straight at 'em. So as I said, I should of known. The cold steel was a Smith & Wesson Model 10. The gun Jane ran off with the day we met Mr. Coeslak. But she was back now, doing what she always did—getting me out of a jam.

I gripped Mitt's gun, slippery with Jane spit, and without a lot of thought, raised it into a very surprised face and shot *his* ear off. The right one.

"There," I said, "Now you're a matching pair."

35

I was really going to have to ask Mrs. Willingford about her past. Sooner rather than later. A good PI ought to know this kind of stuff about his partner. For instance, who taught her that holding a guy's arm behind his back, up high and hard, would work the way it did?

Mrs. Willingford marched the Candle and Blood Club's Master back from where he'd gotten to and forced him to stand on the little stage. First she had to yell at Big Ivy to get the fuck off, but as soon as she did, up he went, bleeding all over his evening clothes.

Big Ivy still hadn't got the big picture. Ruby was back holding one arm, Kitty Anne the other. Big Ivy was yelling about suing us for lost wages. Only Kitty Anne and Ruby were listening. And me. But just for a second.

If things were strange enough, something stranger was happening. The room, only moments ago a black wave of frantic party guests, had gone still and silent. I would of thought most of 'em would of escaped by now, gotten into their cars and beat it. I was wrong. They'd stopped, turned, gone quiet, folded their hands. They were watching the Master.

Damn, but idolatry makes you stupid. The Master's lover turned away from me and my dog and my gun, yelling, "We have to call a doctor. He's bleeding to death. Can't you see he's bleeding to death, you bitch!"

That last bit was addressed to Mrs. Willingford.

She said, "Could be. You should see you."

"Me? I don't matter. Only— oooh, don't feel at all well." That was the end of that conversation. Legs scissoring, body gracefully turning, the Master's lover corkscrewed slowly to the floor and quietly left us for the time being.

That's when things got ten times worse.

The front door was suddenly filled with loud holes. In one second flat, it wasn't a door anymore, it was a shattered mass of wood that screamed as it tore away from its hinges and fell flat on the floor. And when that happened, to a man and a woman and a dog, we also dropped to the floor, as blinding light flooded the black room. Some dropped to save themselves, some dropped because they couldn't save themselves. Only one fell and that was the cameraman. He went right over the balcony rail and landed with a nasty thump on a red divan.

If any were dead, it was probably him. But now wouldn't be the time I'd find out.

Backlit like Boris Karloff or Greta Garbo or the James Gang, Mickey Cates, Sweet Davy Malloy, Mullan and every man jack of their fearless Irish crew, strode through the new hole in the front of the bullet riddled house.

Aside from the war, which didn't count since war always meant weapons, I'd never seen so many guns.

I still can't remember how I did what I did next. I was down and on one side of the room with Jane and two guns, and then I wasn't. From shielding Jane, I was upright in the middle of the room with two guns. Jane at my side—who could stop her?—we were standing square in front of the Master who was sprawled bawling in front of a crouched Mrs. Willingford which put me and my dog smack between

Mickey and his target.

"Russo. You and yer dog, get out of the way," said Mickey. He said it gentle. He said it soft. But he said it and he meant it.

"And if we do?"

"Me and mine, we're after killin' those who killed Caitlin."

Sweet Davy Malloy added, "Every guilty soul in this room."

Every guilty soul in the room cried out, then either moaned or sobbed. Gee, so sad.

"So if the whores would leave," said Mickey, "and you, Sam Russo, and your one."

"Your one" meant Mrs. Willingford. Jane was a given.

"I can't Mickey. I'm no hero but I can't stand by. You're not the law. I'm not the law."

"Fuck the law. What's the law done for us?"

He had me there.

"So if yez'd all stand away from the Grand Poobah there, we'll be gettin' on with our business. Take Mrs. Willingford and that fine dog of yours, take the working girls, and wait outside. No need for ye to see this."

"No."

"Ah, Sam. Ye'll have to. In time, ye'll have to."

"Sure, Mickey." I'd gotten a good grip on Jane's collar. No telling what she was planning. "But not before you do."

"Ah, Sammy, me lad. What'll we do with ye? You'd be protectin' the man who stole our lovely girls off the street to use 'em and watch 'em die, the same as ordered your Holly killed helpless in her wee bed, the same as hid in his hole with that one on the floor there so she'd never see him and squeal?"

"I'm not protecting him, Mickey. I'm protecting us. You too."

"Ah, a noble man. I admire ye and yer noble stupidity. You, Mrs. Willingford, will ye at least go?"

"I'll go," said Big Ivy. Kitty Anne and Ruby didn't say anything; they were already gone. Big Ivy disappeared a second later.

"No, Mickey." Mrs. Willingford was standing now. "I won't. You shoot all these, you'll have to shoot me."

Mickey smiled. Sweet Davy smiled. The rest didn't have a smile between them.

"What we have here," he said, taking off his hat to fan his face, "is what is called a stalemate. I don't want to shoot ye."

"I don't want to be shot. I sure don't want Mrs. Willingford shot."

"No more do I. It's a deal we'll have to be making."

"What deal?"

"Something to satisfy us all."

The lover was beginning to come round. He lifted his head from the floor, heard all the moaning, the weeping, the chattering of teeth, saw all the blood, some of it *his* blood, saw a mob of armed Irish folk, and fainted again.

I looked at Mrs. Willingford and she looked at me. A deal. Could we do that and live with ourselves? If it was the right deal, I could. I read it in her eyes. If it was the right deal, so could she.

"You have something in mind?"

Mickey held up a finger. "Let me confer with my friends."

In a heaving sea of red blood, black hoods, white faces, Jane and I waited for Mickey. I couldn't see her, but I knew Mrs. Willingford waited too. What Edgar Hubbard, New York City's Queen of Quotes and the Master of the Candle and Blood Club, was doing was probably shitting himself. I would be. Mickey Cates wasn't known for his sense of humor.

The Irish mob broke their huddle.

"Here's how it'll be," said Mickey, "yez'll give us the head nance on the box there, the one who leads this infernal club, God curse it—also the nance on the floor. We'll be wanting as well that one who sapped ye in the basement, that fine figure of a woman there. If ye ask Mrs. Applegate, she might return Holly's silver locket."

Mrs. Applegate wasn't more than a few feet away. Even now, she was made of stone. I'd buy Holly a new locket.

"We'll also require Kunze the doorman with his master passkey, the very one who tipped your man Billy over the balcony." Over the ridiculous noise of Kunze the doorman denying everything, Mickey kept going. "The poor fat bastard discovered the club through Kunze helpin' himself to that car. He wanted in. Kunze told Hubbard. Our master here couldn't be havin' a weakling as a member, now could he? And finally the butler, Blackwell, who helped Mrs. Applegate get to Holly. Six will sit well for our Caitlin."

Looked like I wasn't the only one who'd nailed it. How he nailed it, I make book I'd never know. But I didn't mind. What counted was the nailing.

"You're after forgettin' the namin' of one, Mickey," said Sweet Davy Malloy.

"And who might that be, Davy?"

Sweet Davy searched the drained faces staring up at him, eyes wide in the car headlights flooding through the door. His shadow was long and thin, an Irish shadow cast over the doomed like the magic staff of a fairy lord. He pointed. "That one."

We all looked. Who could help it? Mickey and mob put on a swell show.

"No!" screamed BeeBee Nash, rising from the floor. Of them all, turned out BeeBee was armed with more than a silver dagger. She had a small silver pistol aimed at Sweet Davy's heart.

I was holding Jane for all I was worth. The hum in her chest was loud enough for any to hear. She would of gone for BeeBee—and BeeBee Nash would of shot her. I'd had enough of that to last me a lifetime.

Mullan found his voice first. "Duck Davy lad!"

Too late. Mrs. Willingford's friend got off only one shot before Mickey gunned her down. BeeBee the book reader sank back into the sea of black, but her one bullet was a true one. Sweet Davy spun and fell back.

The women warriors went with him, pulling off his coat, opening his shirt, ripping their own for bandages.

"Well, lads, there's one gone," said Mickey Cate. "Too easy for her, but that's death for yez. Five will be suitin' us." He looked down at Edgar Hubbard. "If Davy dies, not the number, but the manner changes. Dyin' won't come as easy for ye."

Edgar Hubbard, lately master of all he quoted, began to cry. "You can't do this. Not to me. I'm famous. I'm rich. I'll pay you. Name your price."

Mickey turned on him, the Mickey I'd watched for years,

not a Mickey I'd want turning on me. "Ye've heard the price, divil. And ye'll be after paying it this very night. Those who won't be dyin' just yet can stay if it suits yez. Even watch. After all, yez come for a killin'." And when he said this, he turned on me. "Is it a deal, Sam Russo, or will ye be wantin' to up the ante?"

Before I could open my mouth, Mrs. Willingford said what I would of said. "It's a deal. Let's you and me go now, Sam, you and me and Jane. Woody is waiting to drive us home."

Sometimes I wonder about who I am. I know I'm not Bogie, not Sam Spade, not Philip Marlowe. But if not them, then who?

We were picking our way back through the woods to where Woody waited in a Willingford car. Leaving behind horror, we could hear others starting up cars, backing up cars, gunning the engines of cars, mad to be gone from the house in the woods. I caught a glimpse of Mitt's replacement bolting for the deepest part of the darkest trees.

We knew what was soon going to happen to the Master and Mickey's chosen ones, and all I could think was: whadda ya know, Holly and Jane and I weren't going to miss the Belmont Stakes after all.

And Mrs. Willingford could listen too.

**Enjoying the adventures of Sam Russo,
Private Eye?**

**Turn the page to preview the first chapter of
Sam's next case:
DEAD ON THE ROCKS ...**

**DEAD ON THE ROCKS and other books in the
Sam Russo Mystery series are available from:**

www.eiobooks.com

And your favorite bookseller.

Follow Ki Longfellow on the Internet:

Blog kilongfellow.wordpress.com
Facebook Ki Longfellow
Twitter @KiLongfellow
Official Website www.kilongfellow.com
Sam Russo www.eiobooks.com/samrusso

Mrs. Willingford sat bolt upright in bed. "Stop whining, Russo."

"I am *not* whining. I am stating a fact."

"Which is?"

"I don't like boats."

"Two days out, two days whining."

"What a load of— "

"Even Jane's had enough."

" —hooey. She has?"

"Only a man who can whine as much as you, could have missed that."

She had me there. I'd missed it. Jane had enough? I looked round. No Jane. Things, already unsteady, were getting rockier.

"I'll stop."

Mrs. Willingford bit my neck. I bit Mrs. Willingford's neck. It was an hour before I whined again.

It was the tipping over of the ship that did it. Did we hit something? A reef? A raft? An iceberg!

I grabbed at the headboard and held on. "What the hell was that! I saw *Lifeboat*. Are we sinking?"

Mrs. Willingford slid off the bed, a big comfy bed bolted to the floor, and all mine for the duration.

From down there, she said, "If we are, you're chubb."

Joker Willingford's wife'd showed up in some kind of flowing rosy red silk thing, all long droopy sleeves and Fu

Manchu collar. She was back in it and out my cabin door before I got another word out.

I lay there and steamed.

Jane was gone. Mrs. Willingford was gone. I stared out my window, a big rectangular thing with a great view—if all you wanted to see was the sea.

All I had now was me.

But the rest of the Willingford yacht was crawling with wildlife. Out there somewhere, charming the whole bunch of 'em, was Jane.

I never felt less like Bogart in my life.

The last time I was stuck on a ship, me and a lot of fellow survivors were shipped home from the Pacific front. Sam Russo, alumni of the exclusive Staten Island Bin for Thrown-away Kids, came back in one piece.

A lot of others didn't. Some didn't come back at all.

Four years in the Philippines getting bombed, strafed, machine gunned, mined, starved and sent on suicide missions, I wasn't sure one piece was good enough. What I *was* sure of was it couldn't get worse.

And then I ran into my first typhoon.

Somewhere out in the gray and endless ocean, every man jack of us sick and tired, all of us homesick and most of us changed forever, all hell broke loose. The sky, already dark, grew darker. The wind, already blowing, blew harder. The waves, already waving, rose higher and higher and higher, high enough to tower over the tallest building on the main street of Stapleton, Staten Island, my home town.

A guy next to me, both of us struggling into lifejackets,

said they were fifty feet tall for sure. He said, "Say buddy, lookit that! That one'd take out the Golden Gate Bridge!"

Brother, did that make me gag.

Gripping a ship's plunging rail, staring at a rush of oncoming water, and heaving my lunch, showed a guy what the sea really was.

The sea wasn't like land. You could trust land to stay land. From one minute to the next, the sea could be anything. Not my kind of odds at all.

That day, Sam Russo made a pact with himself—if he lived through this, he'd never leave solid ground again: no ships, no boats, no canoes, not even a rowboat.

At ten, I'd jump off any Staten Island pier anytime. Now I was twenty nine. On a bad day the Staten Island ferry could give me the willies.

It was all Jane's fault. If not for her, I'd be lying around in my one room back in Stapleton. I'd be reading a good book.

Except for the book, so would she.

There was this guy I'd met on my last case who was reading *I, the Jury*. Now I was reading *I, the Jury*. Only I wasn't reading it on my Murphy bed in room 4-A where Bay Street met Victory Boulevard. I was reading it on a deckchair I'd dragged up to some sort of top deck near the wheelhouse. This was as far away from the rest of the Sip o' Sea's guests as I could get.

Jane was lying on the warm deck, her rump to the warm wind, her red fur ruffled, one eye closed and one eye open. She was asleep. She was awake. With those eyes, maybe she was both.

I'd seen it before. The first time was in an actor's bar across from Carnegie Hall. It still made me think—was a Basenji really a dog?

Anyway, Mickey Spillane had nothing on Raymond Chandler and his Mike Hammer had nothing on Chandler's Philip Marlowe, but I liked the plot. I'd always thought psychiatrists were full of hot air. Reading I, The Jury, I was sure of it.

Back to Jane and boats. My being on a damn boat was Jane's fault because Jane was the real invitee. I was just the guy on the other end of her leash. Or I would be—if I could keep a leash on her.

The only thing made me feel better about getting stuck on a boat was the girl in the next stateroom.

Holly was invited along for being Holly. Joker Willingford liked her. Mrs. Willingford liked her. The crew of the Sip o' Sea liked her. The ship's captain, a chisel chinned fellow who'd give Gary Cooper a run for his money in the looks department, liked her a lot. Enough for me to check him out with Mrs. Willingford.

Captain Eigil Moody was OK. He was experienced. He'd captained something in the war. He'd come highly recommended to Joker by Joe Kennedy. I wasn't one for Joe, even less for his friend, that American "hero" Lindbergh, but if Mrs. Willingford thought Moody was decent enough, then I did too.

Until maybe I didn't.

Long enough out of New York City for Cap'n Moody to notice Holly, and long after Holly noticed him, I asked her the obvious question.

Holly didn't know any more than I did what our

captain'd do when he knew. So far, she wasn't telling him.

I said, "I'd leave it that way if I were you."

"But I like him," she said.

I said, "I don't."

"Why would you? He's not your type."

That one went by like Whirlaway in the stretch. I said, "You'll know your moment."

"And if that moment never comes?"

"You've got a friend."

"Not much of a friend if he doesn't know the truth."

"True. But better not much of a friend than an outright enemy."

"Oh, butter," said Holly.

Holly was a girl except he wasn't. Plenty of people knew that, but few of 'em sailed under Captain Eigil Moody.

As for the rest of the Willingford guests—well, hell.

I was close to broke, I owned two pairs of shoes, one good trench coat, a great hat, a decent gun and a lotta pictures of great horses. I lived in Room 4-A in beautiful downtown Stapleton with a view of Manhattan which was never looking back, my best friend was a talking dog, and what I did with my spare time was go to the movies—I was loaded with spare time—read dime novels, talk to Holly who lived in Room 4-B, and pretend I was Bogart.

OK, so maybe that wasn't a clean bill of mental health, but aboard the Sip o' Sea my fellow guests were fruit and nut baskets.

A couple were famous, a couple of 'em were rich, a couple had talent, a couple were in the racing game, a couple of 'em were smart, but famous, rich, talented, horsey or smart, they were all as crazy as bedbugs.

I wasn't sure, but counting me and Jane and Holly, there must be fourteen, maybe fifteen of us and we each had a guest stateroom—did I mention the Sip o' Sea had twenty of 'em, all with private baths?

Two of the bunch were starlets, pretty but not as pretty as Holly. Holly'd checked. They were both bona fide girls. Clara Louise was as giddy as Daffy Duck, the other one wasn't. Heddie Day said she studied method acting back in Manhattan, whatever that was.

I hadn't seen her smile once. Maybe the plan was to replace Garbo.

Then there were a lot of people not in staterooms.

The crew was stuck away somewhere in the front end where when things got rough, they got it roughest. These were the folks who all these fruitcakes needed around to tie their shoes.

Mrs. Willingford's personal maid had it better. Otelie Coleman had her own small cabin next to her mistress. Next to Joker was Daniels, the very same Daniels who'd served the late William Ransom Cunningham the Third before Billy III was tossed off his own fifth floor balcony making a mess of himself on the sidewalks of upper East Side New York.

You had to give it to her. Mrs. Willingford tried poaching Daniels. She tried wooing Daniels. She tried demanding him. It may of taken a murder—the ridiculous demise of the ridiculous Billy Cunningham—but Mrs. Willingford always got her man.

So here we were... me and a boatload of swells and would-be swells on the Willingford's yacht. Holly was happy to be here. Mrs. Willingford looked pleased enough. Half of Joker Willingford's guests hung around old Joker like the smell in a vat at Joker's Special Blend Distillery. The other half hung around Mrs. Willingford like... most men hung around Mrs. Willingford.

I could whine about sailing but I couldn't fault the boat. The Sip o' Sea was white as shaving cream, as sleek as a close shave, it had an engine rumbling away somewhere below, and it was a—how would I know? I knew diddly about boats. All I could say was it'd picked us and our luggage up off a New York City dock—I brought Jane and a battered suitcase, the rest brought the Saks Fifth Avenue Summer Catalogue—and was now chuffing along off the East Coast of somewhere USA headed from Manhattan to Miami.

I'd never been to Florida, never wanted to go—except for one thing. That one thing drew me like a Private Eye to a crime: Thoroughbred horse racing.

We were all going to Miami to watch the terrific filly Fleeting Fancy—born and bred at Joker's Beeswing Farm in Kentucky—race at Hialeah. That's where the yacht came in and how I was back on a boat far enough from shore there wasn't any shore.

I wanted to be striding around Hialeah breathing in horses again. I figured once off the Sip o' Sea, forever off the Sip o' Sea.

The scream threw me off my deckchair. It got Jane on her feet and her teeth bared. The second scream got us both moving towards the back of the boat. The third scream came when we got there. It was Heddie Day. If she was method acting, you couldn't prove it by me, but she sure wasn't smiling.

Heddie was shaking, she was pointing, she was building up for another scream.

Practically the whole boat was crowded round her.

No Captain Moody to take charge, it had to be me, Sam Russo, Private Eye.

I put an arm around Heddie's shoulder, I tilted her chin up. I said, "Stop screaming, Miss Day."

"I can't. I can't"

"Why not?"

"It's Clara Louise."

"What about Clara?"

"She jumped."

"Jumped?"

"Overboard."

Fuck.

Daniels was half over the railing looking down at the sea behind us. Otalie was waving up at Captain Moody and yelling. Everyone was yelling. "Stop! Turn around! Go back!"

Mrs. Willingford was sprinting for the wheelhouse, no doubt to get Captain Moody's attention.

I didn't sprint and I didn't yell.

Go back for what? Like Daniels, I was leaning over the railing. I couldn't see a damn thing behind us except a wake.

If Clara jumped, Clara was gone.